Swag rolled, facing west. For the briefest instant he caught a flash of Bammer, running back up the stairs and colliding with the doorman, both of them falling to the carpeted floor. Then he saw Kat Jones, right in the middle of the sidewalk, ten yards away, a small automatic held in a two-handed combat stance, her black raincoat streaming out behind her in the light summer breeze.

Kat fired, catching the major high in the chest and dead-center of the threat-zoned Kevlar vest. The impact knocked him back, and Swag scrambled forward to grab the Colt still tucked in the waistband of his uniform.

Swag turned and rolled, firing before he aimed. The first shot caught one of the enlisted men in the shoulder; the second round caught another on the hand, spraying blood and bone across the shattered plastic grip of his rifle and knocking it from his useless grasp.

Kat was walking forward now, her eyes wild. She fired twice more, the shots so close to Swag's head, he could feel the air pushing out in front of them. She was right over Swag then, the gun sited in directly at his head. "You die, too," she said.

"Kat, it's me!" Swag tried, raising his cuffed hands in front of him.

She was pulling back on the trigger, standing over him like some angel of death with that black raincoat spread out like wings in the humid breeze. There wasn't even time to bring the Colt up. . . .

FULL CLIP

L.S. RIKER

ST. MARTIN'S PAPERBACKS

FULL CLIP

Copyright © 1992 by L. S. Riker.

Cover art by Steve Gardner.

ISBN: 0-312-92848-3

Printed in the United States of America

St. Martin's Paperbacks edition/November 1992

10 9 8 7 6 5 4 3 2 1

To Melissa Suzanne
Who makes it all worthwhile

preface

Note this and remember it. The history we live moves slowly, like a car crash. The spinning landscape and oncoming traffic slide by on the other side of the safety glass in fine slow motion and detail. And when the impact finally breaks the spell, it is not a surprise, but nearly always worse than we anticipated. The jarring collision, the screech and thud of folding metal, the shattered glass fallen inward, and the bloodied instrumentation along the dashboard—these are the things that cannot be imagined as history's landscape revolves before our eyes.

Years before America crashed, all but the most dimwitted had seen the yellow center lines swerve from sight. They heard the squeal of tires and the panicked blare of horns. And a nation of people stared transfixed and mute, choosing to suffer the inevitable alone. But there was no safety in pragmatic isolation.

Old men, drunk with power and playing with the radio dials, were at the wheel. And the entire country was in the backseat, without seat belts.

Later the people blamed the pols. The politicians, in good suits and with the elegant passion of televised outrage, damned those who crippled the monetary system. But the people had elected the politicians. And the banks were not the soul of the country. Suddenly blame was not important. Accusations, deniability, and retribution were bitter luxuries. Survival was back in fashion.

Now this is the way it was in one town—in *the* town—New York City. The millions who had waited, worked, and dreamed for their turn at the stuff of privilege awakened to face a nasty glaring truth: things would not get better forever. The bright and shining future that was the covenant of the nation had become a cynical lie. And when the dream ended, the nightmare began.

The riots lasted months. It was as if some invisible barrier had melted away. Wolf packs swarmed down from upper Manhattan and the Bronx. They crossed the river from Queens, Brooklyn, and Jersey, drawn by a lifetime of hate and a one-chance opportunity. They were white and black and Asian and Spanish—but they wore one face: the face of the cheated out to even up the score.

The violence was shocking in its viciousness and senselessness.

Few among the wealthy suspected just how very close to the fault line they had lived those many years. Sealed in the unsparing luxury and comfort of homes and chauffeured cars, they never felt the first, slight tremors. They had slept soundly, eaten well, and amused themselves extravagantly. The tremors they should have felt would have been of conscience.

Many of their kind were killed. Their homes were invaded and looted. Their cars hijacked and burned. They were gunned down in the street, their deaths marked by polite conversation in Paris, Geneva, Brussels, and London. "Horrible, simply tragic," was the phrase whispered in a half-dozen languages. But left unspoken was the belief that, after all, they were Americans. And even the best—the richest—were vulgar.

The only law in town was the law of the street. New York became a wasteland of shattered glass, blue police barricades, and unseen snipers. Up and down the canyoned avenues the skyscrapers of glass and steel burned to shells. In the end, the riots left little but acrid smoke and broken mirrors that revealed the horrible truth of it all.

But the horror was not in the privileged dead, or in the shattered architecture of corporate wealth. The true horror lay with draining wounds in hospital wards, in the crowded cages of locked-down cell blocks, and zippered into the thick black plastic of body bags. The horror was that it had been an uprising of children.

The chickens had finally come home to roost with a vengeance. And the spectacle of it was numbing.

A thirteen-year-old boy, the murderer of four, handcuffed and struggling, screaming defiantly on the six o'clock news as armed men in full body armor hustle him into a precinct.

Twenty more kids lined up kneeling in front of Tiffany's, fingers laced behind their heads, ankles crossed, as the khaki uniforms hold Steyr automatic rifles pointed at their heads. The oldest is maybe sixteen. Fifth Avenue traffic barely slows at the sight.

A young society matron raped, beaten, then thrown through a bedroom window and impaled on the wrought-iron fence surrounding her town house. Police snipers shoot down the culprits through uncurtained windows in the building's library as they carelessly drink Armagnac from a Baccarat crystal decanter. They are two brothers, the oldest is seventeen.

Twenty thousand died; more, many more, were wounded, few above the age of twenty-five. This was the horror of it. A generation had been cheated of a future and pushed beyond the reach of everything except the force of the law.

Under martial law many had been shot in the back. Others vanished into government cars and vans to be killed quietly by the newly instated Provost Marshal's death squads. Law and order were returned at a terrible price.

And when the nightmare ended, the adults were forced back into submission by troops, by hunger, by sheer exhaustion, by disgust at the past and the prospect of a bankrupt future. But New York endured. It remained as it always has been, an island of stone built on stone and filled with hustlers, whores, and tourists. All of them looking and scrambling for the main deal.

chapter one

THE PLACE WAS CALLED THE Dead Banker Bar & Grill.
Wedged into the bottom floor of one of the unoccupied
buildings near Wall Street, it was at once shabby and anonymous, like a failing franchise. At one time it aspired to
cater to an international crowd, so the faded sign out front
included French, German, Italian, and Japanese subtitles.
And it was just dark enough to make drinking at noon
pleasant, but not too pleasant. Shaped like a shoe box, the
Dead Banker was a saloon where the downtown bottom-
feeders did their small business deals over watered drinks.

Swag was standing at the bar watching the barmaid top
off his beer under the spigot then slide it over the two or
so feet so that it bumped against the cardboard coaster that
advertised something called the Royale Deluxe Escort Service. He took a long sip through the perfect two-inch head
and let it sit in his mouth for a brief moment before swallowing. It was cold enough to make his teeth ache.

Swag set the beer back down and looked along the wall.
Above the neat rows of bottles were the framed portraits
of past financial greats. Beneath each face was a small brass-
plated oval that listed the names and dates of birth and
demise in neat script. The male faces ranged from mustach-
ioed and top-hatted gents to the serious countenances of
more recent bankers in somber gray or blue suits. These
latter photos, Swag knew, had been filched and enlarged
from annual reports.

At the center of the bar above the cash register was an unusually large portrait of a smiling young man. He was wearing a bright blue Lacoste shirt and standing in front of a cherry-red Porsche 944 Turbo. The place beneath his name read woods "TEX" sawburn, and included no final date.

"Have you heard from him, Kat?" Swag asked, noticing for the first time that Tex Sawburn wasn't so much smiling as smirking. It was the smirk of a spoiled boy with the best toys in the neighborhood.

"Who's that?" the barmaid asked back, turning her attention from bottle straightening to push a stray strand of thick brown hair back behind her ear with two fingers.

Swag indicated slightly by raising his glass.

"Guy was in a while ago," Kat said, turning to study the picture. "Said Tex was doing good in his therapy. Almost got it down where he can change his own catheter with three fingers."

"That's all he's got, isn't it?" Swag asked.

"I seem to remember a bit of a stump on the left hand," Kat said. "Ring finger, I think."

"You would know," Swag said, then studied Kat Jones through the half darkness of the bar. When she was young, you would have called her pretty, perky even. Now that she was thirty-five, she was still good-looking, but in a better sort of way. The years had been good to Kat Jones.

"I would know," Kat said, without a hint of emotion, particularly remorse.

And Swag knew this to be true. If anyone would know which digits Tex Sawburn still had possession of, it would be Kat, because she was the one who shot the others off with a Ruger Mark II. The first shot caught him as he was reading the English edition of the *Nihon Keizai Shimbun* over French roast coffee. The small .22 slug hit him low on his left leg, chipping off a good portion of bone and knocking him from the chair. It was the first time in four years she had drawn his full attention from the Japanese markets.

Once Kat had his undivided attention, she stalked him through their upper West Side condo—from breakfast nook to balcony—firing into the scrambling banker. She shot him as she did everything else, with terrific style and taste, dropping the empty clips behind her as she advanced. When the police finally broke down the door, she had emptied three clips and hit him twenty-six times, mostly in his extremities.

The papers called the young banker's survival "miraculous," but Swag never saw it as miraculous. He saw it as good aim. After hearing the evidence, which included a complete accounting of Sawburn's numerous affairs and his intention to marry another woman, a predominantly female jury acquitted Kat of all charges, except Unlawful Discharge of a Firearm.

Before the incident, she had worked for a publisher. That job quickly vanished, but the owners of the Dead Banker recruited her as their star attraction, which gained the joint a morbid, if not free-spending, following.

"So, why'd you call me down?" Swag asked, then took another sip of beer.

There were a few suits lined up at the bar, talking in the low tones of conspiracy. Kat gave the suits a quick dismissive glance, then leaned over the bar toward Swag. "Remember E. C. Dullen?" she asked.

Swag shook his head.

"Yeah, you do," she insisted. "Everyone called him 'Easy.' Little guy, always on the hustle and always saying 'Hey, I'm easy' whenever he was negotiating."

"Vaguely," Swag answered, remembering a tiny dark-haired guy with bad skin who'd sell anything from Statue of Liberty pens to black-market jewelry. On some nights he could be seen in an ancient Cadillac limo, driving tourists around town.

"He was working over at the Vista Hotel, bell-hopping," Kat said. "Flipped out a few weeks ago, and they put him in Bellevue."

"Should I be interested in this?" Swag asked.

"Only if you want work," Kat answered, then pushed herself away from the bar to refill the suits' drinks.

"What's the deal on him?" Swag said when she returned.

"I'll lay it out for you like it was told to me," Kat answered, then paused to carefully gather the disparate threads of the story. "Easy's working at the Vista hauling Vuittons and hustling on the side. About a month ago he quits, raving to the bell captain and anyone else who would listen that someone's out to get him."

"He probably burned someone," Swag said.

Kat made a small motion of annoyance with her hand for the interruption. "Yeah, but he goes into hiding," she said. "Locks himself in his room, SRO place near Canal Street. Doesn't come out for two weeks. When the manager breaks down the door, he flips out, jumps the guy, bites a piece of his nose off. And it takes six provosts to wrestle him down so they can throw him in Bellevue for observation."

Swag nodded to show he was paying attention.

"So, the docs at Bellevue diagnose an 'acute paranoidal delusional state,' punch him full of psychotropes and toss him back out as 'nonhazardous.'"

"What about the nose biting thing?" Swag asked.

"They chalked it up to malnutrition," Kat said. "He'd been in that room for a couple of weeks, ran out of food. Started drinking his own piss, if you want all the details. Anyway, they toss him back on the street, literally, 'cause he didn't want to leave. And a day later, someone pops him."

"Just because you're paranoid doesn't mean they're not after you, right?" Swag quipped, and reached into the pocket of his Hawaiian shirt for a cigarette. He held it between his lips while he searched his pockets for a match. Thai cigarettes were available that week. Next month it might be Korean, and hopefully not the MK Ultras, which were the government's own brand.

"Yeah, everyone's a little paranoid," she answered. "It's healthy, right?"

"Something like that," Swag said, still fumbling for a book of matches and not finding one.

Kat lit the cigarette with a deft movement from a disposable lighter, taking the opportunity to study Swag for the first time since he'd walked in. "Swag and his Hawaiian shirts." She sighed, pocketing the lighter. "They're like a trademark, right?"

"So, someone wants to know who killed Easy," Swag said, exhaling a lungful of smoke.

"They already know who killed him," Kat said as she retrieved a manila envelope from under the bar and slid it across to Swag. Inside were copies of the provost report, crime scene photos, and witness transcripts. Swag thumbed through them just enough to see the tops of the documents.

Swag ashed the cigarette and asked, "Who?"

"Some guy with a knife," Kat said without a trace of a smile. "What they want to know is the why."

chapter two

It got better. The way the provost reports told it, Easy
was kicked loose from Bellevue at six-thirty at night. It was
twilight, and the streetlights would be on in another hour
or so. Walking fast down First Avenue, he couldn't find a
cab and probably wouldn't have known where to go if he'd
found one. So he bolted and ran down the east side of the
street. A Con Ed crew, repairing a steam main, saw him.

When he spotted a cab at the corner, he kept running,
breaking into a sweat and puffing hard. The cab driver
remembered seeing him as he pulled away to pick up
another fare across the street—a young woman with a
French poodle. According to the cabbie, given the choice
between a guy running away from Bellevue clutching a
clear plastic property pouch and wearing a bar-coded
patient wristband, and a woman with a French poodle, it
was "no fucking contest."

Easy rested at the corner, panting as he leaned against
a lamppost to catch his breath. He must have looked a little
disoriented and scared. According to the Con Ed crew, two
more cabs slowed, then took off once the drivers got a good
look at him.

By the time he had given up on a cab, Easy was at Fourteenth Street and Third Avenue, and near a bar called Jac's.
Jac's was a walk-down basement bar near Variety Photo-
plays—the oldest movie theater in the city. The bar was a
long narrow room, like a coffin with warped floorboards

and a couple of tilting tables. Its original stamped-tin ceiling was so low that even a short guy like Easy would have the feeling he should hunch his head down when he entered.

The bartender remembered saying, "Easy, whattaya drinking?"

Easy wasn't drinking anything. Without answering the stooped, potbellied bartender, he kept right on moving in a bent-over wheezing run toward the men's room.

Jac's was the kind of bar where nobody, especially the bartender, looked twice at goofy behavior. The bartender, like bartenders everywhere, claimed to have seen everything from behind his length of wet mahogany and had a very selective memory. But he remembered his next customer, all right. The guy was short, dressed in a steel-gray tweed suit, perfectly round steel-framed glasses, a striped tie, and jodhpur riding boots. He had dirty brown hair and a bent nose, not busted, but the kind you're born with. And he was wearing a knife hanging down in front, from a thick belt. Except for the knife around his waist, he looked like a commentator on public television.

The bartender remembered looking up, seeing the guy standing at the bar, then looking toward the door and seeing the girl. She was built, but not showy about it, her eyes obscured behind a pair of yellow-tinted shooting glasses. She wore a perfectly white T-shirt, jeans, and a replica Brooklyn Dodgers baseball cap, with her hair tucked up under it. Although the two customers didn't talk, the bartender was certain that they were together.

The guy, the one in the tweed outfit, ordered scotch, no ice. He spoke softly with an English accent, which explained the no-ice order. Then he threw some money on the bar, drank down the liquor, and smiled with world-weary boredom as he headed for the men's crapper.

A lush trying to get the shakes under control as he dug out a franc note from his shoe was sitting in the stall.

"Who are you?" the lush heard Easy ask plaintively as

he backed away, toward the wall opposite the sink, knocking over the trash can.

"Stand and deliver, you contemptible rogue," the little guy in the tweeds said.

"What the fuck? What's this 'stand and deliver' bullshit?" Easy answered.

Peeking through a crack in the stall, the lush saw the little guy slide a hand down and pull the knife from a wooden scabbard.

"Rogue," the tweedy guy said.

"I don't know you, Jack," Easy said. "Why've you been following me?"

"You shall pay!"

"What are you, a fuckin' head case?" Easy said, anger temporarily overcoming his fear.

"Despicable wretch," the little guy answered, motioning with the knife so that Easy had to back up against the rust-stained sink.

"Asshole," Easy shot back, then made a run for the door.

The little guy blocked Easy's exit, then stabbed out with the knife, cutting him on the arm. "Arm yourself, sir," the little guy said.

"Fuck you," Easy said. "I don't need this shit."

The little guy stabbed out again. This time he missed Easy and hit the hard sink. Easy went for the knife hand, but before he could reach the guy's wrist, the knife came up again, catching him in the chest.

The lush remembered seeing the little guy holding Easy up by the knife blade, wedging him against the sink as he leaned in close. The coroner's report showed that the blade knocked against a rib, then passed through Easy's heart.

The coroner's report also showed that the blade, which was approximately twelve to fourteen inches long, was dull, with traces of oxidation as well as a low-acid preserving agent. Microscopic scrapings from Easy's damaged rib and the men's room sink showed near-microscopic metal fragments from a crude foundry. They had been carbon dated at four hundred years.

"Interesting reading," Kat said when Swag slid the reports back into the envelope. The suits had vanished out the door, and Swag was the sole customer.

"It's bullshit," Swag said, pushing the thick envelope back across the bar.

"It's the kind of bullshit that could make you some serious money," Kat answered. "Five thousand francs."

"It's still bullshit," Swag said, and drained off the last of his beer. "Provosts don't want to investigate a murder, they botch the reports. Probably had a laugh doing this one. Maybe Easy burned the wrong guy. Somebody with enough money to buy off the investigation, the bartender, all of them."

Kat leaned far over the bar, getting right in Swag's face. "It isn't bullshit," she said, the tension rising up into her face and hardening around the eyes. "It's weird, but it isn't bullshit."

"Tell me about it," Swag said, searching for another cigarette.

According to Kat, this was the way it was going down. The report she showed Swag was the provost unofficial shadow report. The documents on file showed Easy dead in a brawl by "assailant or assailants unknown." And there had been others, five at least. Two shot with high-powered rifles. One whacked out with an explosive-tipped arrow, the fourth machine-gunned, the fifth downed by a barbed wooded dart tipped with intocastin—a synthetic form of curare. Descriptions of the assailants varied, but the thing that held it together was the woman. In every case there was a mysterious woman at the scene.

"What's your interest in this?" Swag asked, stubbing out the last of the cigarette.

"One of the waitresses, Sandy Mann, took up with one of the bar's owners. Now she's up in Bellevue," Kat said. "Want to know what for?"

"Paranoia," Swag ventured.

"They're calling it something else," Kat said. "'Urban Trauma.' But it's what Easy had. Same thing."

"So what does he want, the owner?" Swag asked.

Kat paused a moment. "He wants you to poke around and find out who's after his girlfriend. They hauled her in yesterday for observation. That's sixty days. She's in a locked-down ward, so she's safe."

"No thanks," Swag said, and started to get up to leave.

"Swag, you're gonna do it. You know you are," Kat said. "So let's just cut the bullshit, huh?"

Turning back toward the bar, Swag saw Kat standing there, hands on hips, smiling. "Pretty sure about it, are you?" he said, feeling himself begin to smile.

"Absolutely," she said, grinning wider.

"Why's that?"

"Because it's weird," Kat said. "And you like weird. The carbon dating stuff hooked you. Tell me if I'm wrong here. And you like money."

"Any other reason?"

"It'll probably piss off the provosts," Kat said. "And you'd like that even more. And you'll do it for me, as a favor."

"And if it's bullshit?"

"Then it's bullshit," Kat said flatly. Then, pulling another envelope from under the bar, she carefully flipped it to Swag. "But the money's real."

Swag picked up the white letter-sized envelope and felt the satisfying weight that an inch of cash has. "So, when do I meet the owner?" he asked, folding the sealed envelope so that it fit in his back pocket.

"You don't," Kat said. "He's a discreet kind of guy. Know what I'm saying?"

"Spell it out for me," Swag answered.

Kat came forward, leaning her elbows down on the bar. "It's like this," she said. "Stop in a few times a week. Talk to me. Let me know how it's going or if you find something out."

"That's the way it is, huh?"

"Yeah," Kat said. "That's exactly the way it is."

Swag left the bar and felt the sudden blast of midday heat hit him as he stepped out on Cedar Street, which was really not much more than an alley. A few blocks to the west were the twin towers of the World Trade Center, and beyond them, failed offices and luxury condos, the West Side Highway, and the river.

Swag searched for another cigarette and looked up at the World Trade Towers as he fished a Thai 555 out of his shirt pocket. The twin towers were a dirty gray, standing out vaguely against the haze of the afternoon sky. Way back when, they were filled with sixty thousand people. Now they were just one more low-rent operation in the sky. Cheap office space and expensive tours. Up to the fifteenth floor the towers were filled with rentable space. You could rent a flash and splash office for a week, a month, or a year to impress European or Rim suckers for a business deal. A concession in the lobby sold brass plaques with magnetic backing. But mostly the occupied floors were filled with low-rent cubicles called flats, where hustlers worked ancient phones, moving merchandise and services that ran from gray market to black, and every shade in between.

The Japanese and Koreans still loved the tours. Germans had bought the elevator franchise. There was talk of opening a casino on the top floors once the new gambling laws went into effect.

Lighting the cigarette, Swag turned right, up Cedar, and began walking the slight hill toward Broadway. This was the old part of the city, laced with quirky one-way streets and winding alleys that showed cobblestone where the asphalt had worn through.

You could chart the architecture of America's boom years here—the twenties, with ornate gray granite and sandstone; the sixties' glass and flash; then the high-tech boxes of tinted glass and darkened steel of the eighties.

This was the part of town built by middlemen. First goods from Europe, then stocks, commodities, then money. Later, the high-priced hustlers and pitchmen made nothing but deals, and even they were shoddy. Twenty-five thousand big money lawyers, money men, and corporate hustlers, their meters running like a taxi from Hell, all of them doing piecework deals that fell apart faster than cheap suits.

Swag took a last drag from the cigarette and dropped the butt in the unswept gutter. The streets were shadowed in this part of town. Even on sunny days the crowded buildings on either side of the street obscured the sun as effectively as a jungle canopy.

Dodging the light traffic on Trinity, Swag kept moving toward Broadway. He was trying not to think about the guy he was going to see. Sam Narcadia was a fixer—maybe the best in the city. If you needed something, anything, he either had a name on file or could get one. He could put together investors for a limited partnership lawsuit or find a mule to carry a million black-market francs across a border, any border. Street legend had it he was either a lawyer, accountant, or broker before the crash. And Swag could believe it; all three were harder to get rid of than roaches. They never vanished—just moved from room to room, office to office. Now he had a shabby one-room office in the Equitable building, working a bank of fifteen phone lines from a head-set, and speaking in a code so obscure that Berlitz couldn't teach it.

But that's not what people remembered about Narcadia. What they remembered, those few who saw him—was that he was quite possibly the ugliest man in the city.

A few bike messengers were lounging around the lobby drinking coffee and soda—and making their secret deals before a beeper sounded. Swag had no doubt that they worked for Narcadia. His company was called Protyle Ltd., which acted as holding company for ten or twelve others, which in turn made loans to and held majority positions in maybe forty more, which invested in deals that would have only two purposes—make money and keep city, state, federal, and international investigators working.

The tenant index in the lobby of the building listed over two hundred tenants—something like a third in the same suite. But that didn't matter. Whatever number you dialed, Narcadia picked up.

Swag dropped a coin into a pay phone and dialed the Protyle number from memory. Sam picked up in one ring.

He answered the phone the way he answered all his phones. "Talk."

"It's me," Swag said, not offering his name.

"Talk some more," Sam instructed. "Tell me a joke."

"There's two guys walking down the street," Swag began. "And they see this dog licking his balls. One guy says to the other, 'I wish I could do that—'"

"The other guy says, 'I'd pet him first,'" Sam finished. "You should have told me one I haven't heard."

"I got one you haven't heard," Swag said.

"I'm listening," Sam said.

"It's too good for the phone," Swag answered.

"Then you better tell me in person," came the response.

chapter three

NARCADIA'S OFFICE WAS ON THE fifteenth floor of the Equitable Building. The building, now almost a century old, had changed the city far beyond the shadow it cast over the financial district. It stood forty-one floors on just less than an acre of land, containing within its bland shell something over a million square feet of office space. Even in a city where greed was never a stranger, the thing pissed so many people off that New York adopted the first zoning laws in the country.

The building stood as an unapologetic marvel of the city's rapacious history, and reminder that maybe the good old days weren't all that different after all. But to others it was a landmark and inspiration for the city's hustlers, offering the best plausibly deniable defense ever: "It wasn't against no law when we done it."

Swag took the ancient, slow-moving elevator up to the topmost inhabited floor, the fifteenth, and stepped out into the narrow hall. Narcadia was the sole tenant on the floor, though he used only a tiny office.

There was a green and white plastic Welcome mat in front of the frosted-glass door to the left, and Swag stepped on it with both feet.

Before he could knock, the door buzzer sounded.

Turning the shining brass knob, Swag stepped into a small Lexan cubicle no deeper than a telephone booth and framed with riveted steel at the joints. Its floor was covered in thick black rubber. From beyond the clear plastic entrance he could see Narcadia, his back to the door, looking out the window. The fixer was in his shirtsleeves and had sweated through the back of his blue oxford shirt. The dark stain resembled a soggy exclamation point that ran down his narrow back.

He was standing behind his desk, a gray-metal monster that took up nearly the entire office. It was the kind of desk that an anonymous bureaucrat in an anonymous government office would passionately covet as a totem of power bestowed from the powers that be, if not the gods themselves.

The desk was completely empty except for the telephone control console, a slanting black thing the size of a shoe box, with three thick cables running from its ass end.

Narcadia had a telephone headset fastened to his head, its thin wire cut around from his jaw, under the left ear, across a slicked-back head of hair the color of pencil lead. The cord ran down his side, connecting him to the box on the desk, like a life support system. His sleeves were rolled up so that Swag could see the platinum Blancpain watch on one wrist, a wafer-thin beauty that you would have said cost about ten bucks, if you didn't know any better. On his other hand there was the flash of a three-carat diamond pinky ring, which looked too big to be real. Both shone dully from the light streaming in through the filthy window.

Although Swag couldn't hear a thing, he was certain Narcadia was talking, by the way his head moved slightly. Then, with unexpected swiftness, Narcadia turned to switch lines. The sight of his face took Swag completely by surprise. No matter how many times you saw it, *were expecting it*, the shock always hit the same, coming up in a reflexive expression of revulsion, which Narcadia seemed to perversely revel in.

What Narcadia had was *neurofibromatosis*. What he didn't have was a face. Tumors the size of grapes, some larger than golf balls, gathered at the front of his head, from forehead to chin, obscuring his eyes, nose, and lips. Their bulk pulled the skin taut, elongating his face and adding considerably to the horror.

Swag felt his mouth twist up a little at the sight. The tumors, like the rest of Narcadia's skin, were sickly gray from lack of sunlight.

Narcadia punched down on a button on his console with his left hand and help up his right index finger, indicating he would be with Swag shortly. When he began speaking again, he looked directly at Swag, his head nearly perfectly still. From somewhere within the bunching mass of tumors, two crafty eyes gave Swag the once-over, calculating within their shadowed lair just how much the next deal was worth. For all Swag knew, Narcadia might not even have a call. He could just be staring, working out the next move in what he clearly knew to be a seller's market.

Then he pushed down on two more buttons and Swag heard the voice sound from the plastic cubicle's speaker. "You're wearing a piece, friend," Narcadia said. "Let's see it."

Swag reached behind slowly and drew out the Colt Delta Custom 10 with one hand, holding it up for Narcadia to see.

"Put it in the box," came the next order.

Swag pulled down on a small door cut into the clear plastic and slid the pistol in. When he shut the door, its magnetic lock clicked into place.

Narcadia pushed the button again and studied the small light on the panel. "Okay, come in," he said, when he was satisfied Swag wasn't armed.

The lock on the door buzzed open and Swag pushed through the three-inch-thick barrier. A spring on the door pulled it shut behind him, and the magnetic locks clicked secure back into place.

"You got a joke for me or what?" Narcadia said as he sat down behind his desk.

There wasn't a seat in front of the desk. If you saw Narcadia in person, you remained standing. Just like a fast food franchise. "I've got some questions," Swag said.

"Domestic, government, offshore, what?" Narcadia asked, reciting the menu.

"Street crime," Swag said.

Narcadia answered by lifting a finger, then punched up a number on the console. "Talk."

Swag watched as the tumorous head tilted to one side, listening. Then Narcadia lifted a hand wearily and pushed two fingers through the tumors surrounding his eyes to massage what Swag supposed were closed lids.

"Yeah, yeah, yeah," Narcadia said, speaking into the mouthpiece. Then he extracted his fingers from the cramped eye sockets and studied them casually. The tips were slick with sweat. "Fuck 'em. It's a limited-time offer. Gilt-fucking-edged. And remember, you may already be a winner. You know what I'm saying?"

Narcadia listened intently for a second, nodding slightly, then said, "Yeah," and punched off the line. Turning his attention to Swag, he said, "Yeah?"

"What kind of contract hits are happening?" Swag said.

"You don't waste time," Narcadia said. He was sitting perfectly still, one hand perched near the phone, the other now resting somewhere under the desk. "What do you mean, contract? Give me a clue."

"Six hits," Swag said. "All of them done strange, an antique knife, for one."

"What? You're talking about that bottom-feeder, Easy?" Narcadia asked.

Swag nodded, trying to keep his eyes focused on the desk. "And some others."

"This is street bullshit," came the answer. "Strictly low-rent. I don't need it."

"Do you need a hundred francs?"

"I need two hundred," Narcadia answered.

"What does it buy me?" Swag asked.

"It buys what I sell," Narcadia said, leaning forward slightly. "Names. Names and addresses."

"I need next of kin, witness lists, enemies. How long?"

Narcadia looked at his watch, then raised his head to study the pocked surface of the acoustic tile ceiling. Inside his head countless wheels turned and gears clicked in a clockwork of thought. "Two days," he answered.

While Swag thought it over, Narcadia held up his finger, pushed one of the console's buttons and said, "Talk." After a moment he said, "Check it out. Why would I lie? Do not pass Go, do not collect the two hundred. Allow four to six weeks for delivery. You have a nice day, understand what I'm saying?"

Swag pulled out the envelope Kat had given him, separated ten twenty-franc notes from the neat stack, and laid them in a pile on the desk.

Narcadia eyed the money hesitantly, then punched down on a button. His head swiveled back in the direction of Swag. "Call in two days, okay?"

"Sure," Swag said.

"And remember," Narcadia called as Swag turned toward the door. "You may already be a winner."

The plane's jet engines whined and modulated slightly, changing their pitch as the aircraft turned on the tarmac. The heat from the big jet engines sent the swampy landscape behind them shimmering in the diminishing light as the plane taxied off the runway at Kennedy, away from the commercial terminals. It was a large plane, big enough for commercial use, though it boasted no carrier logo or distinctive markings. In fact, the tail numbers identified it as a private charter.

Even before the engines died down and the plane was at a full stop, an ancient white Rolls was already moving toward it across the tarmac. From the opposite direction came the stairs, pulled by a bright yellow Jeep with a flashing blue light.

As the plane came to a complete stop, the Jeep swung into position and the crew hurried to unhitch the stairs and push them up to the forward hatch. The uniformed chauffeur, a young woman in yellow shooting glasses, opened the Roll's door and hurried around to the trunk to retrieve a length of tightly rolled carpeting. The stairs and red carpet leading to the passenger door of the Rolls were already in place by the time the plane's door opened.

It wasn't until the man appeared in the doorway of the plane that the car's occupant took his position at the foot of the stairs. He wore a light, silk summer suit, was thirty or thirty-five, and very tan. A small ponytail tightly bound at the back of his head extended down to the base of his neck in a curl.

One of the plane's two passengers paused briefly in the doorway, studying his surroundings, then proceeded carefully down the steep length of stairs. He was wearing a loose-fitting shirt so ugly it had to be European, and expensive, tan slacks, and thin-soled Italian loafers. He was dressed perfectly for the weather, having been alerted by the captain of current conditions a full hour before landing. He was maybe forty-five and had the slim build and studied, light-footed agility of a man conscious of his health and his age.

Directly behind the gentleman was the plane's remaining passenger, a woman. His junior by fifteen years, she was wearing a bright, tight-fitting yellow dress that nicely set off her high-fashion curves, dark hair, and dark features. She moved more slowly and hesitantly, having nothing to prove in regard to either health or age. She came down the metal flight of stairs at a slight angle, careful of the way her heels met the narrow steps. The whole ordeal of descending the stairs seemed tiresome, boring, in fact.

The man with the ponytail waiting at the foot of the stairs greeted the couple enthusiastically, taking the man's hand firmly and the woman's lightly. He spoke in rapid French with a slight Parisian accent. His smile appeared almost genuine, showing off a great expanse of capped teeth—as if he wanted to get his money's worth from them. Then, without slackening his enthusiasm, he made the introductions to the young woman in the chauffeur's uniform. The young woman didn't smile at all when she said in unaccented English, "A pleasure to meet you."

"Mon dieu!" the woman said to no one in particular. "But the heat."

And the guy in the suit led the pair solicitously to the air-conditioned car.

chapter four

SWAG WALKED UP BROADWAY THINKING that the world moved in peculiar ways when a bust-out lowlife like E.C. got to be worth five large, and dead no less. It was, Swag mused, the kind of serious money that every street hustler dreamed of, talked about, and longed for. *Fresh-start money. Fuck-you money. And get-out-of-town money.*

Now E.C. was dead, but probably smiling down from Hustler Heaven and saying to any skel angel in a cheap sharkskin suit who would listen, "See that there? See that? Beaucoup dinero is moving 'round cause'a me."

By the time Swag brought himself out of his thoughts of Hustler Heaven, he was near Canal and a couple of blocks from the SRO hotel that E.C. had called home. Cutting east down Franklin, he made his way through the narrow streets of abandoned factories and soaped storefront windows. For reasons known to no one, even the sweatshops avoided these narrow streets. The buildings remained abandoned or home to squatters. A few years ago small-time operators sold trinkets to street vendors from the storefronts. Then even they left.

A few blocks over Swag saw the sign for the hotel. The place was called Hubert's, though known to almost everyone as Hubert's Flea Circus, a passing acknowledgment to both the long-gone Times Square establishment as well as the current population of vermin.

A small crowd was gathered out front, passing bottles,

smoking, waiting for the heat to let up so they could head back up to their small rooms. Swag had seen the hotel before and the small gathering, which never seemed to alter its size, like some single organic mass. Every few days when one of the men ran out of money for cigarettes, liquor, or stale bread, he'd break off and head uptown to wash windshields, run the blind-beggar scam, or collect bottles and cans for small change. These foraging absences for necessities virtually always coincided with the return of another of the group's members, pockets slightly weighted with the clink of coins.

It was not the kind of place Swag would have thought E.C. would have for his crib, unless he thought about it. Then it made sense. Because despite his job at the hotel, E.C. was always looking for the main deal—the connection to the Eurocash flow that always sadistically eluded him half a step around the next corner. He was just another half-smart hustler for whom no shot at the money was too long, and no scam, regardless of chance of double-crosses and Byzantine complexities, too farfetched. He left his tips and most of his salary in bucket-shop grain futures, chophouse ISOs, offtrack bets on three-horse parlays, and transparent insurance frauds that never paid off.

Sway moved through the small knot of murmuring men and went up the narrow stairway, where walls covered in plastic woodgrain paneling didn't quite reach the ceiling of blistered and peeling paint. The hall dead-ended at a Plexiglas-enclosed cubicle of the manager's office. A windowless buzzer-equipped door to the side admitted patrons into their rooms.

A hand-lettered sign taped just under the perforations of the window greeted all who ventured up the dark stairway. It read:

NO WOMEN
NO FIGHTING
NO BUSINESS TRANSACTIONS OF ANY KIND

NO MONEY—NO ROOM
NO EXCUSES
NO EXCEPTIONS

Sitting in the small cubicle, his face hovering just above
the sign, was the manager unfortunate enough to meet
E.C. It wasn't hard to spot him: a greasy pile of bandages
covered the place where his nose had been. Despite the
bandages, he wore the bored expression of desk clerks
everywhere.

He was a big guy, and fat. There was a beard of at least
five days growth, sprouting gray. The filthy gray T-shirt he
wore was soaked through from the heat of the small office.
Every inch of him seemed to glisten in a faint greasy glow
of sweat, from his reddish hair to the thickset arms and fat
sausage fingers.

A thick sandwich of gray meat on a roll sat half eaten on
one side of the desk. Four or five flies buzzed the sandwich,
taking turns landing on the protruding edge of chewed
meat. Two cardboard coffee cups, the milk clouded over on
the surface, sat at his other elbow.

"Yeah," the manager said as Swag stepped up to the window. It wasn't a question, it was little more than a nasal
grunt to show life. Then, as if to offer further proof of life,
he shooed the flies away.

"You the manager?" Swag asked.

A slight light of suspicion rose in the manager's eyes.
"Who says?"

"That bandage for one," Swag answered.

"Where you from?"

Swag fished out one of the bills, a franc note, and held
it up, pinning it against the smudged plastic with two fingers.

The manager came up out of the plastic chair. "What you
want?"

Swag already had the manager's attention, now he
wanted some answers. "I want to talk about the guy who
did that to your nose."

"What are you, a fuckin' comic?" the manager growled, moving closer to the plastic barrier. He was so close, Swag could see where the sweat soaked into the bandages, making them peel slightly upward at the edges.

Swag kept the bill pressed against the plastic.

"I'm a friend of the family," Swag said. He wasn't in a hurry.

"He don't have no family," the manager said. As he spoke, a fly ventured up from the gray meat of the sandwich and buzzed against the glass. The manager lifted a meaty hand up and smashed the heat-dazed fly, spreading it against the glass, adding to the smudges, before wiping its mortal fly remains on a pants leg. "There, there's his fuckin' family. The little maggot!"

"You don't want to talk, fine," Swag answered as he slowly brought the bill away from the glass.

"Who are you?" the manager spat. "Who you with?"

"I'm with myself," Swag said, making a show of folding the crisp franc note up.

"Hey wait, don't be walking off now," the manager said. He was leaning over the desk now, so his face was close to the perforated plastic. Even in the heat his breath fogged the glass. "You bring that frog paper back here, we'll talk."

"Buzz me in," Swag said, holding the folded bill up.

The manager reached under the desk and buzzed the door. Swag pushed through the door into another narrow hallway. A steel-reinforced door on his left buzzed and he walked into the cubicle.

The smell of the unwashed fat man was nearly unbearable.

The manager's hand was out before the door closed behind Swag, shutting off all fresh air.

"Gimme the money," the manager said, wriggling his fingers.

Swag held the bill out, but didn't drop it in the upturned hand. "What do you know about E.C.?"

"I know that scumbag bit my fuckin' nose off," the manager said. "Gimme." The whole hand had joined the fingers' anxious dance to attract the bill.

"Not good enough," Swag said. "Why'd he lock himself in the room?"

"He went wacko," the fat man said.

"What was he into?"

The manager looked at Swag with an air of disgusted disbelief. "What was he into?" the fat man spat back, fingers and hand coming to a reluctant halt. "He was into staying in the room, drinking his piss, and biting my nose off. That's what he was into. A real well-rounded life."

"What kind of business was he doing?"

"He was bell-hopping downtown," came the answer. "Hustling tourists on the side. Shit, why don't you ask him?"

"He's dead," Swag said, closing his fist around the money.

"No shit," the manager said, smiling for the first time. It was a greasy kind of smile, showing lots of gray chipped teeth with meat wedged between.

"No shit," Swag answered. "What happened to his stuff?"

"Who took him out?" the manager sneered. "Or did he do it himself?"

"Somebody with a knife."

"No shit," the manager repeated, his smile spreading, creasing the edges of the bandages.

"What happened to his stuff?" Swag asked.

"What happened to the money?" the fat man shot back, the smile immediately fading.

Swag handed him the bill and then pulled out another.

"I got his stuff back here," the manager said at the sight of the new bill. Then he turned and opened the closet door at the back of the room.

Swag watched as the fat man pulled down a cheap cloth suitcase and threw it on the floor between them. Kneeling, Swag ran the zipper around and looked inside. Underwear, a battered polyester suit. A couple of cheap shirts. Two pairs of cracked leather shoes. Buried in one corner was a manila envelope. Inside was a tangle of gold-plated jewelry: Statues of Liberty charms, Empire State Building necklaces, NYC emblems. It was the kind of stuff you could buy by the pound and try to sell on the street.

Swag rezipped the suitcase.

"Some fuckin' estate, huh? You ain't gonna challenge the will, are you?" The fat man chuckled. "There was a bellhop uniform. The hotel sent some people over for it."

"Let's see the room," Swag said.

The manager didn't answer. Groaning slightly from the effort, he lifted the suitcase and threw it back carelessly in the closet. "Okay," he finally said, "let's go."

The room was back at the end of the hall. Swag could see where it was by the bloodstains on the wall. E.C. was a little guy, but he must have put up a hell of a fight. Not all of the blood could have come from the manager's nose. Alongside the door were two or three holes in the Sheetrock at waist level, as if someone had punched or kicked it in.

The manager dug a ring heavy with keys from his pocket and unlocked the cracked door.

Swag pushed the door open and saw the room was already rented, its new occupant passed out on the cot in stagnant air thick with the odor of cheap wine. It was a windowless rectangle, five by ten at best.

"Huh?" the sleeping man groaned as Swag stepped into the room.

"Maid service, ya fuckin' rummy degenerate bastard," the manager snarled, and the sleeping man groaned again, turned over and went back to sleep.

"Police been here?" Swag asked.

"Came by," the manager said. "Same as you."

"How about the provosts?"

"What? Are you kiddin'? They ain't gonna come out over some psycho bellhop."

Swag turned and walked passed the manager into the hall, handing him the bill as he went.

"Was he acting strange before?" Sway asked. "Nervous?"

"The guy was a jitterbug," the manager said, closing the door. "Always running at the mouth. Always trying to get close to the next guy's action."

"How about just before?" Swag said.

The fat man took his time with this one. "You know, he did say one thing," the manager said. "He got like secretive, you know. Said, 'Don't tell nobody I'm here.'"

"Did you?"

"Did I what?"

"Did you tell anyone where he was?"

"Shit, who would I tell?" the fat man answered. "The guy lives here two years, never has a phone call. No mail. Never has no visitors. All of a sudden he's worried about his privacy."

"Maybe he was making friends," Swag said, starting back down the hall toward the stairs.

"Making friends," the manager grunted behind Swag. "Shit, nobody gave a rat's ass whether that guy lived or died."

Swag came down the stairs to the hotel and into sunshine. Pausing to take a breath at the entrance, he heard one of the group of men say, "How you keep a hotel manager from smelling?"

"Bite off his nose," came the inevitable answer.

The town house was on East 68th Street. An unimposing structure from the outside, inside it was decorated in sixteenth and seventeenth century French and English, which meant lots of heavy oak, all darkly stained. Moody giltframed portraits. Dim lighting. The furnishings were flawless, unless you happened to look under a few of the older pieces to see the discreet label of the leasing agent that offered authentic antiques. Other pieces, such as the massive armoire in the master bedroom, would reveal the blackstenciled name of the theatrical rental agency specializing in high-quality reproductions.

Despite the obvious care that had been taken in furnishing the three-story building, perhaps because of it, every room, including the small marble foyer with its elk-horn mirrored hat rack, retained a permanent air of transience.

Upstairs, on the third floor library, the books that lined the two walls were color coordinated. The complete works of Thackeray, Dickens, and Trollope in royal blue. Hugo, Flaubert, Céline, and Proust in red. The Spaniards were green. The Irish orange. Americans light blue. Italians ochre. And the Germans dark gray. Along the third wall, behind a massive desk, were hundreds of books on the subject of hunting.

The young woman, sitting in a large straight-backed chair, kicked off one ranch-grown baby croc slipper with the toe of the other and said, "But it is so hot."

"If you would like, madame, I could adjust the temperature downward a few degrees," the well-dressed man with the ponytail said. He spoke in a heavy French accent thick with obsequious inflection. Then to the T-shirted assistant, the young woman in the baseball cap, he offered a nod. The young woman vanished out the door instantly, scurrying off to adjust some hidden control.

"Nonsense, Madeline," the older gentleman said. "It must be sixty-five in here. Go take another shower if you're hot." He spoke English with the blandness of someone who had learned it by tape instruction. The Berlitz-American accent nearly covered his native Belgian French. Learning English late in life was an accomplishment of which he was proud. As long as they were in this country, he was determined to speak nothing else.

"It is hot, stifling," the woman insisted in a well-bred whine as she bent to remove her other shoe. "I can feel it, baking the bricks of the building. It is like an oven. Gerard, you have brought us to this terrible hot place and installed me in an oven for our holiday."

At the floorboards the artfully concealed air-conditioning ducts changed pitch for an instant, then fell silent as a stronger blast of arctic air pushed through.

"But how do they survive it? The people who live here?"

"They are well-accustomed to it," her husband snapped back.

"Quite so," the guy in the ponytail said, looking to curtail a family squabble. This was, after all, a vacation, a sporting one to be sure, but a holiday nonetheless.

The squabble was further squelched as the T-shirted and baseball-hatted assistant slipped quietly back into the room.

"Ah, Erica," the man in the ponytail said, as if greeting a lost comrade. "If you would do the pleasure of introducing Msr. Tibeau with his firearm."

"A pleasure, Monsieur Esterhazy," came the response.

All eyes in the room, including that of the young woman, turned toward the woman as she walked leisurely toward a far wall. Without hesitation she pushed in a polished oak panel to reveal a hidden doorway that opened into another room. A glimpse of guns, neatly racked behind beveled glass, could be seen. A moment later she returned, holding a rifle and an engraved Moroccan leather pouch the size of a woman's handbag.

"This is the Holland & Holland .700 Nitro Express," she began, moving across the room to display the gun to the husband and wife.

"Superb," the man whispered under his breath. And indeed the gun was superb. The walnut stock gleamed richly in infinite burls and a deep glow. The scroll engraving was the work of patient artisans.

She held the gun out, as if offering it to the man, then stepped back at the last moment, just as the customer's hands were about to come up and reach for it.

"Approximate weight is eighteen pounds," she began. "Barrel length is twenty-six inches of high grade chrome molybdenum."

"Magnifique," Gerard gasped, slipping back into French.

"As you can see, it is a double-barrel, twin-trigger arrangement, with a hinged front trigger," she continued. "There is the standard foresight with a folding moonsight protector and spearpoint block. The rear sight is a wide-V with one folding leaf."

Gerard could no longer control himself. Reaching up, he nearly begged to hold the gun.

But the young woman continued, working her hands up and down the different features, like a model on a television game show. "The .700 H & H features the same sidelock ejector as on the firm's Royal Deluxe series. That is to say, it also has the standard English fore end, leather recoil pad, and pistol handgrip."

"Please, mademoiselle," Gerard said, his eyes glowing like a little boy's.

"This is the most powerful big game gun ever manufactured," she said, handing the rifle down to the Frenchman, then walking back to the large desk and retrieving the leather satchel. "Only a handful were ever produced. The first was the product of more than four years of R and D and was shipped to a California collector back in eighty-eight."

Gerard took the gun greedily, running his hands along the stock.

The woman, too, admired it, her eyes glowing.

"It fires these," Erica said, her words drawing the Frenchman's head up like a puppet on a string. "This is an exact replica of the original Woodleigh cartridge; a thousand-grain jacketed bullet. Almost ten thousand foot pounds of muzzle felocity at two K per second."

The Frenchman stayed entranced at the huge three-and-a-half-inch shell she held between widely stretched thumb and forefinger. "Mon dieu," he gasped.

"This here is your backup cartridge," she said, bringing up another shell in the other hand. "A thousand-grain jacketed, with explosive tip. A quarter ounce of plastique. You could bring a commercial airliner down with it."

The Frenchman reached out for a cartridge. Erica safely handed him only the nonexplosive bullet as the Frenchman's wife moved over to get a closer look at the weaponry.

"I trust everything is to your satisfaction," the guy in the ponytail, Esterhazy, said. He was standing back, near the far wall, a thin smile on his face.

"Oui, oui," Gerard answered, examining the massive shell. "What precisely will I be hunting? Do you know yet?"

"Why, of course," came the answer. "Erica, do you care to inform our guest what his quarry will be?"

"A waiter," Erica said. "You'll be hunting waiter."

chapter five

SWAG TURNED EAST ON Canal Street. The sidewalks here were lined with peddlers hawking wares in tri- and quadlingual chants. They stood in front of cardboard boxes, battered card tables, tipped milk crates, and blankets loaded with merchandise. Others used open suitcases and shabby briefcases to display their wares.

The offerings were a senseless blur of scavenged artifacts from the crumbling city and next-to-worthless tourist trinkets; look-real gold jewelry, cheap souvenir ashtrays, novelty pens, plush animals, misprinted promotional gimme baseball caps, used clothing, boxes of tangled wires leading into nests of partially assembled tape decks, disk drives, speedometers, ancient Hoovers, and broken televisions. Plastic milk crates held grease-laden gears, aluminum armatures, shining carburetors, lengths of hosing, nuts, bolts, cheap tools, and cracked and anonymous printed circuit motherboards, fat with chips whose purpose was long forgotten.

Others offered art—"urban folk art," as the guidebooks charitably called it—the most common variety being skylines of glass shards glued on cardboard, along with charcoal renderings of street scenes, caricatures, and prison-style montages of glossy magazine photos glued on plywood.

And between them all, patches of counterfeit Gucci, Hermes, Movado, Grundig, Vuitton, Tiffany, Cartier, Scassi, Ebel, Ferragamo, manufactured by cheap labor in cavernous sweatshops and spread out from the gutter to mid-sidewalk like some bizarre garage sale of the apocalypse.

Swag walked slowly, feeling his wallet riding smoothly in his back pocket and the comfortable weight of the Colt in the back holster as he paced himself with the crowd. Instinct brought his shit-kicker boots in pace with the browsing shuffle of the sweat-sticky three-abreast river of people that flowed along the narrowed concrete midway through this low-rent carnival of commerce.

To step off the sidewalk did no good. The street was clogged with cars, taxis, and weaving scooters, motorcycles, bicycles. On the other side were indoor bazaars set into the ground level of shop-house storefronts, alleyways, and con-demned freight elevator shafts of sweatshop lofts.

This was the place where tourists came for bargains and the *authentique*. All too often, as the European guidebooks cautioned, things got way too authentique. Pickpockets, rip-off artists, and three-card monte players flourished down here. It was not uncommon to see some overweight German tourist huffing and puffing—camera bouncing against his chest—as he ran red-faced through the crowd in failed pursuit of a petty thief.

Up at the corner a small group of tourists jammed the sidewalk, watching a cross-legged black guy with dreadlocks cutting aluminum soda cans into small lamps; a dozen slices along the sides with a razor, then pressure at the top separating the ribs. But the crowd-gathering trick wasn't in the craft, it was the fact he was blind. Twin orbs of flawless white eyes, smooth as porcelain, stared up at the gathering as he worked.

Two or three Get'em Kids worked his crowd. Pint-sized steerers, their trick was to press a small trinket—earrings made from smooth glass, or rings of braided wire, into the tourists' hands with sincere wide-eyes pleas of *begabt, regalo, cadeau, gratuit, omake*, and free gift. Each kid steadfastly refused to take the slum merchandise back, and thereby obliged the tourists to listen to their pitch for the cheapest, best bargains in town for anything. Each Get'em worked for two or three stores and a handful of bars. Their ages topped out at twelve, thirteen max. Chosen for tenaciousness, they used their age as a weapon, the youngest of them concentrating on women tourists.

Swag didn't rate a second glance from the kids. Imprinted somewhere on his face or in his walk was the mark of a local. The Get'ems could smell it. To work a local was a waste of time. They worked for a flat fee for each customer they brought in and were known to follow uneasy Europeans and Japanese for blocks, running or childishly skipping alongside as they listed off their sources for the best trinkets, authentique 'merican, Italian, Thai, Spanish, Indian, and Pak meals, and cheap videos. Just darling little street urchins, trying to make a franc.

But if the tourists walked stonily ahead, the Get'ems would change attitude, shifting effortlessly to corrupt street kids and offering authentique just-fell-off-the-truck fashion, imported gold watches, bootleg cigarettes, hardcore porn. A half a block later they'd be offering beaucoup beautiful women, boys, little girls, triplets, and specialty acts. "Anything you want, anything," was their universal cry. "Français Nombre-fuckin'-une!"

Ignoring them would do no good—they had the persistence of a summer cold and operated on the carved-in-stone assumption that everyone wanted something for cheap. The only sure bet to escape their chanting, pleading offers was to hand over a franc or mark note.

A few blocks later Swag was on the border of Chinatown. A small knot of five or six Chinese teenagers loitered at the intersection. Members of the six or more gangs that acted as muscle for the tongs, they were done up in latest Chinatown fashion, slicked back retro-Elvis haircuts and Kevlar-reinforced leather jackets showing bare chests beneath. Their attitudes were uniformly those of bored predators; even the two girls who stood, hip-shot, at the center, looked bored in their tight plastic skirts. The leader lounged against a big bike, a thousand cc's or more, stripped of all chrome and brand name logos, and painted matte black. He effortlessly worked a butterfly knife in a blur of clicking motion, eyes never leaving the shuffling crowd that banked in a loose circle away from his group. Swag knew they were security for either the On Leong or Hip Sing tong, guarding the streets against unwanted peddlers in Chinatown. If you wanted to set up shop on their turf, you paid, *sans* negotiation. Not a single printed paper fan, back scratcher, or incense burner changed hands in Chinatown without the tongs getting their cut.

Swag crossed the street against the light, walking slowly between the jammed traffic. The opposite sidewalk was a wall of discount jewelry storefronts, Chinese restaurants, and discount electronics stores. In the center of the block was a short strip designated a cooperative trade zone by the tongs and Italian factions. As Swag understood it, the tongs collected their mandatory, weekly businessman's association dues, while the Italians shook down the street peddlers at around the same rate.

Coming through the line of peddlers, Swag moved sideways, heading toward the doorway next to Lung Rouge Restaurant, a Chinese place that catered to the French tourists. Inside the dark stairwell he paused; three Chinese symbols in red spray paint faced him on the opposite wall. Six feet high and two feet across, they could only be a warning. He headed up the narrow stairs toward the first office on the right. A faded index card provided the name in precise hand lettering—Green Lady Productions.

Swag knocked, felt the blow absorbed nearly soundlessly by the slab-layered steel beneath the gray-painted tin veneer, and knocked again, louder. A tiny peephole clicked open, revealing a pinpoint of light for just an instant before it clicked closed again.

When nothing happened after a few seconds, Swag gave the door a solid kick with the toe of his cowboy shit-kickers. The peephole clicked again.

"Emery Chen," Swag said, speaking loudly to make himself heard through the two inches or more of steel.

"Go 'way," a heavy Chinese accent called back. "Go 'way now!"

"Emery Chen," Swag repeated.

"Go 'way, no here," came the impatient reply.

Swag kicked the door again. And again came the voice, "Go 'way."

Swag was about to kick the door again when someone spoke out of the gloom of the shadows. "Maybe you better start walking."

Turning, Swag saw the young girl sitting up on the steps to the floor above. She was a gang member, no doubt about it. Not more than fifteen, but looked younger. She wore a light, black leather jacket and perfectly round mirrored glasses. Her hair was cut short and her chin stuck out in confident challenge; so did the chrome-plated automatic she held casually in her lap.

"It's okay," Swag said, taking a step away from the door. "Emery and me, we're old friends."

"Don't look that way," the kid said, stating fact. "Don't sound that way either."

"Give it a second, he'll open up," Swag said.

A half-dozen more kicks brought the peephole open again, this time for maybe ten seconds. Then the door opened.

Emery Chen was a good six-one and not more than 150 pounds. The silk Hong Kong suit he wore was the same light aqua-green as the custom shirt and the dyed ostrich shoes.

He was an Amerasian trick baby just turned thirty. According to legend, promoted chiefly by Emery himself, he was the product of a high-ranking Pentagon official and a Chinese prostitute from Canton turned restaurant hostess. Even if the story wasn't true, he had inherited enough crafty genes from somewhere to make it more than just a little plausible.

"What do you want, Swag?" Chen asked. His tone cut dead center between murderous suspicion and the nostril-twitching scent of a deal. Swag didn't take it personally; it was the same tone Emery used when ordering dinner.

Swag took his time in answering, carefully studying the room from just inside the door. The place was a maze of gray steel shelving, from linoleum floor to stamped-tin ceiling, leaving aisles so narrow that even a thin guy like Emery had to turn sideways to negotiate them. The shelves themselves buckled slightly under the weight of thousands of statuettes, all miniature reproductions of the Statue of Liberty.

Swag stepped into the nearest aisle and began walking, casually strolling down the claustrophobic maze. The maze, he knew, was a security precaution. If anyone uninvited came through the door, say the provosts, the maze would buy Emery maybe another eight or ten minutes.

"What do you want, Swag?" Chen repeated. "No, don't even answer, just tell me where the fuck do you think you're going?"

Swag took a right, then a left, and came out facing the only sizable break in the shelving at the front of the room. Lined up against a bank of grimy iron-framed windows, where chipped paint advertised a long-defunct martial arts school in Chinese and English, were a half-dozen silver propane tanks, topped off by crude cast-iron pots. No more than ten gallons each, they were filled with a grayish molten alloy that bubbled and fumed steadily.

An ancient Chinese guy tended the pots, adding scraps to each one. He worked slowly, measuring each handful of wheelweights, bar solder, tin snippings, and other scraps from the buckets that were lined up in front of the burners. The old guy paid no notice to the lead fumes that an old window fan labored to push out one of the open windows. Rather, he moved hunched and patient between the pots, feeding and skimming dross, and worrying over the molten metal like a chef.

Across the wall nearest the old guy was a group of three or four young ones, working the casting area. Swag watched as they broke open the sand molds to release a half-dozen newly minted Statues of Liberty, no more than six inches high.

"Still like the lady, huh, Emery?" Swag said.

"Just like I had the fucking copyright on her," Emery said. "She's been good to me. Everybody wants a copy of the green lady."

Swag watched as the four young guys began stringing the newly minted statues up across a length of stained doweling, hanging them by framing wire hooks, then dipping them into a tin trough that dyed them coppery brown.

"What, Swag? Why'd you come here?" Emery asked, nervous, maybe even with reason. The last time Swag saw him, a half-dozen young toughs were getting ready to kick Emery's ass in a Mott Street alley. Swag intervened, but now the favor had come due, and Emery knew it.

Swag didn't answer, rather, he turned slowly, heading back into the maze.

"Now, where the fuck are you going?" Emery hissed, falling in behind Swag. "What? What is it?"

It took him a little while to find it, but he did. Coming out on the other end, he found himself facing a wall lined with gray steel shelving filled with yet more statuettes. Cut into a narrow break in the shelving was a door. A square of one-way mirror was set into it at eye level, and just below that, a shuttered gun port, like the kind you'd find on an armored car.

Behind the door was Emery Chen's real business. Swag knew that on the other side of the vault-thick portal was a U.C.-Berkeley graduate metallurgist in a gray lab coat. The metallurgist presided over the best, if not the largest, black-market foundry on the East Coast. In another section of the room a dozen jewelers labored at tables, plying their craft in eighteen-carat gold and sterling silver.

Behind the door, snatched chains, stolen watches, boosted silverware, antique tea services, weighty silver tureens, rings, brooches, belt buckles, tie clips, earrings, cuff links, and any other form that stolen precious metal takes, vanished into a pot, to emerge as something else that could be sold in one of Chinatown's thousand jewelry stores or molded into an exact replica of the Statue of Liberty that would easily pass customs.

Emery, noticing Swag's gaze settle for an uncomfortably long time on the door, pulled his coat back to reveal the .38 wheel-gun at his hip. The gun was solid gold, except for the ivory grips. "No more fuckin' around, understand? What do you want, Swag?" he repeated. "You had the nickel tour, now start talking."

"You remember E.C.?" Swag asked. Behind them water hissed as the old man performed some secretive smelting task.

"Yeah, real good customer," Emery replied. "Used to buy a gross, gross and a half of the statues a month. Lay them off at that hotel he worked at. Had a deal with the gift shop."

"When was he in last?"

Emery took a step back, moving his hands up in front like a pedestrian stopping a taxi running a light. "Hold on there, Jack, you're not a cop anymore."

Swag put on a hurt look. "You don't want to cooperate, Emery. I'm shocked and disappointed."

"I said, you don't have any more juice," Emery tried, his voice rising in pitch. "You hear what I'm telling you?"

"Is that the bathroom?" Swag asked, nodding to the gray door.

"Yeah, but it's for employees only," Emery said. Swag could sense the nervousness rising up inside of Emery, a reflexive jumpiness born out of childhood, of growing up in the secretive kitchens and basements of Hunan and Mandarin restaurants along Pell, Mott, and Doyers streets.

Swag cupped his hands on either side of his face and peered at his own reflection in the one-way mirror.

"What the fuck do you want, Swag?" Emery said, his anxiety turning quickly to annoyance. "You want to buy some statues, I'll give you a good deal. You can hawk them on the street. Sell 'em to your clients."

"How about a tour?" Swag asked. "You got some real artisans here. Real old-world."

"That's it, you're out of here," Emery spat, his right hand flying back down to go for the gold piece.

Before Emery could reach the fourteen-carat .38, Swag grabbed him by the wrist. It was so thin, Swag's fingers met in an almost closed fist around it as he brought it back up between them.

"Hey, Emery, now don't go getting urban on me here," Swag said. He stepped closer, putting Emery's back to the back room's one-way mirror. No doubt there was security posted there, probably some gang member with a sawed-off. "You understand what I'm telling you?"

"What is this bullshit?" Emery said, his voice unexpectedly low as he struggled to get his hand back. "I don't know nothing."

"When was he in last?" Swag said, getting right in Emery's face.

"Shit, do I look like his business manager?" Emery said. "Whyn't ask him?"

"He's dead," Swag said.

Emery's struggle ceased immediately at the news. "No shit?"

"No shit," Swag answered, and released his grip.

"That's fucked up," Emery said, genuinely mournful as he shook circulation back into his wrist, then began rubbing it lightly with his other hand. "What happened?"

"Somebody stabbed him in a bathroom," Swag said, leaving out the best part, about the four-hundred-year-old shiv.

"No shit?" Emery asked.

"No shit," Swag confirmed. "The bucket-shop guys are wearing black armbands; six bookies slit their own throats."

"Yeah, I know what you mean," Emery replied sadly. "I kinda feel like wearing one. That guy was a piece of work. I made some money when he was around. We did some investments together, you know?"

Swag knew that Emery was probably wearing some of

E.C.'s investments right now. Probably got the money on some gold mine in the south of France, or a very limited partnership in a Jersey vineyard with black-market vine clippings that produced Secaucus Sauvignon. "When was he in last?"

"Month ago, maybe," Emery said. "Maybe a little longer. I had a real sweet deal for him. Want me to fill you in on it?"

"No," Swag answered. "What was he like? Nervous, pissed off, what?"

"He was happy, man," Emery said. "We were going to do a little side business, you know, we'd all get well. Want to hear about it?"

"What about before that?" Swag asked. "He talk about anyone? Any other deals he was doing?"

"Naw, nothing," came the response.

"Now I'm going to ask you something and I need an honest answer," Swag said. "If I find out you're lying, I'll come back and kill you."

"What is this come-back-and-kill-me bullshit?" Emery said, feigning an insulted attitude. "Just ask the question."

Swag paused for two beats, then said, "E.C. do any other business with you? The pennyweight kind?"

"Not his style," Emery answered seriously. "He was a guy with a passkey to a hotel, you think he would, but he didn't."

Swag eyed Emery carefully, looking for a hint of a lie and knowing he wouldn't see one if E.C. had been hauling in boosted jewelry in wheelbarrows.

"Look, nobody'd want to kill him," Emery said. "It'd be like robbing the bank where you kept your own money."

It was all so very tedious, the woman thought. Inevitably, a man's passions are enough to bore the dead. It was pursuit without reason. Competition toward no goal. Even the money, after a time, of course, seemed not worth the trouble. But nothing he did now seemed worth the trouble or expense. Elephants in Kenya. Wild boar in Bengal. Brazilian jaguars. If there was a country that was hot, uncivilized, and grubby, then he would find it. And think of something to kill in it.

But worse, the boredom for his hunting had infected her. Even shopping held no pleasure. The designs were so retro and naïve. The jewelry so predictable. She felt as if she had seen it, and worse, bought it all before. Nothing held any pleasure. And, she wondered, with a certain jolt of fear, would she end up like those old women, who gossip and natter in the Riviera cafés, their skin baked like leather, their eyes numbed by the sun and a lifetime of shopping?

True, the young man that Monsieur Esterhazy had arranged for her had proved an amusing diversion—charming even, in his own primitive way. But that was only an afternoon, and she surprised herself with no desire to see him again.

She looked across the table at her husband eating his food—grilled snapper, delicately browned, and covered in mushrooms—thinking of the names of good divorce lawyers.

Her husband glanced up, caught her eye across the table, and smiled. "Quite good, no?" he asked.

"Yes, very," she answered. Then she looked down at her plate of veal for the first time since it had arrived and examined its artful arrangement amid miniature vegetables. The veal bored her.

They finished the meal in silence. When the white-jacketed waiter returned to take their dessert orders, her husband looked up at him slyly, then back across the table as he gave the order.

The woman shook her head slightly. Dessert too, for all its forbidden calories, was also tiresome.

"That's him," her husband said.

"That is your latest prize?" she asked, turning her attention to the retreating waiter. He was neither short nor tall, fat nor thin.

"Yes," came the answer. "We begin the hunt soon."

"Do tip him well, then," the woman answered.

chapter six

SWAG HEARD VARIATIONS ON THE SAME STORY all over town. Everyone, it seemed, had an Easy story. They were like old jokes, repeated again and again, changing only slightly with each retelling. Easy's investments, hustles, and scams were the stuff of legend—street apocrypha that circulated freely and were told almost wistfully, as final and conclusive proof that yes, there was a sucker born every minute. Shares in a Vegas warehouse filled with Jerry Lewis memorabilia had been bought sight unseen to unload in Paris. Stock options in Wyoming Silver Mines had been sold. The recipe for synthetic truffles, purportedly long-suppressed by the French government and recently purloined from an embassy safe, had been sold. Diamonds smuggled out of a mine in Arkansas, beneath the noses of the German owners, had changed hands, only to turn to glass the moment Easy touched them. He'd purchased a shipment of genetically engineered giant shiitake mushrooms, but received instead the bill of lading for the shipment.

Easy's only problem was cash. He'd sleep on the street and steal food from the hotel slop trays for a month to save the minimum buy-in to the next deal. But even then he barely scraped together the ante.

For two days Swag checked on Easy and found no motive for murder. He was a man beloved by every low-rent hustler, con artist, investment broker, and bookmaker in the city. Who, after all, could hate a guy who'd put money into any proposition—the longer the odds, the better—then pay up in cash when the deal inevitably fell through? Easy was that rare breed of loser who didn't learn from his mistakes, except how to make better, more spectacular choices of bad judgment. He was always one step away from that big score—the one that would put him on top. But for all of that, he was small-time, even in his own small-time world.

By late afternoon Swag was out of options and stranded at an East Side coffee shop in the mid-thirties. He dialed the number from memory, then listened as it rang a half-dozen times.

"Talk," Narcadia said.

"You want to hear a joke?" Swag said.

Narcadia was a long time in answering. Swag pictured the tumorous head on the other end, the concealed lips pulled tight beneath the bulbous growths. "No jokes, my friend," he said at last, using words as if he had paid cash for them.

"You have anything to tell me?" Swag asked.

Again there was a long pause, the faint sound of wheezing echoing through the pay phone's receiver, like background noise when the line's put on hold. Beneath the sound of the labored breathing, Swag could almost hear the wheels of Narcadia's thoughts clicking into place. And then Swag thought, no, not wheels, but the clicking beads of an abacus measuring the percentages. "Stay where you're at, my friend," Narcadia said at last. "Somebody'll be by."

"You know where I'm at?" Swag said, already knowing the stupidity of the question. Narcadia would have the phone rigged with an incoming call-number display. No doubt he'd also have it computer cross-referenced to the phone company's records of every pay phone, cellular, and private line in the city.

"Have a cup of coffee," Narcadia said. "Chill for ten minutes."

Swag began to answer, but the line was already dead. Ten minutes later a bike messenger came through the door, carrying the thin gum-rubber wheel of a racing bike in one hand and the *Times* in the other. The kid took his time, sitting at the counter, ordering a burger, fries, and a soda. He ate slowly, not touching the paper by his side.

Swag watched him warily, ordered a third cup of coffee and smoked a cigarette. Young, not more than fifteen, sixteen, but street smart. Dark hair, thin nose that showed a slight bump from having been busted. Steady feral eyes. He was entirely forgettable, the type who could get lost in an empty elevator.

When the kid got up to leave, he picked up his nylon shoulder bag and bike wheel and walked three or four steps, leaving the paper on the counter, then walked back to it. The maneuver was flawless, just a kid forgetting his paper, then remembering to go back for it.

As the kid passed Swag's booth with the paper under his arm, he paused again, searched his pockets in vain, patting them hurriedly. "You got a cigarette?" the kid asked.

Swag held up the pack, shaking one out. "Take two," he said.

A momentary expression of confusion spread across the kid's face, like a well-rehearsed actor thrown off his timing by a piece of ad lib. He took one cigarette. "Thanks," he said. "You want a paper?"

"Sure," Swag said, reaching out for it.

The kid nodded grimly, then left. Outside, he tossed the cigarette in the gutter.

Swag found what he was looking for on the op-ed page. The page was newsprint, Narcadia's report done up in the same justified type as the original; even the day's headlines were authentic.

The first dozen graphs summed up and repeated the information that Kat Jones had given him. The remainder outlined twenty-three additional murders within the last six months with the same victim profile—no family, no friends. The bodies had been identified through criminal records, hospital records, and place of employment. Most had worked in bars, restaurants, and hotels. All of them anonymous joints without a steady clientele. None of them would be missed. There were seven additional possibles, three hookers and four low-rent scam artists.

Half of them had been under observation at Bellevue for Urban Trauma. Four had some run-in with the law within a week of getting zotsed by "assailant or assailants unknown."

Recaps of the coroner's reports give only the briefest rundown of the cause of death, which varied from "multiple gunshot wounds" to "asphyxiation." But Swag knew that the real story wasn't written out on autopsy reports. The key was in the weapons used.

All had been turned over to the city authorities for cremation out on Hart Island. The police and provost records mirrored those Kat Jones had provided.

Swag threw some money down on the counter, refolded the paper, and walked back to the pay phone.

Kat picked up on the second ring. "Dead Banker," she said, above the din of a busy bar. The background noise was patently false, an electronic enhancement to lure unsuspecting customers downtown.

"It's me," Swag answered, watching the scattering of traffic on the street.

"What can you tell me?" Kat said, her voice relaxed. "It's been a couple of days, you know."

"Sounds busy there," Swag replied. "I'll call back later."

"Hold on a second," Kat said, and almost instantly the sound of clinking glasses and laughter was cut short, like a television laugh track.

"No need to chase everyone out on my account."

"Quit fucking around, Swag," Kat shot back. "And tell me what you know."

"That girl, Sandy, she have any relatives? Friends?"

"No, nothing like that," Kat said, making friends and relatives sound like luxuries or liabilities. "She's a kid off the bus, but likes some of the same games as the owner." Kat paused for two beats, then said, "At least she pretends like she does."

"What kind of games?" Swag asked.

"The kind you play in costume. What, you want to see the videos? It's kinked, but not serious. Not even painful."

"And nobody knows about them, right? Not the games, the fact that they're playing them."

"Look, this isn't exactly what you'd call a secure line," Kat said. "You want to chat, come on down."

"I want to talk to the girl," Swag said. "And the guy who's paying."

"Nix on the second," Kat answered immediately. "You want to see the girl, be at the hospital in an hour. Go in through Emergency. I'll set it up for you."

"I'll be there," Swag said. But Kat had already hung up.

Bellevue always had the reputation as the world's foremost rubber Ramada. Forget that it'd always been a city hospital, from influenza and TB right on through. Say Bellevue, and you'll get a quick flash of suspicious recognition.

The old Bellevue is what people remember, a square red-brick building with a chunk lopped out of it. Surrounded by a high brick fence and a moat of dead grass and trash, the old building stood as an imposing sight on First Avenue. But that facility was long out of service. Relegated to a warehouse for those too frail, infirm, or stupid to find a squat or to build shelter down by the river, the old building now offered dormitory-style housing for thousands.

The new facility was farther back. Built in neat light gray cubes of identical windows, it called to mind not a hospital, but a maze of offices and perfect cubicles. If the old building conjured images of pre-electroshock and water-therapy horrors, the new one instilled a fear of bureaucratic hell—printed forms and ringing telephones left unanswered.

Outside were a scattering of gawkers and hawkers. They began to line up early in the afternoon, but by midnight the sidewalk around the emergency room and ambulance bays would be thick with spectators, anxious to see whatever horrors the EMS buses sirened in from around the city. Gun and Knife Club groupies, they gathered by the E.R.

entrance and adopted the medicos' lingo. "They swooped and scooped a guy down in Chelsea last night. GSW." "Head?" "No, through and through, in upper quad. Brought him in with sixty over forty." "Still viable. Bleeding like hell." "All bleeding eventually stops, right?"

Swag strolled warily up through the parking lot as two buses whizzed by on either side. By the time he reached the entrance, the EMS guys were hauling out two men—their hands in plastic bags, which meant felony shooting suspects. Probably shot each other.

As he approached the door, the groupies had already flocked at the E.R. bay, anxiously looking over the victims, shooting Polaroids and talking up the team. "You boys are busy today," one of the groupies shouted from the crowd. A couple of Polaroids flashed in the shadow of the building.

"We got blood on our hands and smiles on our faces," one of the attendants called back as they wheeled the two men into the E.R.

Swag walked through the ambulatory entrance, the doors humming open in front of him with a medicinal wave of just slightly cooler air.

A nurse behind a glass partition pushed a gray plastic tray through the opening and nodded slightly toward a hand-lettered sign that said, "EMPTY POCKETS OF ALL ITEMS."

Swag hesitated, looking behind the closed door next to the nurse, toward the metal detector.

"You want to see a doctor?" the nurse asked. "Then empty your pockets."

"I want to see a patient," Swag answered.

"Around the other entrance," came the crisp response.

"She's expecting me."

"That's nice," he nurse answered, pulling the gray plastic tray back, without any thought. "Around the other entrance."

"Her name's Sandy Mann," Swag said, leaning forward on the sliver of desk. "She's in observation."

The nurse's head snapped up and she eyed Swag suspiciously. "One moment please," she said, then lifted the phone and punched in three digits.

She said something Swag couldn't hear and set the phone down. "Someone will show you up," she said.

Two minutes later a couple of orderlies, one black and one white, came up behind Swag, walking soundlessly on crepe soles. They didn't look like any orderlies Swag had ever seen. They both wore their hair short, military style, and stood ramrod straight, muscles bulging out from the white short-sleeve summer uniforms. The smaller one, the white guy, was six-five and 250, the bigger one was a darker mirror image with two inches and twenty-five pounds added on.

"Swag?" the bigger orderly asked quietly.

"Yeah," Swag answered.

"Come on, then," the other said.

The nurse buzzed them through the door. As they passed the metal detector, it sounded for an instant, snapping the uniformed security guard's head up. When he saw it was the two bruisers, he returned to his doze. Swag bet that the alarm would have sounded if the orderlies had walked through by themselves.

They walked three abreast down a hall smelling of vomit, urine, and disinfectant. The orderlies hung back a careful half step, ready to move if Swag tried anything funny—or even remotely humorous.

For the length of the hall, patients waited in a nightmare of emergency room triage. They were lined up along both walls, sitting slumped and dozing in wheelchairs, stretched out on gurneys, sitting on the bare tile of the floor. Old men, young men, mothers with children. Young women staring straight ahead, and older ones nodding gently to themselves. A few sweated in fevers, huddled in tightly wrapped blankets. Others bled quietly into homemade bandages or ventured a look at an infected wound.

At the end of the hall was the waiting room, the dead gray eye of a television staring down on the crowd that filled the neat schoolroom rows of molded plastic chairs. Swag tried for a count of the patients, but couldn't guess. Two hundred at least, probably more. Used to be, you'd wait two or three days to see some bleary-eyed intern or resident. Now the wait was up to a week.

There was a small group waiting for the elevator. When it arrived, the larger orderly hustled Swag to the front, urging him forward with a hand on the back, while the slightly smaller one discouraged the others from entering with an outstretched hand like a traffic cop.

"You don't like to be crowded, huh?" Swag asked.

"Do you?" the big one answered, deadpan.

The smaller one brought out a ring of keys, punched one into the control panel and turned it. The elevator came to a smooth stop between floors.

"Against the wall," the bigger one said. "You know the position." His voice was smooth, bored almost.

Swag eyed them carefully. They weren't crowding him. No intimidation and nothing personal, they were just doing their jobs.

Swag turned with a slight hesitation, placed two hands above his head and leaned into the wall, feet spread.

The search was fast and thorough. When the smaller one found the Colt in the back holster, he pulled it out slowly, politely almost. "Nice piece," he said, hefting its perfect balance with appreciation. "You'll get it back on the way out."

"What about a receipt?" Swag asked, coming around in time to see the small one tuck it into the front of his pants, then cover it discreetly with his shirt.

"Is that a joke or something?" the small one said, turning the key to restart the elevator.

"Yeah," Swag answered.

"That's real funny," the big one said to Swag. Then to his partner, "You think that was funny?"

"Yeah, it was a laugh riot," he answered dryly.

"You're not laughing," Swag noted.

"On the inside I'm busting a gut," came the deadpan response.

The elevator stopped on the twenty-first floor, a locked

unit. The three of them moved easily through the double swinging hospital doors, buzzed through by a pair of guards. Patients wandered about, some in street clothes, others in knee-length hospital gowns. They watched Swag and the two goons as they passed, trying to classify the three into the well-ordered world of the ward.

The doors to a couple of the semiprivate rooms were open, and Swag looked in as they passed to see more patients, stretched out on beds, killing time, smoking and reading yellowed paperbacks.

Always the smoking, Swag thought. Hospitals and prisons kept the cigarette companies going. They smoked out of boredom and loneliness, with entire miniature economies and manners arising from the need. The prisoner who bums a cigarette from an inmate to test attitude. The endless card games played for cigarettes. And finally, the shopping list of small pleasures bartered for a pack or a handful.

A couple of doctors, residents, passed by, looking up from their clipboards just long enough to administer suspicious stares to the bogus orderlies that flanked Swag. The two seemed not to notice.

"So, what are you guys, orderlies?" Swag asked.

"Physical therapists," the big one said.

"Yeah, we're board-certified physical therapists," the other put in. "Licensed in the states of New York, New Jersey, Nevada, and South Dakota."

Swag decided to let it go at that.

Turning a corner, they came to the final door on the hallway. This one, stenciled KEEP THIS DOOR LOCKED AT ALL TIMES, marked the entrance to the locked-down, secure back ward. A high-security section reserved for the florid psychotics. A Thorazine theme park.

A guard on the other side buzzed them in, and they walked through, the door clicking closed, catching them in a small elevator-size room between two doors. The second door buzzed open, and they went through.

Swag started briefly at the sight when the heavy doors

were flung open. Then he realized there weren't any patients on this ward.

"Where is everyone?" he asked as they walked by the first half-dozen rooms.

"Coffee break," the big one answered.

They passed the empty nurse's station and came to the last room. The only door on the ward that was closed.

The smaller of the two goons knocked on the door.

"Who is it?" called a perfectly sane voice from the other side.

"Visitor, Sandy," the goon said.

"Trés great!" came the enthusiastic reply. "Come on in!"

chapter seven

THE ROOM WAS A SMALL box, just big enough for the two
beds, writing desks, and chairs that it was built around.
What someone had done was to remove one of the beds
and replace it with an elaborate sound system, large screen
HDTV, wet bar, microwave, and compact refrigerator.
Where one of the desks had once been bolted to the floor,
there was now a three-mirrored vanity, with enough
makeup to paint, powder, and scent every high-dollar pross
from Chambers Street to the Bronx.

. Next to the bed on the hospital-issue desk was a high-
speed fax, a cellular phone with digital readout, and a wrist
pager. Swag noted that the institutional venetian blinds
were partially obscured by tasteful blue and pink curtains.
The small single window looked out over the FDR and
across the river to Queens.

But it was the girl that held Swag's attention. She was
sitting up in an adjustable hospital bed on pink and blue
silk sheets, her feet curled under her like a cat, writing in
a thick Hermès day organizer. She was wearing a pair of
tight-fitting French jeans, a blood red silk shirt, and matching lipstick. Her face was the showstopper. She had a face
out of some Renaissance portrait, heart-shaped, with large
dark eyes and a lower lip that drooped just enough to look
like it quivered easily. He also thought that it took a special
type of person to keep an active day organizer in a mental
institution.

"You must be Swag," she said, closing the notebook. "Pull up a chair, why donchya."

The voice didn't go with the face or the outfit. It was a voice right off the street, as hard as curbstone in winter. It was the kind of voice that Swag had heard a thousand times before. The one that belonged to some girl who stepped off the bus at Port Authority five or ten years ago, looked long and hard into the shark tank, and felt right at home for the first time in her life.

Swag pulled the spindle-legged chair out from the vanity and sat down. He hadn't known what to expect; maybe secretly he'd expected some dizzy chick straight off the farm—the latest model of disposable chippies that the city had consumed at an astonishing rate since the beginning. But he was wrong, and the girl sitting in front of him, with those flat gun-metal eyes, made as much sense as anything.

She studied him for a moment, then focused on a point just over his shoulder, her eyes growing slightly wider.

"We'll be outside," the bigger goon said.

"That's good," the girl said.

Swag didn't turn to watch the goons leave, but listened for the sound of the door closing to start talking. "Nice room," he said. "More people would check in if they knew what the accommodations were."

"Frances Farmer goes tasteful, you mean?"

"Who?" Swag asked, his attention suddenly drawn to a pair of animal eyes staring out from under the bed. Too big for a rat, too small for a person. Swag decided it must be a dog. And by the way they looked, feral and unblinking, he could guess that no tail was wagging back there in the darkness.

"She was an actress, went nuts, with a little help from friends and relatives," Sandy Mann said. "You'll see her in old movies sometimes, later-night stuff. I'm a sucker for old movies. Can I get you something?"

"Like what?" Swag asked, thinking of a glass of water.

"Well, let's see," she replied, swinging her legs over the side of the bed and reaching over and opening the drawer to the vanity. "We've got haloperidol. Thorazine, Prozac, Librium. Here's some French stuff, I don't know what the hell it does. Probably makes you saner than shit."

Swag watched as she started digging around in the drawer, fishing out plastic bottles and dumping them amid the makeup. A small vial, its label peeled off like a bottle of beer, held a sluggish liquid, Prolixin.

Shaking his head, he said, "No thanks, I'm fine."

"Don't be too hasty now," she warned, and continued emptying the vials onto the table. "What have we here, ten mil caps of Librium, double-grain phenobarb, Noludar, Clozaril, paraldehyde. And here's a blast from the past, buncha benzodiazepine and psychotrope tranks—Valium, Xanax, Ativan, Halcion."

"You've been taking all of those?" Swag asked, disbelieving.

She looked up suddenly, shutting the desk drawer. "Come on, you'd have to be crazy to take all this shit," she shot back. "But they got some residents in here that aren't afraid to use their pads, if you know what I mean? So I figure it's maybe a good investment, for when I get out."

Swag let it pass. Sale, distribution, and possession of black-market pharmaceuticals were capital offenses now, but Sandy Mann seemed to know her business. "Whose idea was this?" Swag said, jerking his head slightly, indicating the room.

"We, I mean. . . ." Here she groped for a word. "My . . ."

"Friend?" Swag tried.

"My friend," she confirmed. "He thought this was more secure."

"More secure than what, some East Side clinic?" Swag asked.

"Yeah. We shopped a few," she said. "They got shit for security and not enough room for our own people. Nobody gets on or off this floor without a good reason. When I checked in, I was strung out, really stressed to the max. But nobody can get to me here. You see those so-called loonies wandering around on the other wing. Half of them are our people."

She talked tough, not crazy like Swag had supposed she might. No disorientation, no paranoia or hysterics, just a barely discernible pulse of fear that put an edge to her words. If she weren't hooked up with some high roller, that fear would have taken over.

"So who's after you?" Swag asked.

Sandy Mann brought her legs back up on the bed, crossed her ankles, and gave the control button a push. The back end purred up into a sitting position. When she was good and comfortable, she said, "That's what you're being paid for. To find out."

Swag leaned back in the chair, but not putting his full weight on, for fear he'd shatter it. "Let's start again," he said. "Why do you think someone's after you?"

She sighed. "Shit, you're a real waste of money, aren't you? If I wanted to answer moron questions, I could've gone to the police or the provosts."

"You did, though," Swag said.

Her eyes widened a little, and she cocked her head slightly to one side. "You know that for a fact, do you?"

"Yeah," Swag answered. "I know that for a fact. Just like I know they brushed you off."

"So they brushed me off," she said. "What, is that a surprise? They probably thought I was some psychochick off the street."

"Tell me what you told them," Swag said.

She sighed deeply, gave Swag another good once-over, to make sure he was listening, then began in a bored voice. "Okay, so I get a phone call about three weeks ago," she said. "Some guy said I was dead. Big fuckin' deal, huh?"

Swag shrugged.

"Yeah, well right," she said. "That's how I took it. You work in a bar, you're gonna get threats. So I go home, and there's a note on the door to the apartment. It says, 'Good speaking with you today. Till we meet again,' or some shit. Nothing to take to the police."

"But now they know where you live," Swag offered.

"Right," she answered. "They fuckin' know where I live. Then I walk in the door, and there's this laser sight, a red dot, trained on my hand, so I'd be sure to see it. It's coming in through the window."

"But they don't shoot?"

"No, it just kinda follows me around," she answered. "I lift my hand it stays with it, then runs up my arm and clicks off. So I bolt. Check into a hotel under a phony name. Ten minutes later there's a fruit basket, bottle of wine, and a note that says, 'Till we meet again.'"

Tension started creeping into her voice with the memory of it. Swag could hear the fear rising in her, straining at her throat.

"Next day, everywhere I go, there's a note or a message," she continued. "The grocery store. The bar. I walk down the street and a kid comes up and hands me a note, 'Till we meet again.'"

"How long?" Swag asked.

"After the first couple of days I just say fuck it," she said. "But I can't shake it, you know? I mean it's every single day, four or five times a day. It was driving me nuts."

Swag nodded, encouraging her to continue.

"So I called my friend," she said. "He sent out a couple of guys, to follow me."

"And?" Swag asked.

"And nothing," she shot back. "Not a fuckin' thing. They disappeared. Nothing, nada, not a trace. About then I started to get a little schizy, you know. Couldn't eat. Couldn't sleep. Couldn't take an order or write a ticket at the bar."

"Okay, here's the basics," Swag said. "I gotta run them by you."

She nodded, as if tired.

"Any enemies?" Swag asked.

"Nobody this sick," she answered. "Some customer complains I poured light on the scotch, he's gonna do this? This is real wacko stuff we're dealing with here."

"Friends?"

"Yeah, I got dozens of them," she answered.

"Name five," Swag asked. "Five who know where you live."

"Get real here, you don't go telling people where you live," she said, sneering. "I don't need people ringing my buzzer. Calling me on the phone."

Swag let the comment pass. She had no friends. Maybe she had a couple of dozen acquaintances, but nobody she'd let watch her back. "What about family?"

"Naw, no family," she answered. "I guess I'm just a girl who's all alone in this world."

"Owe anyone money?" Swag asked. "Anyone owe you money? Got any side deals going?"

"No, no, and no," she shot back.

"What about the guy who set you up here?" Swag continued. "You getting along okay? He have a wife? Any other side action going?"

"Whattaya mean, side action?" she snapped. "He don't need no side action."

Swag started playing it tougher. The answers were coming too fast. She was too sure. "Everyone's looking for strange, new, different," he said. "You know what I'm talking about?"

"I know what you're talking about," she said, reaching into the desk drawer and pulling out a pack of cigarettes and a lighter. "And I'm telling you now, I'm strange, different, new and improved. He's not going to stray. And I'm not going to fuck it up with some bullshit, like putting the squeeze on him."

Swag watched as she lit a cigarette, inhaled deeply and sent a stream of smoke toward the ceiling. "What about Dullen, E.C., you know him?"

"Just as a guy who was around," she said, bringing the cigarette away from her mouth. "No contact, business, nothing. And I didn't know any of those others, either."

Swag was out of questions. He didn't expect any answers

in the first place. Mostly, he just wanted to see who he was working for.

"So, what? You got this thing wrapped up, talking to me?" she asked sarcastically. "Whyn't you hit the bricks, walk around, make me feel like you're worth the money?"

Swag got up slowly from the chair. "Real pleasure meeting you," he said as he turned toward the door.

"Yeah, it was the high point of my fuckin' life," Sandy Mann said. "A real thrill."

Swag had his hand on the door when it opened from the outside. The two goons had been waiting to escort him back down.

George could feel them closing in. He could feel them getting closer now, even in the tiled chaos of the kitchen. It was odd, the way everything was so normal—yet different. The backs of the three chefs—Phillip, Clive, and Dane—hunched over the burners of the stove, cooking. Their assistants moving about the stainless prep and garnish tables. The revolving order carousel, filled with check dupes. It all seemed so *normal*, yet he knew it was different. They were coming for him.

George lingered in one corner by the dishwasher, feeling the steam rising at his back. His hands were shaking so badly he had to hold one in the other or jam both into his pockets to still them. The sweat that soaked through his uniform shirt was clammy and cold.

Once again he pulled the neatly folded paper from his wallet and read the suicide note. A note written in his own handwriting, which he had received in the mail that morning.

Going to the police was useless. He would have to leave forever. But he needed money. Putting the sheet of paper away, he felt in his pocket for the gun. It was a tiny automatic he'd bought only the day before. And now he knew what he had to do. His motorcycle was just outside the back door. A small bike by city standards, a rebuilt 350, but it would get him through the tunnel to Jersey and then, well, then he'd find something. Maybe head for Cali or the Rim—go back to chauffeuring.

But he'd need money. Not a lot of money, but enough to start a new life. And suddenly it was so simple. Walking stiffly past the double sinks filled with pots, he pushed through the swinging doors and into the back hall. The doors swung closed, muffling the kitchen's noise.

As he walked down the cement floor of the corridor, he saw that the office door was open. A radio was playing inside; easy listening music, something with a lot of strings.

As George withdrew the gun, he felt his chest tightening. He could feel the sweat pouring down his face, gathering across his upper lip. Suddenly it was very difficult to breathe.

George forced a deep breath and pulled the gun from his pocket. Then, clicking off the safety, he walked into the office. He held the gun low against his leg, waiting for the manager to look up.

"I need money," he said, voice quavering.

The manager, an old man in shirtsleeves, began to say something, then thought better of it and laid a ballpoint down on the desk.

"I need money," George said. "Please. . . ."

The manager's mouth snapped shut as he quickly began pulling rubber-banded rolls of dollars, francs, marks, and credit card receipts from the desk drawer.

"Why?" the manager asked as George began stuffing bills and credit card slips into his pockets. When his pockets were full, he pulled off the shin-length apron and made a bundle of it to gather up the remainder. He worked frantically, using one hand; the other kept the gun, shaking, in the general direction of the manager.

"They're going to kill me," George spat back, folding the apron and clutching it to his stomach. "I can feel it! I haven't slept in two days. They're out there now! Now!"

"Don't do this," the old man said, trying to speak calmly. "We'll work this out. Take the night off. We'll forget it. The whole thing."

"Yeah, you'd like that, wouldn't you?" George answered, stepping back toward the door. "I bet you'd like that. How much did they pay you? How much!"

Then George was gone, closing the door behind him and running toward the back exit. His bike stood in the alley just as he'd left it. The gas tank, he knew, was full. Struggling with the keys, he unchained it and climbed on, hastily jamming the apron filled with cash and credit card receipts under the seat. It came to life immediately, rumbling low, as George let out the hand clutch and took off.

George saw the white Cedric when he hit Park Avenue at 33rd Street. The car followed him, flashing its lights as it gained, despite his weaving through the light traffic.

As he approached Grand Central, George twisted the throttle back full, feeling the engine howling under him as he toed his way up through the gears. There was a sharp turn where Park Avenue wound around Grand Central; he could lose the car in the turn, then head crosstown toward the tunnel.

As he sped up the ramp and crossed the 42nd Street overpass toward the statue of Vanderbilt, he leaned forward into the wind. Behind him he could hear approaching sirens. Looking into the rearview mirror, he saw a man, his gray hair blown back by the wind, emerge from the car's sunroof. Then, as if in a dream, the man had a rifle pressed to his shoulder.

George pulled his gaze away from the mirror and the image of the man in the sunroof and saw the immense back end of Grand Central and the stern, looming countenance of Vanderbilt rushing toward him. Glancing down at the speedometer, he saw that he was going nearly seventy with the tach red-lined. He wouldn't even have a chance to turn, and the realization brought him bolt upright in the seat.

The blast of the .70-caliber explosive load hit George square between the shoulders, sending a spray of blood, bone, and flesh across the speedometer and front fender, opening a wound a longshoreman could stick an arm through without staining a sleeve. The force of the huge

shell ripped his grip from the handlebars and sent him tum-
bling head first over the front of the speeding motorcycle.

He bounced once across the asphalt, then the front wheel
caught him on the hip, sending the bike careening upward
and sideways through the air as the second shot hit the gas
tank. The motorcycle exploded in a fireball, its momentum
propelling it fifteen feet or more above the asphalt and battered guardrail to smash into Vanderbilt's patinaed groin.
Then the white apron broke open, sending a shower of cash
and credit card receipts upward, many burning and lifting
skyward in the partially flame-obscured face of old Vanderbilt.

As the Cedric roared past, turning slightly to avoid the
body at the center of the road and easily taking the hairpin
turn, the young woman in the backseat turned to the older
gentleman seated next to her. "Quite theatrical," she said.
"Very."

"Excellent shooting, sir," the driver, a young woman in
T-shirt and baseball hat, exclaimed, not taking her eyes from
the road. "Excellent!"

"Thank you," the older gentleman replied, smiling shyly
and removing a cigarette from a platinum case. "Yes, it was
good."

"The best I've seen in some time," the driver said. They
turned east, heading for the Midtown Tunnel. The car
smelled of cordite, cigarettes, and expensive perfume.

"Yes, worth every sou," the older gentleman answered,
putting a cigarette into his mouth and touching the flame
of a Cartier lighter to it. "Magnificent, really."

"She's already, specifically, said you did well," the woman
answered, bored. "Please, don't be a bore and belabor the
point."

"Your bags have already cleared customs," the driver said.
"The plane is fueled and waiting. I've taken the liberty of
ordering a late supper to be served on board."

"How convenient," the woman sighed.

chapter eight

"DEAD BEFORE HE HIT THE GROUND," Kat Jones said, tossing the beige folder with the printout of the provost report across the bar toward Swag. "Blew out his spine, heart, lungs, ribs, sternum. Just about cut him in two."

Swag took another drink of beer and looked down at the folder. The dark gray edge of a crime-scene photo peeked out from one corner. He pushed it back in with one finger.

Kat's eyes, slightly narrowed, rose from the folder to Swag's face. "Well, aren't you going to read it?" she asked.

Swag answered by setting his beer down at the folder's center. "Suppose you just give me the short version."

"What do I look like, *Reader's* fuckin' *Digest*?" Kat said, then sighed. "Okay, read it later. Here's what I saw in it. Guy takes down the restaurant where he's working, real jitterbug number. Takes off on his motorcycle. A police unit picks up the call from the manager and chases him up Park Avenue. By the time they catch up, his guts are splattered halfway to Jersey."

"Maybe it was a lucky shot?" Swag offered, bringing his beer up off the folder for another drink.

"Lucky with what, a cannon?" Kat said. Grabbing the folder, she pulled an eight-by-ten photo from its plastic sleeve and held it up for Swag to see.

He tried to look at the picture impassively, but it was hard. It showed the naked torso of the waiter laid out on a morgue table, and a hole so big blown through him that

Swag could clearly make out the stainless steel on the other side. A gloved hand held a ruler next to the wound for scale. The hole dwarfed the hand, measuring a good eleven inches across. Around the wound was the collateral damage caused by the fall from the motorcycle.

"So whattaya think?" Kat asked, still holding the photo up.

"It's great," Swag said. "I think I'll have a bunch run off and use it for Christmas cards this year."

Kat gave the photo a final grimacing look before putting it away. "So whattaya gonna do about it?"

"I'm going to finish my beer," Swag said slowly. "Then I'll go through the file."

"And then what?" Kat asked, but before Swag could answer, she was walking down to the other end of the bar to pour scotch for a couple of Middle Eastern businessmen in shiny suits and bad ties.

Swag read through the file slowly. First the reports from the first officers on the scene, then witness statements, followed by the crime lab stuff, and finally the autopsy report. He read every word, slowly and carefully. All of it written in that unmistakable cop language of official phrasing and stripped-down fact. The real stuff, the stuff that would mean anything or offer any speculation, was spelled out in the notebooks and in the heads of the investigating detectives.

When Swag finished reading and looked up, Kat was standing in front of him, leaning against the back bar, a small smile spread across her face. "So?" she said.

"So, I'm going to take this," Swag said, slipping one of the two dozen photos from the jacket out and rolling it carefully into a cylinder.

"You think they're connected, don't you?" Kat said. "Easy, this waiter, and Sandy?"

"I'll tell you in a couple of days," Swag answered. Then he drained the rest of his beer and walked out into the heat and midday sunshine.

*   *   *

Longford opened the door hesitantly, glaring at Swag with his good eye. His bad eye, the left one, was covered with a black eyepatch. A storefront clinic was in the process of rebuilding enough of a socket to support a glass eye in the deep scarring that crisscrossed his face like a county road map. But there was nothing they'd be able to do for the thumb and index finger that he'd lost on his left hand.

Swag grimaced at the first sight of Longford, in part because he felt responsible for the loss of the eye and fingers. They'd been blown off when Swag asked him to check out some custom-loaded ammo. Longford's new appearance was a little more threatening, making him look like a six-foot-six pirate.

"Swag," Longford said emotionlessly, his voice rumbling up like an echo.

"How you feeling, Long?" Swag asked.

"The fingers, they give me trouble on the small work," came the answer as he held up the raw pinkish stumps. "It's difficult sometimes. I'm going in next week for the bone graft. They'll be taking it from the hip."

Swag nodded apologetically, watching as Longford pushed the remaining three fingers through the curly head of steel-gray hair.

"Come in," Long said finally. "We'll talk."

Swag stepped through the steel-reinforced door into the narrow hallway. Longford shut the door behind them with a solid click.

"I finally managed to trace those cartridges," Longford said as they started down the hall to the workroom. "Interesting. They were designed by a Dutch armaments firm. Subcontracts for propellant and explosives in Switzerland, cartridge in Korea, projectile in Bonn," he said. "Never did find out where they were assembled."

Swag listened as they came into the workroom. A spotless shop filled with tools, lathes, and dominated by a steel workbench inlaid with wood.

"Funny thing," Longford said without a trace of humor. "No patents on any of it. I wrote it up for a tech journal, under I. G. Farben. Got a letter back saying I was crazy, that it'd never fire. Then about thirty Feds came around, asking questions at my mail drop."

The workroom was cool, the low hum of the air conditioner the only sound filling the space in the long pause.

"Listen, Long," Swag said carefully. "I need you to look at something for me."

Longford hesitated, his face tightening slightly. The last time Swag asked him to look at something, he'd lost an eye and two fingers. "What is it?" he said finally.

"A cartridge casing," Swag said, then began reaching into his back pocket.

Longford's shoulders hunched and he took an involuntary step back, his worst fears realized.

"It's a photo, Long," Swag said, withdrawing the tightly rolled eight-by-ten and handing it over.

Longford took the tube of photographic paper as if he expected it to explode and awkwardly unrolled it, the fingers on his left hand giving him trouble. There, in sharp detail, was a four-way split image of a cartridge casing from all angles. A millimeter ruler was shown next to each angle for perspective.

"Have you ever seen one?" Swag asked.

"Long time ago," Longford said, his voice not more than a whisper.

"What is it?" Swag asked. "Military issue?"

Longford shook his head slowly, still studying the photo. "Hunting."

Swag moved in closer to get another look at the photograph. "Hunting?" he asked.

"No, that's not quite right," Longford said, walking over to the workbench. "Collecting, really."

"Collecting?" Swag asked, following.

"This is a .70-caliber rifle shell," Longford said, setting the photo down and securing one end with a digital micrometer and the other with a rat-tail file. A partially assembled Llama M-82 lay nearby under the extended arm of a fluorescent-lit magnifying glass. "From Woodleigh, a Brit company. No military application."

"Tell me about it, Long," Swag asked, leaning in closer to the photo.

"Three-and-a-half inches in length," Longford said. "Designed for a thousand-grain jacketed bullet. Nine thousand and fifty-odd feet of muzzle energy and two K per second velocity."

"What do you shoot with it, elephants?" Swag asked.

"Elephants, Cape buffalo, rhino," Longford whispered back. "I suppose you might. But the experienced hunter would use a .458 Winchester Magnum, the Weatherby .378 or .375. At tops, they'd go for a .470 H & H Nitro."

"So, what the fuck is this?" Swag asked.

"Ordnance oddity," Longford said calmly, turning to face Swag.

"What are you telling me, Long?" Swag asked. "That this is a another custom load?"

Long reached up to scratch his cheek with his left hand, remembered the missing digits and switched to the right hand. "No, I've read about this," he said, speaking slowly. "Back in the sixties, Holland & Holland sold what they called 'The Last .600 Bore.' Then in 'eighty-seven or 'eighty-eight a Californian, naturally, called them up and asked for a big rifle, or rather a larger one. The .700-bore Nitro Express."

Longford tilted his head, catching Swag's attention. "It took something like two years for cartridge and barrel development," Longford said. "They built the thing on the company's standard Royal design, with a bolstered frame and twenty-six-inch double barrel. There was a three- or four-year wait once you ordered the rifle. Each was a custom order, maybe they ran a hundred or a hundred and ten thousand, in 1988 dollars."

"People hunted with these?" Swag asked. It didn't surprise him that people had actually paid a hundred grand for a gun. Back then people bought strange things, real estate, for instance.

"I believe that they built fewer than a dozen," Longford answered. "Almost exclusively for collectors. I don't think they ever anticipated these things going out into the field much, if ever. After all, what would be the point? There's a decline in effectiveness once you get up into the larger calibers. The old .600 was a holdover from back when the sun never set on the Brits and all of that."

"Could you fit these with an explosive cartridge?"

Longford gave Swag a hard look, his neck craning slightly. "It's a .70-caliber projectile, you could mount it with a load of C-4 or anything you wanted. But why? What would the point be?"

"To whack someone," Swag answered.

Longford seemed genuinely taken aback by this, as if the idea of shooting someone with a gun had never occurred to him. "Fifty caliber at most," he said finally, in a tone of voice that indicated Swag was wasting his time. "A sniper's rifle would be a .50. None of the old H & H's were built for sniping or long distance shooting—very British, sportsmanlike, you understand—'get as close as you dare, then two paces closer'—that sort of thinking. These rifles had standard foresights with a folding moon and a wide-V rearsight with a folding leaf. They were designed for hitting large animals at a hundred, a hundred and fifty yards. And I suppose they did that well enough."

"For the sake of argument, who would shoot someone with this bullet with an explosive tip?" Swag asked, pointing to the photo and drawing Longford's gaze downward.

Longford sighed. "I know firearms, not people. But if I had to guess, I'd say someone quite rich, with a very big ego. Also, it would be someone who knows his sporting arms, fancies himself an aficionado. Has hunted big game, possibly. What they used to call an 'enthusiast.'"

Swag refolded the photo and was about to leave. "Longford, you wouldn't happen to know anything about knives, would you?"

The big man turned a heavily lidded eye to Swag,

brushed a hand through the mat of gray curly hair on his head. "Only that you place them opposite the fork."

"Do you know a guy, maybe?" Swag asked.

"There used to be someone who worked in the armory section of the Met," Longford answered. "Before they sold off the collection. I have his number. He does work for me every once in a while. Acts as an agent, for certain collectors."

chapter nine

WHEN SWAG CALLED THE KNIFE GUY Longford recommended, the guy sounded nervous, but greedy. He had those well-mannered speech patterns of someone accustomed to dealing with a kinder, gentler, and simpler world. But that didn't stop him from offering a meet on Madison Avenue in the mid-twenties—within the hour.

Catching a cab uptown, Swag got off two blocks south of the meeting and began walking. He had no trouble spotting the guy—he was tall, not less than six-three or -four, and rail thin. He had a head of thinning gray hair, and thick steel-framed glasses. His baggy English suit had gone shiny and frayed with constant use. And he was leaning on a cane of black wood. All in all, he looked like a professor at a not-very-prestigious midwestern college—someone who read Chaucer with great pleasure and was at a loss as to why the world, particularly incoming freshmen, were incapable of the same enjoyment.

Swag approached the guy from behind, taking his time in sizing him up. "Burton Clark?" Swag asked when he was close enough.

The guy turned around slowly, his eyes blinking as the birdlike head rotated above the frayed collar of his shirt. Only when he was facing Swag did he talk. "Yes."

"I'm the guy that called before," Swag said. "About that knife."

"Yes," said Burton Clark again.

"Yeah, well, I'm trying to get a little bit of history on it," Swag said. "It was a knife used in a murder."

"I understand that," Burton Clark said.

Swag pulled the pages of the provost shadow report that dealt with the murder weapon. "These will probably help," he said.

Without saying a word, the thin man hooked the handle of the cane on his left arm and held out his right hand. Swag unfolded the three sheets of paper and handed them over.

Burton Clark looked at the papers carefully, then handed them back. "Baselard," he said at last.

Swag took the pages and said, "What?"

"Baselard," Burton Clark repeated. "The weapon used was a Baselard."

"What is it? Like a sword?"

"A dagger," came the answer.

Swag reached into his pocket and pulled out the five francs they had agreed to on the phone. "Tell me what you know about them," he said.

"Everything?" Clark asked.

"I'll stop you if I lose interest."

Clark carefully refolded the money and took a deep breath. Both acts seemed to tire him. "The Baselard family of daggers is commonly thought to derive its name from Basel, Switzerland, where it first made its appearance in the thirteenth or fourteenth century. From there it spread throughout western Europe, where it gained popularity as both a civilian and foot soldier's weapon of choice. It was also quite popular among knights. They were most commonly worn on the right side or suspended in front. There is documentation to the effect that it was sometimes suspended from a baldric slung over the right shoulder. Portraiture of the period tells us this much."

"What does it look like?" Swag asked, having a taste of what he was in for. The guy could have been Longford's long-lost brother—where Longford had an undying passion for firearms, Clark clearly had an insatiable appetite for knives.

Clark took another deep breath. "The handle resembles a capital letter I. The blade tapers on both sides, evenly down to the point. It's a double-edged weapon. Hilts varied according to the owner's financial circumstances. Some were very elaborate affairs. The vast majority were ivy, box root, bone, or horn. The grips were the width of the tang."

"How long?"

"I assume you mean the blade," Clark said. "The one mentioned in this report is fourteen to eighteen inches in length, just as the medical examiner surmised."

"Who would have used this?" Swag asked.

"Anyone, really," Clark answered. "That's the beauty of knives, they're entirely self-explanatory."

"I meant, who would choose to use it?"

"Ah, now, there you ask a different question," Clark said. "That's an entirely different question. May I quote a poem?"

Swag saw no use in arguing. "Knock yourself out."

"It's from the fifteenth century," Clark explained.

"There is no man worth a leke,
 Be he sturdy, be he meke,
 But he bear a basilard."

"That's it?" Swag asked.

"I didn't say it was long poem," Clark answered snootily. "I presented it merely to offer historical perspective on the weapon about which you inquire."

"What about a guy who would wear one today? Tell me something about him."

"He would know his weaponry," Clark answered. "Probably European."

"Why European?"

"Americans generally know or care little for history, beyond the week previous. If they care at all, their appreciation lapses altogether somewhere in the eighteenth century, when this particular trend had long passed."

"Where would I buy one of these?"

"Buy one?" Clark answered, somewhat taken back. "They're extraordinarily dear just now."

"Who would buy one?"

"An avid collector; someone with impressive resources and a—shall I say—passion for such things."

"An enthusiast?" Swag tried, using Longford's word.

"Precisely," Clark answered. "A very well-to-do enthusiast."

Clark vanished around the corner, walking slowly and exerting little pressure on the cane. Swag watched him go then flagged down a cab.

The thing that bothered him first off was the choice of weapons. Easy had been killed with some knife that nobody ever heard of, and the waiter was shot with a rifle meant for big game. Both obscure and expensive weapons—which meant that whoever was doing the killing wasn't local and wasn't off the street.

But then again, the other victims had all been small-time—and small-time doesn't draw out of town heat. As the cab cut west across Fourteenth Street, Swag realized the second thing that bothered him, which was the car that had been following him since he left Longford's on East Tenth.

The car was a red sporty number, an Italian two-door convertible with the top up. Eighty-five degrees, with humidity so thick the mannequins in Bergdorf's windows were sweating bullets. It couldn't have been more obvious. Imagine, Swag thought to himself, trying to follow someone in a red car. Reaching behind him, he pulled the Colt from its back holster and tucked it into the front of his jeans. Safety off, a round in the chamber.

The cab turned right, then began heading up Park, moving in starts and stops in the mid-afternoon traffic. As they approached 23rd in the right lane, the cabbie began accelerating, trying to sneak through the changing light on the corner.

"Stop at the light," Swag called through the partition. "I'll get off at the corner."

Swag slid the money through the partition's swivel tray and headed for the sidewalk. The red convertible was three cars back, halted at the light. Swag walked quickly, doubling back, his mind counting the seconds until the light changed. He passed the red car without glancing at it. Then he turned back into the street, cutting around the rear of a delivery van.

As he moved into the street, he could see the light about to change. The three or four pedestrians crossing at the corner hurried their pace to avoid the oncoming traffic. Swag took the last dozen steps at a run, reaching to his waist for the Colt as he came up on the red car's driver's side. He caught a glimpse of two hands on the wood-grained wheel, then pulled the Colt out in one smooth move as he dropped low, just behind the car's driver.

"Don't fuckin' move," he whispered, shoving the gun in through the open window so that it touched lightly at the back of the driver's head, just behind the ear, the barrel resting across the top of the seat. To the surrounding cars it looked as if he were chatting with the driver.

The car in front, a black sedan, began to move forward as the light changed. From behind, the sound of impatient horns sounded.

"License and registration are in my purse," said the familiar voice.

Swag relaxed his grip around the trigger as Kat Jones turned slowly to face him. A wan smile broke across her lips. There wasn't any fear in her look, just a vague hint of embarrassment.

"Damn it, Kat," Swag muttered, pulling the gun back through the window and slipping it into his waist. Behind him a half block of cars began laying on their horns.

"Want a ride?" Kat asked.

Swag didn't answer; rather, he walked around the front of the car, which he now saw was an ancient Alfa Romeo, and slipped into the passenger seat. "So what's the deal?"

he asked, closing the door. "Just out for a little spin or what?"

"What do you want to believe?" she answered, letting the clutch out quickly and feeding it gas, so that the car jumped ahead. The light was about to change again, but by the time they had traveled the thirty yards or so to the corner, she already had the car in third and sailed through.

"That's what I want to believe," Swag said. "I want to believe that you were out for a ride and just happen to see me. But just for the hell of it, you know, why not tell me the truth?"

"The truth's this," Kat said. "Things are falling apart at Bellevue. They're gonna boot Sandy out by the end of the week—that's three days. For what she's paying there, you could rent a floor at the Plaza. Every resident, orderly, med tech, and nurse in the joint has their hand out now. She's already got half the staff on the pad. And it's a ballbreaker of a payroll."

"So, what's that got to do with me?" Swag asked.

Another light came up, and Kat came down on the clutch and braked to a sudden stop, leaving all of three or four inches between the Alfa and the van in front of her.

"She's a little worried that maybe you're not motivated enough," Kat said, turning to smile at Swag sweetly. "I told her that was bullshit. And that you had motivation to burn, tons of it."

The light changed to green and Kat shot the car forward again, slamming Swag's head back against the headrest. He reached out and held on to the dash with one hand. "What? She wants her money back?" he answered.

"No, nothing like that," Kat said. "More like she wants me to work with you. You know, two heads being better than one. Many hands make light work. That kinda thing."

"No deal," Swag answered. Then the car shot forward before he could think of anything else to say.

Kat was in the middle of the intersection and shifting into second when she cut the wheel sharply, sending them east down 34th. "Now, that's not a very cooperative attitude," she said, taking a whole two or three seconds in third gear before shifting into fourth. Swag could guess that third didn't see a whole lot of use in this car, except maybe when she was parallel parking.

"Still no deal," he repeated, seeing the rear end of a bus rushing toward them.

"You're not going to give me some bullshit about it being dangerous, are you?" she asked, noticing the bus and down-shifting to second, then careening around into the opposite lane. Thankfully, there was no oncoming traffic. The engine roared as the tachometer's needle flew into the red zone. "Like in the movies. You know, when they say that in the movies, the girl always goes along. Even saves the guy's ass now and again."

But Swag didn't answer. A couple of kids on motorbikes, messengers, had been riding two abreast in the opposite lane, probably chatting. Now their faces were painted with sheer terror as the red sports car bore down on them. They both cut a hard right, the one on the far end jumped the curb by the abandoned movie theater. People on the street had stopped, their faces frozen in anticipation of seeing some crushed metal and blood.

Kat shifted back up into third and zoomed through the light that may have been red and crossed Lex. "So whattaya say?" she asked, her voice unnaturally calm.

"Jesus Kat, where'd you learn to drive?" Swag asked, his fingers tight on the black vinyl of the dash.

"Jersey," she said as they approached Third Avenue. The light was already red, a line of cars waiting. Swag could feel it in his gut that she was about to cut the wheel and fly around them, swerving again into the opposite lane and straight into the traffic on Third. He could see the uptown bus creeping across the intersection.

Fear shut Swag's eyes. Then he felt the car jolt to a sudden stop. When he opened his eyes again, they were behind a taxi, and so close that Swag could see the fear in the driver's face reflected in the rearview mirror, right through the back window and plastic passenger partition.

"So, what's the deal?" Kat asked, turning to Swag and smiling sweetly.

"I didn't know you were from Jersey," was all he could manage.

"Yeah, well I am," she said. "Just don't spread it around."

The two men stood on the overgrown lawn of the Oyster Bay estate surrounded by elephant-hide luggage. They watched in silence as the reconditioned Hughes 500MD helicopter moved slowly, seemingly tentatively over Long Island Sound, its suppressed rotors flattening the calm water. When it was a hundred yards or so from shore, the chopper banked gracefully and then gained altitude as it receded into the distance.

Behind the two men stood the ruins of a neo-Tudor mansion. What remained of the house was more than enough to suggest its former life and the moneyed anglophile who'd built it. Its leaded windows had long been shattered, vines struggled up its stone walls, and neglected maple trees cast it in shadows even at midday. The slate roof had been scavenged, as had every salable item from its interior, right down to the plumbing, light fixtures, and paneling. The house, like so many others, was a suffix of a number-coded land parcel that belonged to an obscure Delaware firm, a subsidiary of a Liechtenstein-based holding company whose owners—many of them other holding companies—were scattered throughout Europe's common market.

That is what happened to the suburbs. The defaulted mortgages held by banks and tax liens obtained by cities had long been bundled and sold. Few were rented, some were squats, but all were subjects of obscure international tax laws and all but forgotten—paper assets to be traded and depreciated—as distant as next year's grain futures. Split-level ghost towns.

Rats had long claimed the moldering domain within the stone walls of the house. Fifty generations of them had added their own smells to the scent of unhurried decay. They moved ceaselessly through the dust-laden motes of dim sunlight that fingered in through the smashed windows. They gnawed lazily on the insulation of wire hidden deep within the walls, and sniffed suspiciously at a bar of Crabtree & Evelyn bath soap that lay miraculously still fragrant in the back of a hall closet. Now, two of them sniffed and twitched in the window seat overlooking the water, hearing for the first time the sound of human voices.

"'Elluva good ride, that," one of the men said, as the chopper at last vanished. He was maybe sixty, red-faced and potbellied. He sweated profusely in the humid air. "Jolly good, a hundred and fifty kilometers per, not four feet off the water. Bloody exhilarating!"

"So glad you enjoyed it," the other man said. He too spoke with a Brit accent, which would have proved patently false to anyone but another poseur, which his companion was. Taken together, they were a Frenchman with a talent for language, specifically accents, and a businessman from London's East End with a flair for fast food chains, the management of slum housing, and pretensions to the plummy-voiced upper class.

"Immensely, really," the older gentleman replied. "Nothing like speed to get the blood pumping."

"Then I dare say you'll enjoy your trip into the city," the younger man said as he began walking down the gentle slope of shin-high weeds. His tightly wrapped ponytail bobbed with each step.

The older man followed obediently, like an overfed puppy. When they were a few yards from the crumbling dock, he let out a low breath of air, which his companion hoped was the sign of appreciation and not an oncoming stroke. "I say," he said at last. "My word."

Tied to the dock sat a wood-hulled boat, gleaming with varnish and brass fittings. On its stern was the gold-leaf script that read: *Miss Tea Leaf.* Waiting, just to the leeward side of the dock was the young woman. This time she wore a dress-white captain's jacket that fell far north of her knees and showed off her legs to good advantage. There was a preponderance of gold braid along the epaulets, sleeve cuffs, and across the front. A white-peaked captain's hat, with yet more gold braid, sat rakishly on her head, doing little to stem the flow of bright red hair.

When she saw the men approach, she saluted smartly, and with not a little good humor.

"She is a beauty, isn't she?" the older man said, quickening his step down the hill.

"A classic," came the wry response from his companion. "Beautiful lines, she's seen very little use. But I warn you, she's built for speed."

The small joke elicited a hearty if slightly wheezing chuckle from the older man, who was now covering the last steps at a fat man's trot.

"Gentlemen," the young woman said, smiling widely in greeting.

The two men stopped in front of the young woman. "Erica, why don't you provide a little background for Mr. Hollowbutton."

"A pleasure," she responded, then added another smile followed by a slight turn of the leg and a graceful sweep of the hand, like a game-show hostess. "This craft is a 1928 commuter. They first came into use in the early twenties, and continued through the mid-thirties by businessmen from this region who used them to travel to and from their offices in Manhattan."

"Impressive, don't you think?" the young man asked conspiratorily.

"Quite, quite," the older one answered, trying his best to rise to the joke.

The young woman turned slightly and edged out onto the dock. Her white deck shoes moved without hesitation over the rotting boards. "As the trend continued, commuters began competitions across the Sound, and increasingly the boats were built for speed. Wagers on the outcome of these competitions were not unheard of."

"Quite a bit of fun, I imagine," Hollowbutton replied, his voice now a bit tremulous as he attempted to follow her out onto the docks.

"You'll notice the brass exhausts," she replied, indicating the gleaming seven-inch diameter pipes. "Originally the boats were powered by either V-12 Lycoming or Packard engines. Needless to say, they made very good time."

"A bit more comfortable than the racers today, I imagine," the older man said, indicating the twin-leather seats, and finding to his great relief that the dock did not collapse under his considerable weight.

"A great deal more comfortable," the woman said, leaping gracefully from the dock into the cockpit to stand behind the controls. "Now, as I mentioned, the originals were outfitted with V-12s. This particular craft, however, has been fitted with a Miller V-16, one of a half-dozen such engines known to exist. And the same model that won both the 1929 Gold Cup and President's Cup."

"You don't say" Hollowbutton answered nervously, feeling the dock begin to rock. Behind him, on solid ground, stood his companion, smiling.

"Yes, indeed," the woman replied, then pushed the starter button. The huge engine roared to life, then began rumbling. The sound was a deep, menacing purr, which even at an idle seemed wholly irresponsible in its potential for power.

"Beautiful, isn't it?" the younger man called from the edge of the dock.

"Shall we go for a boat ride, Mr. Hollowbutton?" the woman asked.

"Yes, indeed," the fat Brit answered, clumsily boarding the craft. "And do call me Reggie."

The younger man moved out onto the dock then, and cast the lines off the tilted pilings.

"Are you ready, Reggie?" the woman asked from behind the controls. She did not take her eyes from the tach even as she pushed the nickel-plated lever into the forward gear and pulled back, bringing the throttle back to increase the RPMs.

"Did I mention I'm to be knighted?" Hollowbutton said as the craft eased off from the dock.

"How fascinating," the woman answered, casting a quick look back to check the lines. Then she kicked in the throttle a bit more, sending the boat plowing out over the water.

The younger man watched alone from the dock for some time as the boat, like the helicopter, vanished in the distance. Then he pulled a small cellular phone from his pocket and pushed the auto-dial button. "Asshole," he said, meaning Hollowbutton, in an accent now American. Then added in French, "*Fou gogo.*" Crazy sucker.

chapter ten

SEEK YE PATTERNS. SWAG COULD SEE the letters floating before his eyes. He could see them just as clearly now as when he saw the police academy instructor scrawl them across the blackboard so many years ago. Find the pattern—the link. That was the first rule of multiple homicide investigation. The pattern would point to the perp.

The pattern was clear enough. The victims were all dead ends. None of them would be missed. They were all nobodies. In a town full of nobodies, they were prime examples. Taken together, all of their possessions would fit in a couple of large shopping bags. Whatever computer file the police, provosts, or Feds had on them wouldn't fill the memory of a digital watch.

Then there was the suspect that waxed Easy. A blond Brit wearing a tweed suit. And the waiter had been shot with a Brit gun. But then there were the others, preliminary M.E. reports were all over the place, citing traces of Asian skin under the fingernails of one victim, and red hair in the mouth of another. And the weapons were all over the lot; one died by a blast to the head from a pistol; another strangled by a length of wire; and of course Easy, stabbed with an antique knife.

The only thing that connected their deaths was the panic. A steadily rising hysteria in the last days before their deaths. If they'd all received the taunting notes, the mysterious stranger following them, then they had good reason to panic. Panic, flight, then death. That was the pattern.

He'd been on the case two days, Kat working with him for half that time, and together they'd managed to turn up nothing. They ran themselves ragged, from hotels to high-rise squats and back again. Nobody heard nothing, saw nothing, knew nothing on the street.

"Swag, damn it, are you listening to me?" Kat said, pulling him back from his thoughts.

"No, not really," Swag answered truthfully and picked up the beer that she set down in front of him. At four o'clock business at the Dead Banker was just beginning to pick up. A couple of Middle Eastern types huddled at one of the corner tables, talking quietly. A half-dozen or more low-rent stock operators were lined up at the bar, nursing drinks and bullshitting each other about how good business was.

"Well, you better start listening," she said. "Sandy's hitting the street tomorrow, and she's not happy about it."

"We'll get her out of town," Swag said.

"If you'd been listening, you'd know it's taken care of," Kat answered sourly. "And she's not leaving town. There's a suite booked at the Plaza."

Now there was a bad piece of news. The Plaza was home to the Provost Command—specifically, Colonel Bammer. The good colonel would bust Swag for a wrong look.

"She figures it'll be safe with all those provosts running around," Kat continued.

"Europe would be safer," Swag offered.

"Yeah, well, Europe isn't going to happen," Kat shot back. "In her situation, absence doesn't exactly make the heart grow fonder. As if that were the piece of anatomy we're talking about."

Swag took another drink of his beer. "What does absence make it, *exactly*?"

"It makes it start cruising midtown bars, looking for replacements," Kat said.

"We're not talking true love here, huh?" Swag asked more than a little sarcastically.

Kat didn't answer; rather, she hustled down to the end of the room, where a small group of Japanese businessmen had bellied up to the bar. Swag watched as she poured them a round of *mizu-wari*; blended scotch with much water and ice. The time-honored sararimen special.

A brief argument broke out among the men over who was paying. Kat waited patiently as they decided. When the argument ended, a pile of yen appeared on the bar. Kat took the money and rang up on the sale on the ancient register, then returned the change in dollars. Hard yen for soft dollars.

"One of the businessmen began to protest, insisting on "*En! En!*" meaning yen, with much finger pointing to the small tray and stack of dollars.

"*Ei, doru.* No, dollars," Kat replied in a bored voice. Swag could see she was hoping the bluff and impolite use of the word no would get her through. It did. The sarariman backed down and pocketed the dollars carelessly, like a bunch of used Kleenex.

She strolled back to Swag with a small smile of triumph spread across her face.

"Nice score," he said, figuring she made about two thousand yen on the deal.

Kat ignored the comment, forcing the smile back where it came from. "So, what were we talking about?" she asked.

"True love," Swag answered, downing the remainder of his beer.

"You want to see true love, watch a late movie," Kat answered.

"Little early in the day for cynical, isn't it?" Swag asked.

Kat settled behind the bar, then leaned over the polished surface on her elbows, getting right into Swag's face. "Look, first off we're not talking about love," she said. "Right now we're talking about moving Sandy from Bellevue to the Plaza without getting her shit blown away."

* * *

Hollowbutton hated to wait. He hated to wait for any-thing, planes, meals, money, or women. He detested long books, long movies, and slow trips. Everything had to be fast, particularly the money. While many would call his impatience a curse, he personally viewed it as a secret asset. Without it, he always felt as if he'd still be back in that mis-erable broken-down house on Vallance Road.

He'd been in the city two days, and the time passed slowly. He longed to be on with it. The suit fittings, the meals, the small entertainments that had been provided, did nothing to ease his sense of time wasted. Even the woman, Erica, was of little distraction. Speed was what he longed for. Speed and the thrill of the hunt.

Hollowbutton rose slowly from the chair, pulling his weight up with a slight grunt, and walked to the window. On the street in front of the town house a line of cars crept toward the corner. Any of them would do. But this Esterhazy seemed to know his business. He had promised something extraordinary, and by God, he better deliver it.

Erica came through the library's door, looking cool and confident in the blue suit she wore. Not a proper woman's suit at all, Hollowbutton thought, more like a man's suit, cut slim at the waist. Even the starched white shirt was more like a man's.

"And how are we today, Mr. Hollowbutton?" she asked, still walking toward him. She wore a tie of silver and gold wire braided together so that it formed a subtle regimental pattern.

"Damned impatient," he answered, noticing her hair was put up in a tight bun at the back of her head and that she was carrying a cap. It was a peaked cap, not unlike the one she had worn on the boat, though this one was free of trim.

"And what do you fancy yourself to be today?" he asked, as she stopped just in front of him. It was another damned costume, he thought. In the past two days she'd dressed in everything from outright loony Milan fashion to silk jumpsuits. And that was only in public; in private her tastes ran to the outright unconventional, which was golly inter-esting, at first anyway.

"Why, your chauffeur, of course," she answered. Then, as if to prove the point, she set the cap jauntily on her head.

This was a new twist; for the past two days hired cars had driven them about town. Hollowbutton arched a bushy eyebrow suspiciously. "Esterhazy running a bit short, is he? Has you pulling double duty?"

The young woman smiled. "Not at all," she said. "But I'll be driving today."

"Cap and all," he said.

"Cap and all," she echoed. "It's always been my under-standing that a proper English gentleman would never trust a driver who didn't wear a cap."

"Quite right," he said, then followed her from the room.

The drive was not a short one from the town house. Hollowbutton fidgeted in the backseat of the Citröen nerv-ously, glancing over a day-old copy of *The Financial Times* as they made their way west. He never cared much for French cars. Too damned noisy.

"I say, it would be nice to know where we are going, wouldn't it?" he asked, more than a little annoyed.

"Don't worry," she called back, turning her head slightly to catch his eye in the rearview. "I know exactly where we're going."

He did have to admit she was a marvelous driver. Even in the hazardous New York traffic, she wound her way in and out with great aplomb.

Presently, she turned onto 42nd Street and continued west.

"Not another damned sightseeing trip?" he asked, seeing the river.

"No, not quite," she answered, her voice close to a laugh.

Then they were right at the water. Ahead of them he saw the docks where the sightseeing boats were tied up. The rusting bow of a half-submerged tour boat protruded from the water at the northernmost dock, its red, green, and white paint chipped. Damned filthy river, he thought to himself. Makes the Thames look like Lourdes.

She slowed the car only slightly as they negotiated the entrance, weaving around the chain-link fence, then up the ramp to the pier that held a three-story concrete structure.

Hollowbutton felt himself tense. Yes, finally something was going to happen. He saw now that the building in front of them was a parking garage.

The attendant spotted the Citröen as they approached and activated the electronic gate. Erica gave the car a little gas, and they moved through without stopping.

She drove through the garage at thirty, squealing the tires around each turn. When they reached the top level, she headed to the very end. Hollowbutton leaned forward in his seat, gripped with expectation.

At the end of the garage, waiting beside a large black car, he saw Esterhazy. Erica pulled neatly into the spot next to Esterhazy and the car, which looked familiar, but he couldn't quite place.

"Here we are, sir," Erica said.

Hollowbutton studied Esterhazy as he waited for the woman to come around and open the door for him. Esterhazy was wearing a light raw-silk suit, sans tie, and leaning ever so lightly on the front bonnet of a car whose paint had been stripped down to base metal, smoking a John Player Special. There was an air of total ease about him; even the small ponytail, which Hollowbutton had lately come to hate, seemed relaxed.

The girl opened the door as smartly as any doorman at a King's Road club, and Hollowbutton pulled his bulk from the cramped backseat. "Now, what's all this, then, eh?" he said, by way of greeting. His voice echoed slightly in the empty garage.

Esterhazy dropped the half-smoked cigarette and ground it into the oil-stained concrete using the toe of his John Lobb shoe. "Your vehicle, sir," he replied warmly as he stepped away from the box-shaped car.

Hollowbutton studied the car with some interest. It

could have been a Rolls, but wasn't. Damned old, though. The wheel caps provided no clue—there weren't any. And not a hint of chrome on the thing. "This thing!" Hollowbutton said at last. "It must run better than two tons. No speed."

Esterhazy turned, walked slowly to the driver's door—on the right, very British—and opened it. "Bentley, Turbo R," he said, revealing an interior of polished wood and Connolly hide.

"My word," Hollowbutton said, now stepping closer to admire the classic. "I haven't seen one of these since—"

"The fastest luxury car ever produced," Erica put in easily, stepping around Hollowbutton. "Factory standard was a 7.75-litre V-8. Zero to sixty in 6.8 seconds."

Hollowbutton studied it in greater detail. The familiar B logo was nowhere to be found, not even on the bonnet badge. Likewise, someone had altered the vertical grill, replacing it with a cheap chrome version of an American standard. "A bloody shame," Hollowbutton sighed. "What you've done to it. Bloody shame."

"The car was originally fifty-three hundred pounds," Erica said flatly, continuing the tour. "Our people have managed to trim that down to forty-eight hundred. We've also rebored and refitted the engine. Boosted the torque a bit. And it's been outfitted for defensive driving."

"Bloody 'ell," Hollowbutton said in a sigh. "What defensive driving?"

"Any unforeseen circumstances," Esterhazy put in.

"Now, this is the best part," she continued, leaning into the car. "Do you see that button there?"

Hollowbutton nodded slowly.

"Nitrous charge," she said. "A little of that and nothing will be able to touch her."

"What can she do?" Hollowbutton asked.

"I've track-tested her at one ninety," Erica said. "And she still had more."

"My word, I wasn't expecting this," Hollowbutton said.

"Not at all. A Ferrari, something red and Italian, or one of those German cars, but certainly not this. I must say. . . ."

Erica and Esterhazy exchanged a small awkward glance. The car was chosen specifically for Hollowbutton, and not only as a point to cater to country and Queen loyalty. The prospect of Hollowbutton cramming his more than generous posterior down into some Italian or German machine was more than a little painful to consider.

"This is a gentleman's car," Esterhazy offered diplomatically.

"A gentleman's car capable of some ungentlemanly speeds," Erica added.

Hollowbutton stepped back from the car, skepticism fading. "Yes, yes, I dare say you're entirely right."

Then Esterhazy came around one side of Hollowbutton, while Erica came around the other to flank him. "We wanted you to see her, before," Erica said.

"Before what?" Hollowbutton.

"Before the yellow cammo goes on," Esterhazy finished.

chapter eleven

THIS IS THE WAY IT WAS GOING TO RUN. Sandy's two physical therapist goons would drive her from Bellevue to the Plaza. Swag and Kat would work backup in another car, the trailer. They would make the trip late, two in the morning, to avoid traffic and delays outside and inside the hotel.

Swag dropped in at the Dead Banker a little before nine. The gray security gates were down on the windows on either side of the door. The neon script of beer brands hung silent and dull on the other side of the dirty windows. Inside, a dim light burned at the back of the narrow room. Swag, peering into the gloom, knocked lightly on the front door. Kat stepped out of the shadows, moving cautiously forward, a little off center. When she saw it was Swag knocking, she relaxed and picked up her step to get to the door. It was only when she was right at the window that Swag could see the matte-black .380 automatic in her hand.

"You're early," Kat said, opening the door and securing the .380 in a back holster. She was wearing loose fitting jeans, a loose dark blue silk shirt, and old-fashioned sneakers—black canvas hightops. Except for the sneakers, she would have blended right in at some Eurobeach weekend where tan people barbecued burgers in an unwitting parody of bygone suburban days.

"There's just a bunch of things bothering me," he said, stepping into the stale-beer smell and shadows of the closed bar.

Kat was already walking back into the shadows. She answered without looking back. "Like what?"

"Like the money, for one thing," Swag said. "There's money all over this thing. The five K I got from you. The hospital setup. The whole thing."

"It all spends, doesn't it?" Kat replied, opening the door to a darkened office at the back of the room.

"Yeah, it all spends," Swag said. "Except it's spending too damn fast."

"If you got it, then why the fuck not, huh?" Kat said, closing the door as they stepped into the room. For a split second they were in the dark, then Kat flicked on the light to reveal a nearly bare room, save for a folding aluminum card table stacked high with papers.

"Where's it coming from, Kat?" Swag asked.

"It's money," she said. "Sometimes there's a bunch, sometimes there's a little. You know, money."

She pulled up a folding metal chair, turned it so she could sit resting her arms across the back. If it was anyone else, Swag would have written it off as "chick macho," the kind of pose some blonde confection would imitate for a perfume ad in a glossy magazine. But with Kat it was completely natural. She was the one those high-priced models were imitating in the ads.

"What's that, a half-assed economics lesson?" Swag asked, pulling up a chair for himself. "You left out the part about supply and demand."

Kat fixed Swag in a hard stare, rubbed the palms of both hands along her legs, and brushed her hair back with them. "Look, entre nous, maybe you've been working the hotels too long, huh?" she said. "You know, walking those tourists to restaurants and shopping. It's done some serious damage to your thinking. Maybe you forget what the real deal is down here with us common folk hustling for that hard currency, huh?"

The office was suddenly cool, chilly cool. If Swag didn't know better, he'd swear the chill was coming off Kat. When he spoke, he half expected to see his breath come out in clouds. "And you're gonna tell me, is that it?"

"Same as it always was," she answered, now a bit tired. "Flash, cash, and trash."

Swag gave her the long stare, but she just sent it right back. "This thing is kinky as hell," he said finally, to fill the cold silence. "It sucks, big-time."

Kat kept the grim expression for a full two-beat count before answering. "You got the money."

"Yeah, I got it," Swag answered warily.

"So we got a few hours, want to play some cards?"

He knew he wasn't going to get more out of her. Swag nodded, and Kat reached over to the cluttered table and dug out a deck of gimme cards from a Japanese beer company. There was a picture of a pretty Asian girl on the back, kneeling in the foaming white surf of some black sand beach. She was smiling and holding a sixteen-ounce bottle of dry beer.

For three hours they played poker. Kat dealt from the bottom. She dealt seconds. She crimped and nail-nicked everything that came into her hand. When Swag started cutting more judiciously, she dealt out from the center to beat the hop. And that was only what Swag noticed. Every hand she dealt was like some mail-order video on card mechanics, only without the slow-motion replay and explanations.

When they finally quit, Swag figured he would have lost about twenty francs if they were playing for money. "Come on, let's get out of here," he said before she could throw some more cards his way.

"Loose enough?" she asked, cutting the cards smoothly with one hand.

"Bored," he answered. "And you are too, you're not even bothering to cheat anymore."

"Even cheating gets a little dull, you know?" she said. "If it wasn't for the money, nobody would put in the effort."

"You made a pretty good effort," he said.

"A girl's got to stay in practice," she answered, pulling

a red queen from the deck and studying it with mild interest. "Keep her skills sharp."

"Waiting for Mr. Right, are we?"

She folded the queen back into the deck and rose out of the chair, stretching. "No, just the right Mr. Stupid."

Swag had expected to see the convertible when Kat walked him down the block to the World Trade Center garage. In the last level, three floors down, was the car. Swag saw a half-dozen other cars nearby, all with private livery plates. Kat walked past the convertible to the far wall toward a black Jag Sovereign. When she was fifty yards away, she stepped casually behind a concrete pillar and pulled a small plastic rectangle from her pocket, punched in a code and waited.

The light at the top of the security device flashed from red to green a half-dozen times, then settled on green. She moved out from behind the pillar then, pushed another button, and there was a slight click as the doors unlocked.

"Nice ride," Swag said as they took the last few steps to the Jag.

"Your basic transportation," Kat answered, heading for the car's trunk. "But don't be too impressed, it's gray."

Swag knew what she meant. Gray-market cars were common enough. They brought them in by the boatload. With the luxury models there was usually something missing, an engine, transmission, interior. They came in cheap that way, shipped as scrap to avoid taxes.

"The engine isn't original," Kat said, answering Swag's unasked question.

"What's in it?"

"A guy up in the Bronx put in an old four fifty four-barrel," Kat said. "It's been rebored and turbocharged, did a bunch of other stuff to it."

"Like what?" Swag asked.

"Like stuff," she answered, moving around to the trunk. "To make it go fast. *To make it go very fast.*"

Inside the trunk was a small arsenal. Eight or nine nylon

gun cases of all sizes lay carefully arranged on the floor.
Three others were secured right on the underside of the lid.

"Okay, you're riding shotgun, here's a shotgun," she said,
going straight for the gray plastic case at the center and
snapping open the locks.

Swag watched with an uneasy feeling as she teasingly
lifted the lid. When the case's top was thrown back, he was
sure. It was an old USAS-12. Even with the new, right-to-
self-defense gun laws, this was way out of the ordinary.
Everything about it was illegal for private ownership.

"Now there's something you don't see every day," Kat
said, staring down at the weapon and top of the case, which
held neat rows of shells.

It was a nasty-looking thing. An eighteen-inch barrel
attached to what looked like an assault-rifle body. The
parkerized metal ended with a black thermoplastic bull-pup
stock. It was outfitted with combat pistol grip and a drum
magazine that held twenty 12-gauge rounds. There was an
integral carrying handle at the top, but someone had
removed the aperture at the rear and front post for the sites.
Across the top of the handle was a high-powered laser site.

"You have a permit for this?" Swag asked, not feeling
guilty about nitpicking. Just being in the same room with
the thing could buy you ten years of state custody.

"Yeah, but darn it, I seem to have left it at home," Kat
said.

Swag picked up the gun. Someone had filed down all the
markings then hammered over the space with checkered
lines. Acid wouldn't reveal anything about the weapon if
it fell into official hands.

"That's a twenty-round magazine," Kat said. "I filled it
this afternoon with alternating rounds of government-issue
fléchette loads. There's twenty-two of the eight-grain suckers in each shell. You got a range of maybe fifty yards."

Swag flinched. It was bad enough the weapon was government issue, the ammo was too. That could double the
years on a sentence. "What's the other load?" he asked, not
sure he wanted to know.

"So glad you asked," Kat said sweetly. "Solid copper. .50-caliber sabots. Two fifty—something grains."

More government issue, Swag moaned to himself. And this one just happened to be the weapon of choice for Bammer's men, preferred even to their Steyr rifles. Genuine roadblock ordnance, they particularly liked its ability to go through things—car bodies, doors, glass, and people.

"Well, just don't stand there with your mouth open, say something," Kat ordered. "You look like a kid at Christmas who got nothing but sweaters."

"How about a kid that just got five to ten in a maximum security slam?"

"Swag, you're such a fuckin' drag sometimes, you know that?" Kat chuckled. "Look, I'll show you something."

She unzipped another bag then. One of the ones secured to the trunk lid. Swag wouldn't have been surprised if she pulled out a small thermonuclear device. "Now, isn't this a beauty?" she asked, pulling out the oddest pistol Swag had ever seen. It was a huge, heavy-looking semiautomatic of no distinct make. A laser site was secured to the top. Beneath it, folded under, was a foreshortened steel stock.

"Shit, now what the fuck is that?"

"It's a Japanese .50," she said. "Won it in a poker game. Beauty, huh?"

"You shoot that?"

"Not too often, you know," she answered. "It needs custom loads. Thing has a helluva kick to it, so I had it fitted with this. Steel alloy, almost light as aluminum." She folded the stock down and attached it to her arm. Three Velcro pads held it in place. Swag saw it was some kind of stabilizer that ran nearly to her elbow, like a prosthetic device. At the far end was a series of springs, presumably to take up the recoil. What she had done was turn her arm into a .50-caliber rifle.

"How many rounds?" Swag asked in morbid curiosity.

"Eleven," she answered, flicking on the laser and sighting in on a far wall, then flicking her wrist up so that the gun flew up and locked between thumb and forefinger, over her wrist, giving Kat use of her hand. A downward flick sent the gun back into her hand. "Load 'em with anything I want. Explosives. Glasers. Hollowpoints. Anything, really. Neat, huh?"

"Yeah, neat," Swag answered.

Kat seemed a little puzzled by Swag's lack of enthusiasm. "Okay then, let's get busy," she said, and slammed the trunk closed.

They rumbled up the FDR in the Jag. Whatever the car looked like from the outside, it didn't sound like a Jag. It sounded like one of the old hotrods kids would race along Brooklyn back streets. The engine sound came into the interior in a deep, throaty growl.

Kat showed remarkable restraint by keeping it under sixty. Traffic was light, but with every car they passed came stares, to which Kat seemed oblivious.

"Okay," she said when they turned off the FDR over to First Avenue. "Here's the way we'll play it. She's coming out the back entrance. The muscle boys escort her to the car. She'll sit in the backseat. Two of them up front. I'll just hang back, anything happens, then we'll step in."

"What's the route?" Swag asked, then reached into his pocket for a cigarette. The burled wood dash of the car had been replaced by sheet metal. There wasn't a lighter.

"Thirty-four to FDR, then straight up to 61st," Kat answered, pulling a pack of matches from her pants and lighting one in a deft one-handed move. "We'll cut across on 59th. Let her off at the side entrance. Once all three of them are inside, we're off the clock."

"What about those bodyguards? Are they any good?"

"Supposed to be," Kat said, parking next to a green Dumpster across the street from the back entrance. A few kids were climbing over it, looking for goodies. Scraps of aluminum shelving, busted chairs, anything they could sell off to the recyclers.

"Speaking of which," Kat said, and nodded to an old black limo that cruised past into the open chain link gate to the back entrance. "Here comes one now. Why'n't you go in, help bring her to the car?"

Swag took it to be an order, picked up the shotgun and walked as casually as he could to the entrance, carrying fifteen pounds of federal-offense weaponry.

He met the bodyguard at the back door. The guy was wearing a chauffeur's outfit with a long-barreled Wildey tucked into a tactical holster. "Don't fuck this up, asshole," the guy said, and opened the door with a key.

"Just do your job, ace," Swag answered. "Just do your job."

The guy gave Swag a hard look but didn't say anything. They stepped through the door into a doorway. Inside, the only light was provided by a cracked exit sign that gave off an eerie red glow. They were inside the last floor of a stairway that smelled of trash. From above came the sounds of talking and the hollow echo of footsteps.

"Here they come," the guy said, and pulled the Wildey out. The stainless gun shone dully in the red light.

Swag dropped the cigarette and ground it out beneath his toe. The voices were getting louder. He could make out Sandy Mann's voice. It was a slurred whine. And the other bodyguard answered an apparent question by saying, "Just one more flight."

Then they rounded the corner. Swag saw that the bodyguard was supporting Sandy as she walked shakily down the stairs. She was wearing a long tan raincoat buttoned up to her neck, scarf over her head, and dark glasses. He wore black leather pants and a T-shirt that said, GUNS DON'T KILL PEOPLE. I DO.

When they reached the last flight, which was maybe a dozen stairs, the bodyguard rolled his eyes back in an expression of pure exasperation.

Swag could see now, even in the strange light, something was wrong with her. She wasn't just frightened, she was barely able to walk. "What's wrong with her?" he asked.

But before the bodyguard could answer, Sandy lunged forward, smiling, determined to take the last steps on her own. For a split instant it looked as if she would make it, then her hand slipped from the railing and she fell forward. Her feet tangled for the briefest instant, then she rolled in a heap down the stairs. The fall sent her glasses from her head and left her sprawled between Swag and the chauffeur bodyguard.

Swag and the two bodyguards looked down at Sandy. She looked back up at them, giggled, then said, "Uh-oh," like a little girl.

"What's she been into?" Swag asked as he pulled her up, and the other two draped a dull red Kevlar blanket over her.

"What hasn't she been into?" the one with the T-shirt answered. "Started this afternoon with a few Valium. Ten mil tabs. By the time we hit happy hour, she was chewing Marinol and Percodan like after-dinner mints."

"Well, at least she's in a good mood," one of the bodyguards said.

She began singing. At first the words were incomprehensible beneath the heavy Kevlar shroud as they half carried, half dragged her across the parking lot. But by the time they had her to the car's door, she had launched into a spirited version of "New York, New York."

The chauffeur-dressed bodyguard opened the door, while Swag and the other one pulled and pushed her into the backseat.

"I want to wake up in the something, something, something," she murmured. "And be king of the something, something, something. If I can make it where, I can make it without a care. . . ."

"That used to be one of my favorite songs," one of the bodyguards said.

When Swag saw that she was completely in the car, he slammed the door. "Okay, let's go."

The two guys got in the front. The car came to life, and through the tinted window Swag saw the bodyguard in the passenger seat give him a wave with the barrel of a shotgun.

chapter twelve

THE FDR DRIVE CLUNG to the east side of Manhattan like an asphalt and concrete skin. In most places there were three lanes in each direction, divided by a three-and-a-half foot high concrete barrier. It was always the closest thing to open road in Manhattan. No lights, like the West Side Highway, only a twisting and curving stretch of road where few rules ever applied after midnight.

They came onto the FDR in the Thirties, the crowded midtown skyline looming large to their left. Kat kept a good distance between them and the limo, skillfully moving in and out of the sparse late-night traffic.

Swag, the auto-loading shotgun at his feet, lit another cigarette and leaned back in the seat. The cool summer air streamed in through the half-open window. The lights across the dark expanse of East River glowed brightly.

"Piece of fuckin' cake, huh?" Kat said, looking over briefly, smiling.

"So far," Swag said. They were just approaching the 42nd Street exit and things were looking good. The midtown skyline grew closer, lit up as it always was, courtesy of the Fed. You could almost believe that they were still working office buildings and not shells. You could almost believe it, except for the bland uniformity. All the lights were exactly the same. Swag knew the windows were lit, every one of them, by government-issue three-foot-long fluorescents. Nostalgia for the tourists.

Across the river was the darkened shell of the old Pepsi sign. Once a landmark of gigantic neon proportions, it was now a mute logo against the dark summer sky.

They were coming to the 42nd Street overpass, a covered section of highway that supported the United Nations above it, when the taxi passed. Swag looked over at the speedometer. They were going fifty and change. The taxi, one of the old checkers so popular with tourists, must have been nudging seventy-five.

"He's in a hurry," Kat said, just to say something.

"Maybe," Swag answered, feeling his stomach go hollow.

Kat saw it immediately, the taxi slowing up, pulling along the passenger side of the limo. She punched down hard on the accelerator, coming up close on the taxi's rear, urging him to speed up.

"Between them," Swag shouted, bringing the shotgun up off the floor. "Get between them!"

"Trying," Kat hissed through clenched teeth. There was less than a foot between the Jag and the taxi. When the taxi didn't budge, Kat eased the accelerator to the floor and bumped him. The impact nudged Swag back in his seat, but the taxi held its position. It was like bumping a brick wall. Then the cab sped up a little, and she bumped him again.

As they emerged from the overpass the limo's driver did exactly what he should have—he jammed on the brakes. The big car's tires squealed unmercifully, its long body drifting out into the right lane to first hit the taxi, then the Jag, with the sickening sound of scraping metal. From the corner of his eye Swag caught a glimpse of Sandy's face pressed up against the fogged glass. The Kevlar blanket was still wrapped about her head, but her face poked out a center hole. She was smiling, like a kid on a carnival ride.

Kat fought to bring the Jag under control, easing down on the brakes and cursing as she pulled hard against the wheel. The landscape spun briefly. Swag looked back, forcing his head around, and saw the limo straddling two lanes.

Luckily, the road was empty ahead, but the taxi had slowed up as well.

"Sonofabitch! What kind of bullshit is this?" Kat hissed. She had just gotten the car straightened out. In front of them the taxi was speeding up. Kat came down hard on the gas and took off after it.

They were under the pillared entrance to the 59th Street Bridge, a completely dark tunnel of concrete that lasted for two blocks. That's when it hit. The blast of light was so sudden, it seemed to explode at the back of Swag's skull, blinding him completely. Kat too caught its full power and jammed on the brakes. This time she lost control of the car and it drifted right, running along the wall and leaving a trail of paint and sparks.

Swag's vision came back slowly. Somewhere within a landscape of floating red and purple dots he saw the taxi pass them, heading the *wrong way* down the FDR. It was going back for the limo.

"He's going back!" Swag shouted.

But Kat had seen it too. She began pumping the brakes hard. When the car stopped, she threw it into reverse, yanking the wheel around in a three-quarter turn that sent their back end crashing into the wall as she shifted back into drive and straightened the car out. "There's some shades in the glove box," she said.

Swag sprung the lock and fished out the cheap wraparounds from a tangle of papers and debris. Then he reached over and slid them on Kat.

"Can't see shit," she said.

They were coming up fast on the cab. It let go with another blast from the rear lights, but this time Kat kept going. She rammed it twice. The second time, it recovered within a split second of hitting an oncoming motorcycle. Ahead of the cab was the limo, traveling fast on the inside lane.

As the cab approached the limo, Swag saw a hand holding a gun which began firing from the cab's back passenger seat. The limo's back rear window shattered, and the driver slammed down on the brakes.

"Okay, asshole," Kat hissed, and punched down hard on the accelerator as she turned a hard left into the outside lane. By the time the cab flashed the rear lights again, they were right alongside, both cars flying upward on the incline near 42nd. Swag had the shotgun poking through the window, his finger wrapped tightly around the trigger.

If another car came up the FDR, they were dead. Swag would have to shoot fast. As they began to pass the cab, he let go with a three-round burst. The gun jumped in his hands, its recoil driving the butt plate into his shoulder, the muzzle rising with each blast.

The first shot slammed into the side of the driver's door, ripping open a nasty hole. The second shot, a solid brass slug, caught the window high, shattering it with a fist-sized hole, exiting through the roof and knocking out the wiring for the FOR HIRE sign.

The cab hit the brakes and the Jag shot by, Kat cutting the wheel hard to the right, missing an oncoming car by maybe three inches.

"Get ready," Kat mumbled as she turned the car quickly. They were in the inside lane, but at least they were heading in the right direction.

Ahead the taxi had turned around, too, and was passing the limo. Once again the hand with a gun came out the back window and fired two rounds.

As Kat passed the limo it was almost a blur. "Don't do it," Swag said. "Go back for Sandy!"

"Fuck it," she spat. "I'm gonna take this asshole out!"

They eased up on the cab at the edge of the 59th Street overpass. Kat flicked her left wrist, the gun's grip snapping down neatly into the palm of her hand, the laser site clicking on.

The cab sped up as Kat came up alongside. Using one hand, she pulled the wheel hard left. The Jag bounced off the cab but didn't move the car an inch. "That's not a nor-mal cab," Kat whispered, her voice tight in her throat.

"No shit," Swag said.

They were going maybe seventy, now passing the 61st Street exit. She cut the wheel again, getting so close she could have touched the passenger window. Then she extended her gun hand partially out through her window. The laser's red dot bounced up from the door and settled dead center on the fogged glass of the cab's rear passenger window. She fired, the blast deafening in the car. The bullet hit at an angle, smashing the passenger window and going on through to the windshield.

Then the cab hit a pothole and the glass fell away. Inside the darkened interior Swag could see an old red-faced guy. And he was smiling. *Smiling!*

The cab shot ahead and Kat's second shot pinged harm-lessly off the hood.

They were approaching the Seventies now. The buildings rose sharply on their left. Across the river on the right Swag caught a glimpse of a passing tug, its running lights zoom-ing by in a blur. The cab gained distance, putting fifty or more yards between it and the Jag as it moved into the left lane. Kat, her face a mask of determination, pushed her foot all the way down on the accelerator. Something deep in the engine opened up, and the Jag began closing the gap.

"Get on the roof!" Kat ordered.

"What?" Swag shouted back over the din of the engine.

"Lean out the damned window and shoot over the fuckin' roof," Kat said, her voice more than just a little nuts. "What? I gotta spell it out for you? You can get a clean shot."

Swag glanced at the speedometer. It was nudging ninety. "You get on the roof," he said. "This isn't some movie, you know?"

"Shit," Kat said. "Whatta fuckin' pussy!"

There was a roadblock ahead. The orange and white saw-horses and flashing warning lights signaled a pothole crew site. The cab veered suddenly left. Kat, seeing her chance, crashed through the sawhorses. For an instant the wind-shield vanished in a mayhem of splintering wood and bursting light. The car plunged viciously, hit the edge of the hole, then bucked upward, throwing Swag back into his seat.

When Swag regained his senses, there was a spike of white and orange wood protruding through the shattered window, aimed at his throat, and they were coming up behind the cab again.

"Okay, take out this motherfucker!" Kat screamed. "Get him!"

Swag pulled the splintered spike from the shattered glass and stuck the barrel of the shotgun through. He fired a quick two-round burst that dissolved the rear window and put another hole through the trunk.

The cab fell back again. Swag pulled the shotgun back through the hole and shot through the open passenger window, letting go with two more rounds. They ripped up the cab's front fender and rear passenger door.

Kat eased up on the gas and the cab slid back into view. They were separated by a lane now. Swag was about to fire again, but suddenly a car fell between them. The car was doing maybe sixty, but the Jag and cab passed it like it was standing still.

When he had a clear shot and was about to fire, Kat cut the wheel hard to the left, bringing them right alongside again. He saw through the last remnants of safety glass that the driver's metallic sun visor was turned toward him. Before he could think of what it meant, he found out. As soon as he pulled the trigger, he was bathed by a blinding strobe light.

Swag fired again, but couldn't aim. His shots were all over the place, ripping into the door, going high over the roof. With each shot the driver seemed to speed up or slow down.

"That car's got more fuckin' lights than a French disco," Kat yelled in frustration. "I'm gonna get close!"

She cut the wheel again, throwing the Jag into the side

of the cab. Again the car didn't budge as metal scraped metal. For a moment they were so close, Swag could have climbed out the window into the other car. Then Kat eased off, pulling back into the middle lane.

Between the strobes Swag saw the fat-faced passenger extend his gun hand through the rear passenger window and begin firing. He moved in a jerking motion, the fat red face first smiling, then grimacing with the effort of aiming the shiny little automatic.

The sound of the gun was swallowed up by the roar of engines. Three bullets whizzed through the Jag and plinked into the door. Swag felt something hot burn across the back of his lower leg with the first shot, then felt the second hit the seat under him. He fired three rounds fast, the shotgun jumping in his hands, and watched as the fat face vanished down beneath the window.

"Fuck! That asshole almost hit me!" Kat screamed, pulling the wheel savagely right. "Sit back now!"

Swag pulled the gun back in through the window and launched himself back against the seat.

Kat was steering one-handed, her left hand bent across her chest as she began firing through Swag's window. Two of her five rounds smashed into the door next to Swag, taking out the leather and wood trim. The three others sailed through the window and into and over the cab.

"Stop it! Just fuckin' quit!" he shouted, his voice sounding tinny in his numbed ear.

They were just passing 110th Street, and Swag could see the Triboro Bridge ahead. If they made it to that exit, they'd be lost in a tangle of roads that could take them to the South Bronx, LIE, and all over hell and back.

Kat eased off into the left lane, keeping an uneven pace with the cab as the fat man kept firing wildly. His face was a big grin. Even in the strobe there was something weirdly familiar about it.

"Just get to his right, don't let them get on the bridge," Swag shouted, his hearing returning slowly. "Get on his ass!"

Kat did as he said, falling behind the car to come up on the right side. Then, as if in a dream, Swag saw himself doing what he didn't want to do. Wrapping the safety harness three times around his left arm, he pulled himself up in the open window. He had the shotgun's sling wrapped around his right hand.

Kat saw what he was doing and eased off on the gas, offering Swag a clean shot at the cab's rear window. They were going maybe eighty, and each pothole threatened to knock Swag from his perch on the window.

Using his left forearm, wrapped in the safety harness to stabilize the shotgun, he let go with a four-round burst. The barrel came up hard, but Swag kept the shots in a tight pattern, peppering the rear of the cab, where he knew the gas tank to be. When he stopped firing, a huge hole had appeared at the cab's rear.

The cab pulled away slowly as they approached the 125th Street exit. The fat hand was stuck through the rear window, firing blindly, the shots pinging off the asphalt.

"Again!" Swag yelled. "Again!"

Kat kept pace with the cab as Swag fired as fast as he could, each shot crashing into the rear of the cab, tearing huge chunks of metal from its trunk and fenders. Two more shots and the rear window exploded in a hail of shattered glass.

As they approached the 125th Street exit, Kat cut the wheel hard to the right and sped up, the two cars colliding as she forced the cab onto the exit. Then the cab's driver did something. The engine pitch changed completely and the car shot insanely ahead, a hot blue flame shooting from its tail pipes.

As Kat fell behind, Swag kept firing, the barrel burning his arm.

When the cab was twenty yards ahead, Swag capped off the last round. The gas tank exploded in a low rumble and burst into flames. Suddenly the driver lost control of the cab. It skidded wildly, swerving left, then hard to the right as the roadway curved. It missed the exit ramp's curve and crashed up over a narrow lot of dirt and broken glass.

For a split second the cab, its rear engulfed in flames, seemed to hang in the air, sailing out into space. Then it crashed, hissing into the East River.

chapter thirteen

WHEN CARS SINK INTO THE EAST RIVER, more often than not, they come to rest in bottom muck upside down. The weight of the engine pulls them nose first into the murky water, and then the momentum flips them over in the darkness.

From the roadblocked exit it was easy to see where the Bentley went into the drink. Even in the semidarkness of predawn, the Triboro Bridge seemed to cast its nasty shadow over the river and shores around it. This was the Hell Gate section of the river. A stretch of water of such treacherous currents that its Dutch name—*Hellgat*, Beautiful Pass—was soon bastardized to a more fitting moniker.

Eight divers, two police launches, a half-dozen Zodiac inflatables, and a fire boat marked the spot. Parked at the water's edge were two EMS buses, a half-dozen NYPD blue and white patrol cars, three unmarked Plymouth detective units, and a dozen provost gray vehicles. All kept their emergency lights spinning, casting a confusing array of light over the scene. Just beyond them, secure behind yellow plastic police ribbon, stood the news vans, the chauffeured limos of news anchors, and a variety of early morning gawkers, including a few fishermen, who sat patiently at the fringe, poles resting across their laps.

Pacing impatiently along the water's edge was Colonel Bammer. He had just arrived, immediately following the near positive identification of the body.

"What the hell is this?" Bammer shouted, his face gone red with rhetorical rage. "What the hell is this?"

"They killed Cap'n Reggie, sir," the young major replied.

"They killed Cap'n Reggie, sir," Bammer mimicked cruelly as he ceased his nervous pacing.

"Yes, sir," the major answered, oblivious, unaware, or too scared to respond to the insult.

"They killed Cap'n Reggie," Bammer said, his voice suddenly much calmer, though still barely under control.

"Yes, sir, you know, Cap'n Reggie," the major answered, hopeful that the rage had permanently passed. So hopeful that he began singing the jingle. "'Cap'n Reggie's fish and chips, the most crispiest chips and delicious-iest fish! Cod and haddock and flounder too, spiced just right, straight from the ocean to you!'"

The young major would never know if it was his rendition of the Cap'n Reggie sea-chant jingle or maybe the bobbing, old salt dance of the commercial that he tried to imitate—whatever it was, it turned the colonel's face a bloodless white with emotion that passed rage and stopped on the doorstep of incoherent paroxysm.

"Major! Stop instantly!" Bammer yelled, spittle forming at the corners of his mouth. "We've lost a goddamned tourist here! A well-known public fuckin' figure! And you're dancing around like an imbecile!"

"I thought it might be useful, sir," the major answered weakly. "For background, as it were. As it pertains—"

"I don't give a flying fuck for background!" Bammer roared as more spittle collected at the corners of his lips, which were contorted with rage. "Do you know who woke me up this morning?"

"No sir," the major answered.

"The bloody British consul himself," Bammer screamed. "Called at 0400, as soon as the body was identified. But I had to put them on hold for the State Department."

The major, wisely, chose not to answer directly. Rather, he pointed toward the water, where the Bentley was rising ominously from the cold depths. This would make the third attempt, the other two failing when the cables snapped under the weight of the massive vehicle. Now they were using a length of cable commonly employed by tugs to pull barges.

The Bentley rose like a soggy yellow apparition from the depths, water falling from its undercarriage and out its windows in great splashing sheets as it scraped up over the rocks toward shore.

There was a flash from the photographers as it came to rest on dry land. Even from where Bammer stood, his neatly pressed uniform safe from danger of stains, he could see the bullet holes. They stood out in sharp contrast in the creased metal. If the eyewitness report of fire was correct, it had not done much damage. Probably didn't have enough time before the car went into the drink.

"Are the news people here?" Bammer asked the major, still at his side.

"Yes sir," the young officer answered.

"Which ones?" Bammer asked, turning now to inspect his hair in the sideview mirror of his unit. His hair, a perfectly barbered head of steely gray, was one of his best assets, second only to his deep, sonorous voice and good posture.

"The major dailies, French, Brit, and German wire services, and two news magazines," the major reported.

"What about the ENGs?" Bammer asked, the acronym for electronic news gathering as familiar to his mouth as any military term, maybe even more so.

"All local stations," the major said, then added, "and three cable."

"National?" Bammer asked hopefully. "Any of the affiliates?"

"All local, sir," came the small response.

Bammer turned from his primping and looked eastward, toward Ward's Island and beyond to Queens. It was just about dawn. The first rays of pink and blue light were appearing on the horizon across the river. Their soft hues contrasted sharply with the dark expanse of water and the black outlines of deserted warehouses, abandoned buildings, and the bridge in the background.

Bammer studied the scene intently, his eyes roaming from the horizon to the car then back again. Then he turned; over in the vacant lot he could make out the microwave antennas of the news vans, shooting straight up like a small grove of leafless trees.

"Sir, is there anything else?" the major asked.

Bammer was a long time in answering, seemingly engulfed in thought. "Yes, bring me Dobbs," he said.

"Yes sir," the major said, and ran off at a smooth double-time trot.

Dobbs, the colonel's head of media relations and crisis management, appeared nearly instantly, walking calmly over the rough terrain at a stroll. He wore a pair of French boating shoes, tan pants, and crew-neck sweater. The round gold-framed glasses gave him a slightly intellectual appearance. He looked for all the world like an untenured Ivy League professor with a fat trust fund. At thirty-eight, there was something still boyish about his slightly plump face. Except for the eyes; Dobbs's eyes were pale green orbs of a cynicism so profound they appeared at turns amused and dead. They were eyes that viewed the world as if through a pair of auto-focusing minicam lenses.

"You saw the report on the computer?" Bammer asked.

Dobbs nodded.

"Then you know how I feel, right?"

"You're mad," Dobbs said.

"I'm really fuckin' pissed off," Bammer elaborated.

"But not *too mad*," Dobbs corrected. "It would be an annoyance if a British citizen weren't involved. A Brit who just happens to be a big asshole buddy of royalty. So this is serious. You're resolute. In control. A leader with a clear objective."

"Catch the motherfuckers who did it, cut off their pricks, and ram them so far down their throats, every time they take a step they'll be fucking themselves up the ass! And—"

". . . To see that justice is done," Dobbs corrected tactfully. "To oversee the orderly and lawful pursuit of justice in regard to this heinous crime. A job, nay a public trust, that you and your men are eminently qualified and sufficiently equipped to carry out."

Bammer digested the description of his mood in its entirety and assimilated it into every cell of his being. This ability, like his hair, was entirely natural. It was his sole genius. "Got it,' he said after a brief pause.

"Even at this moment, your men are following through on several leads. You have every confidence that arrests will be forthcoming, though you would hesitate to predict just when, due to the fact that it's currently an ongoing investigation. You will personally oversee the entire investigative process."

"Got it," Bammer said. "When do we roll?"

Dobbs studied his watch, an ancient Hamilton Reverso. "We'll have sufficient light in twenty minutes," he said. "The cameras will shoot natural light, eliminate shadows and glare. National Weather Service predicted cirrostratus clouds in the east; it should make for a nice shot. And we'll still have time to make the early news. We'll go as a pool story. No one-on-one interviews. No comment after your initial statement."

"I just walk away?" Bammer asked. "Where do I go?"

"Start at the car," Dobbs instructed. "Walk forward, hitting your first mark twenty-five feet in front. Talk the talk, then pause for the photo op. Give it a ten count, then walk the walk. I'll arrange for three uniforms to cluster at your left. That's your second mark, a closer with you deep in conference, skyline in the background."

"Where do I stand?" Bammer asked. "That first mark is where?"

Dobbs made a complete circle, his eyes taking in every detail. "In front of the car. Just to the right of the driver's door. I'll mark it with chalk," he said. "Roll up your sleeves, loosen the collar. You personally have been poking around, searching for clues. Keep the divers and craft in place. I'll arrange for two crime scene techs to remain active in the background, good for effect."

"You want we should dump the car back in?" Bammer asked. "Maybe we can haul it out again for the cameras."

Dobbs considered this for a full ten seconds. "I think not," he said at last.

Behind them the provost catering van arrived, and a white-uniformed attendant began serving up coffee, doughnuts, fresh fruit, and orange juice to members of the press. A few of the fishermen ventured over to the food, but were quickly shooed off.

"There's no national people here," Bammer offered. "I mean no national electronic people."

Dobbs turned slightly to face the colonel. "I know," he said indifferently. "I've arranged for an intercept off one of the locals' microwave. We'll re-edit back at my office, send out three flavors to the nationals."

"That's it, then?" Bammer said.

"Not quite," Dobbs answered, and handed Bammer a sheet of paper with large computer-generated type. "Here's the text of your statement. We can run it off the mini-prompter if you like."

Bammer studied the sheet; it contained twelve sentences, eighteen lines in a neat block of justified type. The perfect sound bite. "No, I can handle this," he said. And then he began reading it. The fact that he moved his lips was barely noticeable.

Back at the Plaza, Sandy Mann slept like a baby in the queen-sized bed. The drugs, adrenalin, and a split of champagne had dispatched her without so much as a backward glance toward consciousness.

Out in the sitting room, Swag, Kat, and one of the two goons mulled their options over room service fare. The other goon sat in front of the television, devouring a bacon, cheese, ham, mushroom, onion, garlic, green pepper, and caviar omelette in great noisy slurps. He was watching one of those early morning news shows, where a serious young woman interviewer was questioning an angry young writer about his latest book.

"You think she gets enough?" the goon in front of the television said. "I mean, shit, it's early in the morning, and she's showing enough leg and chest."

"Shut up," Kat snapped. Then added, "Where's the limo?"

"The Harlem River," the goon not watching television answered, meaning the bottom of the river.

"How 'bout the Jag?" she asked.

"Same," came the answer from the other goon. "Shit, there's so many cars down there, it looks like a used car lot. You think maybe she does it just before she comes on the show? You know, she's always so, like, perky."

This time it was Swag's turn. "Shut up!" he called over his shoulder. "Anybody see you drop her?" He was feeling a slight ache at his calf where the bullet had grazed him.

"Naw, we loaded her into a cab on 44th," the goon not watching the television answered. "No way to trace her to anything."

"How come I never meet no classy gash?" the guy watching the tube bemoaned, then took another bite of the omelette, using his hands to lift the dripping mess off the gold-rimmed plate. "I mean, they must be around. How come I don't never get a shot at something like that?" This last part was spoken with a full mouth.

"'Cause you're a fuckin' moron," Kat said dully.

"Now there ain't no reason to get insulting," the guy said, almost genuinely hurt. "I mean, I don't come down on you, or your boy there in that shirt."

"What? You don't like the shirt?" Swag shot back. "What's wrong with it?"

"I wouldn't bury my worst enemy in it, pal," the guy said, turning to get a view at Swag's yellow, blue, and orange landscape of the New York skyline depicted in volcanoes.

"Quit this bullshit now," Kat instructed. "We gotta get a line on who that asshole in the taxi was."

"Holy shit, will you look at this," the guy by the television said.

"Shut up!" Kat barked. "Just shut up!"

"No, look, it's the guy!" the goon answered, actually pointing toward the screen. "It's that guy!"

Swag, Kat, and the goon all turned toward the television at the opposite side of the room. It only took a quick glance, then they were crowded around it. On the screen was Reginald Hollowbutton, dressed in morning coat, top hat, and smoking a big cigar. At the top of the screen were the words, COMMERCIAL.

"Never give in!" Hollowbutton recited in a deep aristrocratic voice. "Never, never, never—in nothing great or small, large or petty—never give in! Especially when you're in the mood for the best fish and chips in the world. Come to Cap'n Reg's."

It hit Swag in an instant. That's why he'd known he'd seen that face before. Everyone had seen it, in dozens of commercials.

Even as Hollowbutton held up a portion of fish and chips, served in an authentic imitation newspaper cone, the newscaster's voice came on, detailing Hollowbutton's tragic and sudden demise.

"Holy shit," Kat whispered.

Then the screen switched suddenly, from Hollowbutton to a live remote from the East River. The camera panned slowly, settling on none other than Colonel Bammer. He looked professional as hell standing by the yellow Bentley with crime scene techs swarming all around.

"Turn it off," Swag moaned.

"Doncha want to hear what Bammer has to say?" the goon closest to the set asked.

"No," Swag answered.

chapter fourteen

SWAG, BLINKING HIS EYES OPEN, stretched and listened to the commotion in the room around him. While he slept fully clothed on the sitting room couch, the room had been transformed into an office. It was like falling asleep at the Plaza and waking up in the underwriting division of a not-too-prosperous insurance company. There was still a profusion of gilt-trimmed furniture, tactful lamps, and carpeting; these alone reinforced his memory of the night before.

A long buffet table lined one wall. Six overweight middle-aged women, jammed into a rainbow display of polyester, worked the phones and typed into terminals. At the opposite side of the room, two balding fat men, so close in appearance that Swag had to blink to be sure he wasn't seeing double, sweated through shirtsleeves and typed away at twin terminals between bites of mustard-laden, room service corned beef.

Three other guys in shirtsleeves and loud ties paced in narrow circles near the door. They spoke in hushed tones into cellulars while maintaining a pattern tighter than any that ever circled Kennedy or LaGuardia's runways.

Rising from the white and gold brocade couch, Swag took in the scene more carefully. He counted eleven people in all, not including one of the goons—the bigger one, by the double doors to the bedroom. He was wearing a Brit jogging suit and leaning back in a folding chair, reading a paperback, a large automatic wedged under one thigh.

The television in the armoire was turned to a cable financial network with the sound off. A listing of stocks ran across its bottom while a Japanese commentator mouthed silent words before a chromokeyed screen of the latest in battery-operated Bento boxes paraded off an assembly line. It was like a movie so badly dubbed that the words would never appear. Four more televisions were set up on rolling stands around the wall beside the armoire, three tuned to different financial networks, the fourth displaying pay-per-view soft-core porn.

Four high-speed laser printers hummed contentedly on another buffet table near the door, releasing their paper into plastic trays. A small Asian woman gathered the papers from each tray and began distributing them around the room, working her way counterclockwise.

There were three large coffee urns set up on a room service table near the double-door entrance to the room. Swag made his way to it cautiously, unnoticed by the busy workers. The urns included small signs that hung from the spigots: Decaf, Coffee, and Hot Water. A neat stack of gold-trimmed Plaza cups, milk in a silver creamer, and tea bags were artfully arranged at the side.

Swag poured himself a cup of coffee and lit a cigarette. Judging from the sparse light that crept in through the closed curtains, he judged the time to be late afternoon.

The Asian woman scurried by with a stack of papers and nodded politely. Just another day at the office.

Swag was halfway through his coffee when the goon guarding the door signaled him over with a finger. He crossed the room, coffee cup in one hand, cigarette in the other, dodging the workers as he went.

"Boss wants to see you," the goon said. He was smiling.

"Now?" Swag asked, and took another sip of the coffee.

"Said as soon as you got up," the goon answered, then leaned over and knocked, to save Swag the trouble.

Swag, not waiting for an answer from the other side,

walked through the bedroom door. And there was the boss. Sandy Mann was propped up in the huge queen-sized bed, three pillows supporting her back. She was wearing a white terry-cloth robe, the kind hotels offer guests. A cellular laptop on her lap, and yet another bank of televisions along the opposite wall. There were at least six of them; one was tuned to a cable news station with subtitles, the rest to financial channels.

Sitting comfortably at the foot of the bed, curled up on a pillow, was a Lhasa apso. The dog eyed Swag suspiciously. It looked for all the world like Toto—if Toto had been stolen as a pup and raised by bikers.

"You're the boss, huh?" Swag said, kicking the door shut behind him.

"You got it, Jack," Sandy said, looking up from the laptop.

"No mysterious sugar daddy, huh?"

"'Fraid not," she answered. "Just a girl all alone in this world, trying to make good, doing the best she can for herself."

Sandy stretched out one of her bare feet and began rubbing the dog behind the ear with her big toe. The animal nuzzled in closer without taking its small, black-marble eyes off Swag.

"Kat was in on it?" Swag asked. He wasn't fully awake yet, but it was beginning to fall into some kind of order.

"Don't hold it against her," Sandy said. "Kat works for me. It's not like she had any choice or anything like that."

"And all that out there?"

"Support staff," Sandy said, brushing a stray hair behind her ear. "We're what you might call a diversified organization."

"Why'n't you lay it out for me?" Swag asked.

"If you think it'd help." Sandy yawned, stretching. The small dog began to lick at her ankle. She pulled away from the animal, then gave it a vicious kick that sent it rolling off the bed, snarling and yelping.

This is the way it was: Sandy was in the legitimacy business. For a small fee she'd turn anyone from a hooker, to a black-market money guy, to a dealer in hot microchips, legit. Need a business to run credit cards through? No problem, Sandy had a dozen bars all over town that would punch plastic for a straight fifteen points off the top. How about proof of gainful employment for the parole officer? Sandy provided computer-generated pay stubs, tax forms, anything you wanted. She'd set up a front; pay taxes; keep time sheets; make short-term loans; dummy up bills of lading; register a car in a company name; provide new identities in national and local computer networks; offer references. Sandy was in the cleaning business—she washed dirty people and dirty money. Little wonder she left Bellevue—she had a business to run.

The whole operation was run through more than three dozen companies, some of them legit, as in limo companies, bars, restaurants; messenger services; phone sex lines; fast food franchises; and a small cable station featuring soft-core. Other companies she ran existed only on paper with accounts set up in tax havens with secrecy laws. There was also a small offshore bank which she owned outright.

With state, local, and fed computers slowly closing the net around underground money, business had been very good indeed. And she'd played it smart, not greedy. She didn't tell Swag where her money went, but he guessed it would be someplace offshore. The sugar daddy had been a nice bit, something to keep competition guessing and, better yet, just a little scared.

As she continued to lay out the operation in sketchy detail, Swag felt as if he could use another cup of coffee. He settled for a cigarette.

"Okay, I'm telling you this because someone's trying to whack me out," Sandy said, crossing her ankles.

"What about Cap'n Reg? You buy into his franchise?" Swag asked.

"That crap?" Sandy exclaimed. "Fish paste and soy filler. Give me a little credit, I got *some* standards."

"So what's your connection to him?"

"None, zero, zip, nada," Sandy recited. "But I'll tell you this—more than a dozen of my customers and employees got zotsed in the last three months."

"But we're talking about you, right?" Swag offered.

"You got that right," Sandy said. "Besides, fuck 'em, they were nobodies."

"Zeros, huh?"

"Yeah, fuckin' waste of skin," Sandy said, her face emotionless. "You find out who set me up for that fat tea bag and bust a cap in his head. I'll give you five K more for the effort."

"Sorry, no deal," Swag said and turned to the door.

"Whattaya mean, 'no deal'?"

Swag, cigarette still in his mouth, turned back to Sandy. "You didn't play it straight with me. Not from the jump," he said. "I'm gone."

He was about to leave, one hand on the doorknob, when Sandy said, "Rip his fuckin' balls off!"

At first Swag thought Sandy was talking to him. Then he heard the high-pitched growling yip-yip and saw a flash of black and brown fur. The dog made a heroic leap from under the bed, its small jaws clamping down on Swag's leg across the torn blood-stiff section of pant leg that the bullet had torn through.

The pain drove Swag back a staggering half step. The dog lost its grip on the small chunk of flesh, and its teeth snapped shut on Swag's torn pants. Growling and working its back legs, the dog tore Swag's pants from just above his knee to halfway down the polished side of his cowboy shit-kickers.

Swag reached down to where the dog was working on the ripped material, picked the animal up by the scruff of its neck and tossed it back into bed with Sandy.

"Stop," Sandy said, and instantly the dog curled at her side.

"It's been a real pleasure," Swag said, opening the door.

"You wouldn't be saying that if you'd been sitting down. He woulda had your stones for kibble," he heard Sandy call as he shut the door.

The commotion inside the bedroom had apparently gone unnoticed by everyone in the sitting room. The place was still abuzz with activity.

"She introduce you to that dog?" the goon by the door asked.

"Yeah," Swag said, pausing briefly to survey the damage to his pants.

"Some fuckin' pooch, huh?"

"Yeah, a real prize," Swag said, pulling up a flap of his dangling pants, matching it to the other. The pants, a pair of tan khakis, were a total loss.

"Teeth are sharpened. Filed the fuck into points," the goon said, smiling. "Trained by some hick pit-bull breeder on the West Side. Mutt can hang by its teeth from a hunk of raw meat from now till next Sunday."

"Okay, but what about the dog?" Swag shot back, letting go of the twin flaps of material.

"Don't bitch her off," the goon warned. "Just do like she says."

"I'm not going to do anything," Swag answered. "I'm not working for her."

"Yeah, well, that's good too," the guy said. "Hey, listen, do me a solid, huh? Take these coats out to the guy in the hall to dump, okay?"

Swag thought about it for a second, then took the white hospital coats the guy handed him. He walked across the room unnoticed and out the door.

In the hall, the second goon had set up a chair. He was staring down the narrow hallway, a large matte-black automatic resting in his lap.

"You're outta here, huh?" the guy asked, perking up when Swag closed the door behind him.

"Here," Swag said, handing him the white coats.

"Yeah, I gotta get rid of these," the guy said, holding up the coats.

Swag saw that the hospital button pinned to the lapel had changed its color from green to orange. Only a small circle of green remained at the center.

"Better get yourself checked out too," Swag said. "Looks like you took a dose from an X ray."

"What the fuck you talkin' 'bout?"

"That button," Swag said. "Says you're hot."

"I didn't go near no X ray," the guy said, turning the coat over to study the button. "We were on a psych ward, remember?"

"You got a dose somewhere," Swag countered, then began walking down the hall.

As Swag turned the corner toward the elevators, he heard the guard shout again, "We were on a fuckin' psych ward!"

In a well-appointed town house, workmen were moving from room to room, emptying the place of rented antiques as more workmen began installing shogi screens, tatami mats, and low lacquer tables. The change was remarkable. In a matter of hours they had removed furniture, molding, rugs, lamps, books, paintings.

In the master bedroom on the second floor, a new futon was stored in the closet of the largest bedroom and a low table sat at the center of its polished floor. By the end of the next day the house would be completely and entirely converted into the type of luxurious yet utterly traditional Japanese inn called a *ryokan*.

Off to one side, the alcove, which had previously boasted a bronze bust of Wellington, was turned into a *tokonoma*, the bust replaced with a small lacquer table and an artfully delicate arrangement of flowers in front of a sixth century wall-hanging scroll—*kakejiku*—which depicted a summer scene of birds and fish.

Kneeling in front of the alcove, Japanese style, was the tall Frenchman with a ponytail. He was dressed in cotton dinner robe, called a *yukata*. He worked deftly, carefully adjusting the five green stems and two blossoming flowers in the vase. His concentration was complete. He prided himself on his skill at *ikebana*, having studied once with a master of the art. In reality, he was not very good at it. Perhaps as talented as the typical Osaka housewife, if you caught her on a particularly bad day. In origami he was worse and often resorted to scissors and paste.

When he finished the task, he stood up effortlessly to admire his handiwork, nodded, and turned to see four workmen struggling to squeeze the immense—*hinoki furo*—bathtub of scented white cypress through the door. Other workmen, carrying polished stones for the bathroom floor, waited patiently.

Turning to the door, he was surprised to see the woman, arm in a cast, waiting silently. Attached to the top of the cast, just below the shoulder, was a small red-plastic box that sent small electrical charges through the arm to help the bones knit.

"Darling," he said, moving quickly across the room. "You must feel dreadful. What did the doctor say?"

"He said a week in a cast," the woman said. In the silk teal blouse and light summer pants, she looked more like the victim of a less than perfect holiday than someone who less than twenty-four hours ago had been shot in the arm, driven a car off the FDR, then swum two miles downriver before crawling ashore.

"Come, see my *tokonoma*," he answered, dismissing her injuries entirely. "*Fantastique*, no? Tradition places them in the room for the entertainment and delight of the guest."

It was the way he said it that bothered Erica—the stiff way he always talked—as if reciting from a guidebook or into the microphone of one of those cheap package bus tours.

"Easily amused, aren't they?" the woman said, unimpressed. Even her martial arts training and a fistful of painkillers could not kill the dull throb in her arm.

"Ah, remember, *o-kyaku-sama wa kami sama*," he replied in faultless Japanese. *The guest is a god.*

She shrugged by way of answer, which released a new wave of pain that jolted down to her fingertips.

"Ah, mon chéri," the man said, leading her by the good arm through the doorway to the hall. "But you must remember, it is your own fault, no?"

"How do you figure that?" she asked, shaking off his solic-
itous grip on her elbow.

"Did you not deviate from the itinerary?" came the
answer. "We are, you must remember, in the tourist business,
after all. Any deviation, any at all, means disaster. Perhaps
you believe me now."

"You don't seem too upset about Hollowbutton," she
answered back in a conspiratorial whisper.

"Is but nothing," he said offhandedly. "What's one more
dead Englishman?"

"It's going to attract attention," Erica answered. "The
local authorities."

"Ah, in so many ways you are still that same little girl,"
the Frenchman said, sounding as if he were about to start
singing a melody from *Gigi*. "I remember you as if it were
yesterday—a fresh-faced au pair in Tours, first time away
from—what town was that?"

"Queens."

"Yes, Queens," he said.

"Thank heaven for little girls from Queens, right?"

The Frenchman's expression changed instantly, from solic-
itous back to employer. "No, but you should thank me for
that Legionnaire training."

Sensing thin ice under her feet, she said, "I do, really, I
guess I'm just a little off from last night. But we will be
drawing some serious heat over this thing."

The Frenchman's friendly expression returned, the lines
of his face softening ever so slightly. "Do not worry. One
or two more guests and then we are gone."

"Okay, sure," she answered. "Give me a call. You know
how to reach me."

He watched the young woman make her way down the
stairs, leaning slightly in order to balance the cast. "Indeed
I do, mon chéri," he whispered when she was well out of
earshot.

chapter fifteen

SWAG GOT FOUR MESSAGES THE NEXT DAY and a postcard.
The messages were from Kat and delivered by street run-
ners—little kids in gimme T-shirts and plastic shoes who
ran the streets, back alleys, and roofs, making deliveries for
a couple bucks American. The messages were all the same:
"Need to talk," "Need to talk," "Need to talk."

"You got an answer, Jack?" the last runner asked. A tough
little guy in a filthy Evian T, he stood there defiantly.

Swag dug in his pocket for a couple of bucks, handed
the wrinkled bills to the kid. "No answer," he said.

The kid took the money. "The chick's a psycho, you know
that. Jitterbug."

"You have to get to know her," Swag answered and
turned away.

"You get to fuckin' know her, Jack," the kid said and ran
off.

The postcard was from Jim Bob Spurock and left at a
storefront mail drop Swag almost never used. He hadn't
seen Jim Bob in a couple weeks. Now he knew why. The
front featured a badly printed four-color photo of Pitcairn
Island's major exports—pineapples, oranges, and postage
stamps. The meticulous printed ballpoint message on the
back read, "Having a wonderful time. Wish you were
here. Remember, you can do what you want, as long as
you do what you have to. Best Regards, J. B. Spurock."

Swag examined the postcard, which included a patently

false Pitcairn stamp and postmark. Nobody, even Jim Bob, could mail a letter from the South Pacific and have it work through the system in a few days. But it would be just like Jim Bob to pick some place like Pitcairn as a front.

The day after that there were eight messages from Kat. And on the third day, twelve. He got the last message while standing in front of a food vendor on 52nd and Broadway, eating tempura vegetables for lunch. A light rain had fallen, and the streets glistened under a hiss of light traffic.

At first he didn't recognize Kat. She moved out of the crowd of straggling tourists at a fast walk, hunched over as if the rain was still falling. She was wearing one of those cheap plastic raincoats that maybe offered some protection from the rain, but made you sweat unmercifully.

When she spotted Swag, she nearly broke into a run, clutching at the collar of the raincoat as if she were making her way through a January blizzard and not hustling down the street in a humid ninety degrees.

"Goddamnit, Swag, didn't you get the messages?" Kat asked. She was sweating mightily. When she ran a hand through her hair, it slicked itself back across her head, adding to the crazed look.

"Yeah, I got them," Swag said, finishing off the last piece of broccoli and handing the paper boat back to the vendor.

"Well, what's wrong, huh?" Kat asked. "I gotta talk to you; I've been looking everywhere."

"What's wrong is that you didn't play it straight up," he said, turning his back and walking off slowly.

Kat hurried after him, still clutching at the raincoat. "Don't do this to me," she said, coming up on his side.

"I'm not doing shit to you, Kat," he said, stepping off the curb. "Nothing."

"We've known each other a long time," she said, falling in step beside him. "Been friends a long time, right?"

"Right up to when you decided not to play it straight," Swag said, turning the corner and heading up to Sixth Avenue.

"Hey, didn't I tell you that I didn't have no choice?" Kat

asked. "I didn't have a choice, she was the boss. What should I have done?"

Swag stopped short. "Yeah, you mentioned that in message five and nine," he said. "If you'd asked me, I would have told you what to do. Play it straight. I don't have time for bullshit."

"Look, Swag," Kat said, "you gotta give me a minute here, I gotta talk to you."

Swag started walking again. He was nearly to Sixth. On either side were the large buildings. Sixties skyscrapers, they now held the mostly one-floor outposts for sweatshop headquarters, agribusiness conglomerates, and the banks and overseas corporations that held the paper to seventy percent of America's farmland. High-tech farms took less personnel to plant, irrigate, harvest, and all the rest, than to make the deals for the European and Far East buyers.

"Swag, everything's changed," Kat said, almost begging as she continued to follow him, then dodging a group of tourists, Eastern European types. Stout men and stouter women. "The whole thing's changed."

"Like what?" he asked, purposefully not looking at her. If she was lying again, he didn't want to know her. Even if she wasn't lying, he wasn't sure he wanted to know her.

"Sandy canned me," she said, her voice anxious. Swag gave her an opening, and she was using it. "I'm not working for her anymore. That part's over. Fini."

"You're giving me a load of shit here," he shot back. "Sandy Mann burned some guy in a deal or someone's trying to move in on her corner and started whacking her people. The whole thing's tired."

"I'm giving it to you straight up," Kat said, nearly screaming. "I don't work for her since you beat up her dog and walked out of the suite at the Plaza."

They were coming out onto Sixth Avenue now. A group of Japanese sararimen were clustered at the corner, grim-faced and sweating in their suits. Swag always thought the Japanese looked as if they were always thinking of whatever personal or business shortcoming had earned them their TDU—Temporary Dispatch Unaccompanied—to New York, a corporate exile from which few ever returned. Now they were stranded, left to work in this shabby city and to live in gated communities up in Westchester or Connecticut. The French and Spanish businessmen, on the other hand, always looked quite jolly, while the Germans just looked grim and vaguely disapproving.

"Congratulations," Swag said. "I wish you every good luck in your job search and future endeavors."

"They're after me, Swag," Kat suddenly blurted out. "Those fuckers are after me!"

Swag stepped off the curb with the sararies, who cast furtive sidelong glances toward Kat. She was sweating heavily now, her face covered with a slick sheen. Beneath the sheen of sweat he could see uncharacteristic panic.

"Goddamnit, are you listening to me?" she screamed. "Those fuckers are after *me* now."

The sarari suits quickened their walk to escape the scene.

"Who's after you?" Swag asked. "Cap'n Reg is dead. Remember?"

"Them! They, whoever they are," she said. "It started just like it did with Sandy. The letters, the telephone calls. It's just like it was with her!"

Swag stepped up on the curb and kept walking, now heading downtown. He had no thought of where to go, except to lose Kat. But she followed behind, talking the whole time, repeating everything she'd said so far.

"Look, no deal, Kat," Swag finally said as he began crossing 51st. "If you're afraid, hire some muscle. I'm not the guy."

Steam was draining from the manhole at the center of the street. Swag was just stepping over it when Kat grabbed him by the shoulder. He shrugged off the hand, but she held tight, digging her nails in through the material of his shirt and spinning him around.

"You're the guy, motherfucker," she said, hissing.

He saw the gun as he turned. Its barrel poking through

the front of the raincoat and aimed directly at his head. It was an over and under shotgun, cut down to a pistol grip and covered in tape. She had it under the bulky raincoat, secured by the butt and forestock with a length of rope around her neck. She held it one-handed through a hole punched through the pocket of the plastic coat.

"Kat, you're going to get busted for menacing," Swag said, raising his hands slowly. Steam was rising up between them.

"If I get busted, it won't be for menacing," she said. Her face was desperate, half obscured by steam. She was almost crying.

All around, pedestrians hurried to the corners, not staring, just wanting to make it across before the light changed.

"Look, you're upset," Swag said, backing off a tentative half step. The raincoat fell open then, and Swag saw the faded blue material of a Kevlar tactical vest.

"You sonofabitch," Kat said, her mouth twitching down at the sides as the first tears came. "You're damn right I'm upset, you sonofabitch. They're trying to kill me."

"Okay, how's this?" Swag tried, inching back. "We'll go someplace cool and I'll buy you a cup of coffee and we'll talk about it."

"Yeah, that sounds good," she said, the barrel coming down, but not much. "Yeah, that'll be okay."

Then the light changed, and the blare of horns began to sound.

A few blocks uptown at the Plaza, Colonel Bammer was lunching with his second-in-command, a thin major named Aston Martin. Bammer found the name annoying in the extreme. The whole growing fad toward changing a perfectly good name like Phil or Steve or Bill to a pricey consumer item showed, in his mind, a complete lack of class. Already he had six Royces, four Rollies, and seven Dunhills in the ranks of his men. There was also a Dom, but you couldn't be sure about that guy.

"What can you tell me?" Bammer asked.

"The so-called taxi that went into the drink was a Bentley Turbo operating on nitrous oxide when it hit the water. It was the nitrous that gave it the power—even without it, the driver wouldn't have been able to make the turn. The taxi was equipped with antiterrorist devices. High-intensity lighting, reinforced frame and bumpers, Kevlar compartmentalized tires, the works. It was registered to a Cali company that declared bankruptcy six years ago. Somebody sprayed it pretty good with a shotgun," the major said, then paused long enough to catch his breath. "Traces of O-positive blood were found on the driver's side. Hollowbutton was AB negative. Divers recovered a Steyr GB 9 with Hollowbutton's prints on it. Eighteen rounds fired out of a possible eighteen."

Bammer kicked the food cart away from the sofa with one booted foot and rose, the napkin still tucked into his uniform's collar. "Bullshit," he said, with a voice of righteous rage and unquestionable authority. "Almost a week into he investigation and you come to me with bullshit?"

"Hollowbutton died of drowning," the major continued. "The position of the body indicates that he was not able to make an escape through the window. Too fat."

"More bullshit," Bammer said, strolling past his personal guards toward the window.

"We have every reason to believe—based on coroner's reports—that Hollowbutton was not driving," the major continued. "No prints on the wheel. Whoever was driving was wearing gloves."

"Water could've taken care of that," Bammer said, gazing out the window. Down below was the park, its greenery looking cool, even in what Bammer knew was oppressive heat.

"Wasn't in the water long enough," the major answered. "Also, Hollowbutton wasn't registered at any New York hotel. His passport indicated that he had entered the country in Boston. His corporate headquarters confirms this. Says he was in the States to open a new fish processing plant in New Bedford. They indicate that they have no idea what he was doing in New York."

Bammer turned from the window. "What does anyone do in New York?" he asked angrily. "He was here to whore around. Gamble. Maybe get into some trouble."

"Sounds reasonable," the major answered.

"Well then, start with that," Bammer said. "Run his credit cards. Shit, do I have to do every-fuckin'-thing in this joint?"

"We ran his cards," the major said. "Traced his Barclay traveler's checks too. He didn't buy a pack of gum since he entered the country."

"What about his hotel in Boston?" Bammer asked, turning from the window. The food cart had mysteriously vanished. That was the trouble in these classy joints, shit was always vanishing and appearing—waiters and maids always creeping around. It was like a goddamned magic act.

"Not registered in any Boston hotel," the major shot back. "he cleared customs and vanished for a coupla days. Turns up in the river."

Bammer let out a great long sigh. It had been a slow news week, and the papers were playing up the murder. "Okay, here's what you do," he said finally. "Get two of your men, the kind that wear a suit and speak decent, to go back over the basics. British Consulate, his corporate headquarters, the widow, airlines, customs, all that. I want to see a lot of activity there. I want the papers to see it too."

"They're all stonewalling," Aston said. "Nobody's saying nothing. Especially not his widow. His office keeps switching me over to the public information guy."

"Just have them do it," Bammer snapped. "Then you get a couple more men, the kind who don't wear suits and just grunt, you put them on the street. And whatever they have to do down there, have them do it. But I don't want to read nothing about it in the papers."

"Yes sir," Aston said. "Anything else?"

Bammer thought on it awhile, taking his time to cross the room toward the small bar he had installed. "Yeah, get me Dobbs," he said.

"Yes sir," the young major answered and left the room.

Thirty seconds later Dobbs appeared. He was wearing a light blue summer suit and carrying a computer printout. It was neatly packed in a blue folder labeled Confidential.

"What's the word today?" Bammer said.

"Thirty-five percent think the city's safer than two months ago. Thirty percent think it's more dangerous," Dobbs recited. "Sixty-one percent believe with their hearts and minds that the Provost Command is doing a good job. That's a three point positive increase over last month."

"What's the photo op tonight?" Bammer asked.

"Your choice," Dobbs answered. "TB clinic out on Roosevelt Island. A lady who's raising orphans out of a brownstone on Madison. A convention of French police over on a junket."

"Christ almighty," Bammer moaned. "Lungers, orphans, and frog cops."

"We got a promised page three photo for the papers," Dobbs argued. "And human interest segment after national news on two stations."

"How 'bout we just kick down a door somewhere and bust some slime," Bammer suggested. "I'll bring out the ol' Sam Wesson wheel gun and we'll go tactical on some scumbag, huh? Take about ten minutes. In and out."

Dobbs gave Bammer a weary look, removed his glasses and rubbed the bridge of his nose with two fingers. "We do these polls for a reason," he said with strained patience. "Do a few more of these charity things, and I can promise you four points in personal ratings index and six in the safe city category."

"I bet the mayor isn't going to be hobnobbing with lungers, frog cops, and orphans," Bammer whined against Dobbs's solid reasoning.

"He's on a fact-finding mission with the city counsel," Dobbs countered.

"Yeah, where?"

"St. Croix," came the answer. "Now tell me which one you want; I have to phone in for the coverage."

"Ah, fuck," Bammer sighed. "Let's go pet some orphans."

chapter sixteen

SWAG STEERED KAT OFF THE STREET and down the stairs to the old Rockefeller Center promenade. Most of the stores were vacant, their windows soaped opaque or covered in faded newspaper. Those that remained offered cut-rate trinkets, T-shirts, and souvenirs—the kind you'd find at a two-runway airport.

When weather forced the street vendors indoors, they often took up spots along the echoing corridor, trying to catch the scant tourist traffic with wares spread across blankets or a doo-wop rendition of "Heartbreak Hotel" in French.

Swag and Kat walked along the mall slowly, not talking, not looking at the merchandise. One enterprising guy had set up his photo business along the wall. For a few easies he'd snap your Polaroid in front of an enlarged picture of the Rock Center Christmas tree.

The hustles just got stranger and stranger, Swag thought to himself. The city had become a place where weird urban apocrypha lurked behind every hustle and scam. A few days before, he'd spotted a kid, no more than thirteen, selling Genuine NYC Sewer Gators—Florida imports, no doubt, but bleached white to affect albino coloring, and stuffed with shredded newspaper. Another vendor had pulled the same hustle with rats, dying their fur electric blue, yellow, green, and orange, then outfitting them like tourists—complete with miniature cameras—before mounting them in standing positions on blocks of wood.

Swag steered Kat to the Japanese-style coffee shop near the subway entrance. It took much convincing to get her into a booth seat, though no amount of talk could get the sawed-off away from her.

"Don't you know, they're everywhere?" she pleaded, knuckles white around the taped stock. "You saw how they work."

"Kat, the point is, we're not going to get served if you don't put that away."

Four televisions hung from the ceiling, all tuned to the same cable-retail channel, the kind that offered twenty minutes of advertising wedged between reports of smiling newscasters or public domain movies. You used to see the televisions everywhere, fast food joints, airports, doctors' offices. Visual Muzak. It was going to be the hot new thing, until the country fell apart. Now, those remaining units offered recycled news and ads for cassette lessons in French, Japanese, and German, or ads for bottom-feeding lawyers specializing in lawsuits.

"Look Kat, just wrap it in the coat," Swag suggested. "Lay it across your lap."

Kat thought on it for a second, then slipped the rope from around her neck, shrugged out of the raincoat and wrapped the shotgun in it. She kept it in her lap, facing the door. "Yeah, maybe that's better," she said.

The effect wasn't worth the effort. Still wearing the full-body armor, Kat looked like she was preparing for war. A K-bar knife hung in its sheath upside down from her left shoulder. A straight razor was Scotch-taped to her right side, and a line of 12-gauge shells ran around the waist, neatly fitted into the loops someone had sewn on.

"Feel better?" Swag asked.

"Yeah, maybe a little," she offered, her eyes dodging around the room for assassins.

"Look, you have to chill just a little, Kat," Swag said.

The waitress, a young Oriental woman, approached warily, as if this order could be her last. Swag ordered two steamed sweet rolls and coffee for both of them.

"It isn't right," Kat said. "I don't even know why they're after me."

"Maybe the Cap'n Reg thing?" Swag asked, taking a bite of the roll and trying hard to make it all seem normal.

"Nothing to tie me to it," Kat said. "Nothing connects me to the bar either. I'm on the books as a driver for one of Sandy's car services."

"When did it start?" Swag asked.

"The day after you roughed up her lapdog," Kat said, trying to take a sip of her coffee, but shaking so bad she lost most of it across the saucer and table.

"What about her goons? Maybe it's them?"

"No," Kat answered, bringing the sweet roll up to her mouth and taking a small bite. "They check out—who do you think hired them? But it doesn't matter."

Swag took a large bite of his roll and began chewing between questions. "Why doesn't it matter?"

"They both split," she said, staring hard across the table. "Gone. Quit."

Swag saw it then. In the hard fluorescent lighting of the coffee shop he saw the dark circles under her eyes, the skin of her face pulled tight. Her movements were sharp and birdlike. "When's the last time you slept?" he asked.

"I dunno, day before yesterday maybe," she answered, her head coming up fast from where she was staring at her sweet roll. "Been moving around a lot. Catch a half hour here and there. You know, moving target harder to hit and all."

"Shit, Kat," Swag said. "You know better than that."

"All I know is someone's after me," she snapped back.

Swag drained the rest of his coffee. "Okay, let's go."

"Where?" she asked suspiciously.

Swag thought on it a moment. "Raffles, their security is good. You can sleep there."

"That tea-bag hotel," she said. "You figure they can't catch up to me in some Brit hotel?"

Swag got up from the table, pulling Kat up as he moved around the side. She kept a hold of the shotgun, still wrapped in the plastic raincoat. "Come on," Swag said, not asking, but ordering.

They were halfway to the door when the televisions switched from news to a commercial. Spread across the screen was Cap'n Reg, a wide-screen apparition back from the dead and dressed up as a flounder. The costume was complete with top hat and tails which made the portly franchiser look suspiciously like Churchill.

"Never have so many sacrificed so much, for so long, to bring you the juiciest fish and chips for so little," Cap'n Reg intoned. Cartoon bubbles rose from his mouth with each word, and his electronically altered voice made it sound as if he were speaking underwater. It was, by all accounts, one of his less tasteful though most prophetic commercials—considering the facts of his demise.

"Tea-bag sonofabitch!" Kat screamed, stopping in her tracks.

Swag turned just in time to see the shotgun come up. He shouted "No!" as he fell to the floor.

The blast was deafening in the small coffee shop, its ear-numbing report covering the sound of the picture tube blowing out. A second later Swag felt glass falling across his back, looked up and saw Kat lowering the gun with a self-satisfied grin on her face.

The sound of the Cap'n Reg jingle still blared from the other screens. As Kat turned, the sawed-off already raised, Swag came to his feet. He caught her from behind, gripped the shotgun's abbreviated barrel with one hand and tried to work a finger behind the trigger. But Kat was too fast. She pulled back on the trigger, sending the blast nearly straight up. A shower of blown-out acoustic tile and fluorescent lighting rained down on them just as the jingle ended.

"Sonofabitch!" Kat hissed.

Swag wrestled the empty gun away from her, pulling her

around as he pried it, raincoat and all, from Kat's desperate grasp.

The counterman, cashier, and waitress were all shouting at once. All three were holding pistols on Swag and Kat, motioning impatiently for him to throw down the shotgun.

Swag did as he was told, then watched the cashier dial the police on a wall phone.

Detective Sergeant Patrick O'Neal sat in the battered precinct chair across the interrogation table. He was chain-smoking Gitanes like it was a race, lighting one off the other.

Swag stubbed out his own cigarette, clearing a space in the overflowing ashtray, and smiled. It was a smile that was intended to be charming, friendly, conciliatory even. But it fell short by a mile.

"Stop grinning like a fuckin' idiot," O'Neal snapped. "It ain't funny. None of it."

"Come on, what was the damage?" Swag asked. "So she blew out the television. There's plenty more. The whole city is wired like that book, 1984. They're narrowcasting fast-food joints, doctors' offices, schools, banks. They'd put the fuckin' things in crappers if they could."

"Except now they're selling lawyers, soap, and liquor," O'Neal conceded.

"Okay, you got the story," Swag said, then motioned slightly toward the mirror facing him behind O'Neal.

"I gotta take a leak," O'Neal said. He rose and walked out of the room. He came back through the door in maybe fifteen seconds, about as long as it would take to turn off the video camera on the other side of the mirror.

Swag lit another cigarette and exhaled slowly. "How much?" he said.

"What we got is about three hundred for the television, another twenty for the light fixtures and ceiling," O'Neal answered. "Call it three twenty and you and the girl walk."

"Let's call it three fifty," Swag countered. "And you keep the girl in a precinct lockup for two days."

O'Neal nodded and inhaled deeply on the Gitane, burning it down to the filter. "You're my ex-partner, and I love and respect you," he said. "But you gotta tell me what you're into here."

"Cap'n Reg," Swag said, smiling.

O'Neal, cigarette now burned out between his thick yellowed fingers, said, "Aw shit, Swag. Are you fuckin' wacko?"

Swag shrugged his answer.

"Do you know how far Bammer is bent out of shape on that thing?" O'Neal pressed, suddenly remembering the cigarette and dropping it into the pile on the ashtray. "He catches a hint of you nosing around; you're as good as disappeared."

"So you'll keep her in the cage for two days?" Swag asked, ignoring O'Neal's question.

"She's a fuckin' headcase too," O'Neal said. "I'll lose the paperwork on her, but she better not start any shit."

"She'll sleep for most of it," Swag answered. "I guarantee it."

O'Neal pushed his chair back across the floor and rose from his seat heavily. "You put your nose in that tea-bag's murder, you can't guarantee nothing."

Major Aston Martin of the Provost Third Tactical Unit drove slowly along the access road parallel to the West Side Highway. He was driving an unmarked Plymouth out of the NYPD motor pool, rather than one of the flashier provost vehicles.

This was the old freight yards, nearly eighty acres that extended from 59th to 72nd Street along the West Side. Once the lot worked around the clock, accommodating thousands of freight cars for the New York Central and Hudson River lines. Grain elevators, roundhouses, a hundred or more parallel ladder tracks.

Now it was like an abandoned expanse of trash-strewn real estate so out of place in the city as to seem unreal. Martin guided the car carefully up the road, his eyes glued to the rough concrete viaduct on his right and the long line of doors hanging awkwardly on broken hinges, many missing altogether. When he saw the rusted blade of a snow plow, he turned the car gently through the darkness of an open door.

He parked just left of the open door and walked into the dark room, pausing just long enough for his eyes to adjust in the dim light. A huge pile of road salt stood at the center of the cavernous room. Beside it was a Plymouth identical to the one he had arrived in. The walls were covered by ancient graffiti, faded red, blue, yellow, black, and white spray paint. Much of the art were tags—names and street numbers done up stylishly—Wire 84, Sly 125, Psycho 159. Larger works covered the ceiling and upper walls. Frescoes of subways and skylines. Anguished faces with bulging eyes. Water had gotten to some of it, but enough remained to make out the effort that had gone into each stylized rendering.

What was the point? he thought to himself. It wasn't like anyone was ever going to see it. And it wasn't like you could sell it. Just goofy kids with spray cans, doing what every city, state, and federal con since the beginning of time had done, scratching on the walls.

Moving farther into the room, he heard the pleading cries. It was like a chant of "Please, please, please, please, please." Then it stopped, cut short with a croaking thud of what he knew was a rifle's butt striking flesh.

Martin walked cautiously around the thirty-foot-high pile of rock salt. The pleading was more distinct now, echoing slightly in the abandoned space. Above him he heard cars passing overhead.

In the far corner of the room, laid out against the wall, was an old man. Martin sized him up as a skel by his clothes. Old suit pants, filthy with grime. Running shoes held together with tape. His T-shirt, which had once probably been blue, was covered in blood. So was his face. The old man's face was a bloody horror, his mouth a great bleeding wound, distinguished only from the other half-dozen deep gashes along his chin and cheeks by the remnants of broken teeth.

"Please, no more," the old man wheezed, cowering in pain, arms spread against the wall, as if he were trying to pass through the crumbling concrete to escape the two plainclothes provosts who stood over him, rifles held butt up, taunting him with feigned jabs.

Martin approached quietly, shoes crunching down on salt.

"You want us to go, old man?" one of the provosts asked, lifting his rifle higher, the bull-pup stock already dark with blood.

"We own this fuckin' town," the other put in, then turned slightly to acknowledge Martin's approach. "This is *our town*. We love New York."

"Please, no more, please," the old guy begged. "I told you, didn't I?"

"Yeah, you told us," the first provost sneered, then hauled his foot to kick, but stopped short as the old man cowered, pressing himself harder against the wall. "Now tell us again."

The old man stopped his begging then, focusing on Martin, who was now just slightly behind the two plainclothes. "Please, mister," he said, renewed hope coming into his eyes at the sight of a uniform. "They're killing me. Please."

"What did you see?" Martin asked, his voice gentle. "Tell me what you saw."

"Like I told them, I seen it," the old man wheezed. "I seen them run that guy off the road into the river."

"What guy?" Martin asked, easing himself between his two men. "What guy did you see go into the river?"

"That English guy," the old man said hurriedly. "The one on the news, who dresses up like a fish. Please make them stop."

"You lying sack of shit," one of the men behind Martin said, lifting his gun. "You didn't see nothing."

"I did," the old man insisted, bringing a filthy blood-stained arm up to wipe blood away from his mouth. "I saw the car that shot him. Exploded the gas tank."

"What were you doing there?" Martin asked, now kneeling down in front of the old guy.

New hope lit in the old man's face. His eyes, swollen to slits from the beating, darted about frantically. "I lived there," he said. "I got a squat down there. I was a lawyer. Was with C.S. and M. I was . . . almost, nearly a partner."

"Don't tell me what you were," Martin said, his voice as gentle as Marcus Welby in rerun. "Tell me what you saw. That way I can help you."

"I seen two cars," the old man said hurriedly. "That taxi and the other, an English classic. Heard them first. Heard them racing, then heard the shots."

"What kind of English car?" Martin asked.

"Jag," the old man said, nodding painfully. "Sovereign or XJ-S. I had one once, an XJ. I know. Beautiful car. Beautiful. A V-12, you know."

"Tell me about the one you saw," Martin asked, reaching out, but not touching the old man.

"Oh, a beauty," came the answer. "Black with tinted glass. No hubcaps, though. None. No chrome trim either. Oh, but it was fast. Doing ninety at least."

"How many people in the car?" Martin asked.

"It seats four, comfortably," the old man said.

"Tell me how many you saw," Martin said.

"There were two," came the answer. "One driving and the other shooting, hanging out the window. A real cowboy. He was hanging out the window shooting."

"Know what I think?" Martin said, his voice changing, suddenly becoming hostile. "I think you're lying or crazy."

"I'm not, please," the old man begged. "I'm not lying. I'm not. It was a Jag. Two people. I saw it."

"You're lying," Martin insisted, rising up. "I tried to help you, but you lied."

The two bruisers moved forward, menace in each step as they raised their rifles.

"I didn't lie," the old man begged. "Please, believe me. Don't leave. Please."

"Why should I stay?" Martin asked, his voice flat, a small smile playing around his lips. Martin didn't turn back toward the old man.

"They'll kill me," the old man said, crying. "Help, please."

"Okay," Martin answered, taking the Steyr rifle away from his men, then turning quickly to fire a three-round burst from the waist into the old guy.

The shots echoed off the graffitied walls as the bullets ripped into the old man's chest, knocking his back against the wall.

Martin only admired his marksmanship for a moment before stepping closer. Then he emptied the magazine of caseless ammo into the old man's head, focusing on the jaw as he obliterated any chance for anyone to ever match dental records.

When he turned to hand the rifle back, he saw the men turned away in disgust at the sight. Martin cleared his throat, and one of the men turned to accept the emptied Steyr. Then Martin was walking toward the light of the open door and his car.

"What should we do with him?" one of the men called.

Martin turned, standing at the center of the doorway. His eyes already adjusted to the light, he saw only vague shadows at the rear of the room. "Dump him at the sewage treatment plant. In one of those juicy vats," he said, then walked out through the flowing motes of dust, back into daylight.

chapter seventeen

SWAG FOUND NORMAN BUBERE sitting in the presidential suite of a midtown hotel. It was one of those hotels that featured style over elegance, and offered insipid ass-kissing personnel rather than professionals. Built by people from California, the original owners' vision of class lingered like the stench of a dead rat under the floorboards.

But style costs too, and what you bought in this hotel was the chic of the moment, which in this case happened to be a large three-room suite done up completely in white and ivory. The drapery along the three walls was shut, blocking out the sun and casting the room into a strange semidarkness. Swag followed a young woman to where Bubere was sprawled on a long white leather couch, watching a soap opera through a pair of dark, wraparound shades.

Nothing about Bubere could surprise Swag. If you found him at all, he would just as likely be in some five thousand franc a night suite running up gargantuan tabs on bogus credit cards as crashed out on a stained mattress in some municipal subbasement, living on ancient Civil Defense crackers and warm Pepsi. But wherever you found him, he was under the net of respectability—plugged into distant data bases and his own reality.

Now he was wearing a pair of faded Walker-plaid golf pants, stretched tight just under a protruding stomach and held up by a cracked white vinyl belt. He was also wearing a filthy magenta T-shirt with the silk-screened words, YOUR COMPANY'S NAME OR LOGO HERE and a cheap cherry-red plastic watch, which Swag assumed to be part of a matching set, since it bore the same words along its face.

As Swag entered the room, Bubere stayed glued to the soap opera, his concentration intense even behind the plastic lenses. The woman who ushered Swag in took a seat next to Bubere; on his opposite side was another woman. They had that cool, lean look of sophistication generally associated with game-show ornaments. Both of them were dressed in nearly identical white evening gowns, their hair and makeup done up magazine-perfect, as if they were about to go out for a night on the town. This wouldn't have surprised Swag, except it was ten-thirty in the morning.

"So whattaya want?" Bubere said, stretching his bare feet out from the couch and changing the channel with a remote. A wildly cheering crowd came on, the object of their enthusiasm an aging gray-haired talk-show host hobbling along in an aluminum walker among a stage filled with dwarfs.

The women sat there pouting slightly, like a pair of bookends. One was holding a half-eaten processed sausage, the kind they used to sell in delis and from behind bars. The other held a huge tumbler filled with Coke, its surface covered with a layer of bobbing maraschino cherries.

"Looks like you scored big-time," Swag said, walking around so that he was just to the left of the television's screen.

"Better live large," Bubere said, "'cause everyone dies small, right?"

The two women nodded in unison at the sage advice.

"I got a job for you," Swag said. "A little computer work."

"Retired," Bubere answered, bored.

One of the women, the one on the left, lifted the large tumbler of cola and cherries to Bubere's mouth. He shook his head petulantly, like a small child.

"Come on, Normie," she coaxed playfully.

"Since when are you retired?" Swag asked.

"Since last week," he said, scratching at his beard, which somehow perpetually stayed at a three-day's growth.

"Till when?" Swag asked.

The woman brought the glass a little closer, moving it back and forth under Bubere's nose, so he could check the bouquet.

"End of the month," Bubere answered, a little smile playing along his lips.

"Come on, Normie," the girl repeated, bringing the drink in closer.

Again Bubere shook his head petulantly.

"Can we talk here?" Swag asked.

"Sure," Bubere answered, then shook his head at the drink again.

The other woman brought up the sausage stick. Bubere's nostrils twitched at the scent, but he kept his mouth stubbornly closed.

"In private," Swag offered.

The two women shot Swag a contemptuous look, but continued to tempt Bubere with food and drink.

"This is my place," Bubere said. "How much more private do you want to get?"

The woman with the drink brought it up again, swishing the cherries around enticingly. "Open the pod bay door, Hal," she said, deadpan.

Bubere opened his mouth slowly, and the woman poured the drink in, much of it running down the sides of his mouth and along the already stained expanse of magenta T-shirt.

"There's some money involved here," Swag said.

"There's money involved everywhere. Just once I'd like to do something constructive. Something for society, you know?" Bubere answered. Then he quickly added, "That's a joke."

"Open the pod bay door, Hal baby," the second woman

cooed, and Bubere opened his mouth as she rested the stick of processed meat across his yellowed lower teeth.

"Shut the pod bay door, Hal," she instructed playfully, tapping the meat along his teeth.

Bubere bit down on the dancing sausage stick.

"Having fun?" Swag asked.

"Yeah, you know, as a matter of fact I am," Bubere said, head lolling back as he chewed. "You just can't find talent like these girls anywhere, you know."

"So you're not interested in money anymore?" Swag asked.

"There's some real fuckin' talent here, Jack," Bubere said. "Right in this room."

"I wouldn't be surprised," Swag said, leaning now on the cherrywood cabinet of the television.

The women shot him another look that said they wanted him to vanish, and like fast.

"Did I tell ya, I'm starting a new career?" Bubere said, bringing his head back off the edge of the couch.

"What's that?" Swag asked.

"Thinking about showbiz, ya know."

"Showbiz," Swag repeated, waiting for the punch line.

"Yeah, like showbiz," Bubere said. "Gonna be a singer. Listen up to this. Ready, girls?"

The woman on the right sat up just a little straighter as she put the drink down on the floor in front of her. The one on the left put her hands to her mouth, for sound effects for the old-style rap song.

Then Bubere began nodding his head to the rhythm, and starting singing, with a fervor that shocked Swag.

"Now take old Freddy Engels and that homey Karl Marx
    Everywhere there's cap'lists sleepin' in the parks
    You think that they'd be happy, you know, really laughing hearty
    But they be dead as J. P. Morgan—and it kills them not to party.

First the Eastern bloc, those states crashed like
tired whores
    And all our friendly creditors came banging down
the doors
    Now just chill for a minute, 'cause this is gonna
sound funny
    But it's never about politics, it's all about money."

Bubere held his hand up, stopping the song instantly, and
letting out a wet wheeze of a laugh. "You like it?" he asked,
still nodding his head to the beat.

"Yeah, it's great," Swag answered without enthusiasm.
"What about that job I was talking about?"

Bubere leaned forward, grabbed the drink off the floor
and took a long gulp. "Wait," he said anxiously, bringing
the drink down. "We got another. Now listen up. I call this
one 'Bubere's Blues.' Ready, girls?"

Both women leaned slightly forward, ready.

Swag listened as Bubere went into the song.

"Silicon chips outta Bell in New Jersey
    They'd invent 'em on Monday, we'd boost 'em on
Thursday
    RAM from Japan, motherboards from Korea
    No one was safe—a mainframe Crimea!"

The girls picked up the last line, repeating it in a hip-hop
style chorus a half-dozen times before Bubere broke in
again.

"Now they got gallium ars'nide alloys and erbium
amps
    Makes hardwire look slow, like fourth-class stamps
    Todei and Keio, and Herriot-Watt
    Got their optics in parallel, you can't steal what
they got!"

The two girls came in again to joint a repetitious chorus

of "Can't steal what they got," before Bubere picked up the
last verses.

> "They got nonlinear optics linking new chips
>   Photorefractive crystals, all propriety shit
>   They got phase-conjugate mirrors, and quantum
> wells
>   Superlattice processors—chips from Hell!
>   Now the switching's done with lasers and some-
> one's going Nobel—
>   Give them money in Sweden, I'll give them the fin-
> ger in Hell!
>
>   Those pocket-protector posses who couldn't get
> laid
>   Stayed up working all night, so I can't get paid
>   Postdoctoral nerds, they shoulda been dating
>   Not in the lab, checking refractive index grating
>   You know it ain't right, the way they busted that
> move
>   But that's why I'm singing them old Bubere blues."

Once again the women came in on the chorus, repeating,
"Them old Bubere blues."

When they had repeated the line no less than eight times,
Bubere tipped his head back, focusing on some minute spot
on the ceiling, and wailed, rock and roll style, "Roll over
Tom Watson! Tell ENIAC the news!"

Bubere had his head back on the couch when they finished, a small sad smile playing across his lips. "You like it?"
he asked, pushing the wraparounds up over bloodshot eyes
with one pudgy finger.

"Real top-ten material," Swag said. "What the fuck does
it mean?"

Bubere carefully rearranged his glasses, then let his hands
fall across his lap. "It means, Jack, that the game's over," he
said. "Called on account of progress."

"What are you talking about?" Swag asked.

"Two patents filed last week," Bubere said. "English and Japanese. Both for optical systems. All switching done with light. Light-based chips. Grew out of fiberoptic telecom research. I saw part of the plans, the précis, they got it wired like a fuckin' human brain. Another year before they go into full production. But they have orders up the whazoo—banks, corporations, every government on the planet is jockeying for the first systems."

"And you won't be able to get into them?" Swag asked.

"Get in? *Nobody's getting in*," Bubere said, annoyed. "Five years minimum before this stuff hits the streets. By then they'll have those fuckers on phone lines. Spit out an analysis of every time some schmuck dials up the weather. Add voice recognition, no one in this country, or any other, is gonna be able to work under the system. The net just got a whole lot tighter. I figure I got eighteen months. After that, I'm outta business."

The two women looked glum as Bubere, their lips set into nearly identical pouts.

"Yeah, well, I'm real sorry about that," Swag said. "What about that job I got now?"

"You ain't seen sorry until they plug them monsters into the system. Total fuckin' optic-compatibility off the fiber lines. And get this—the things can see! Plug in a video camera, the things can recognize and analyze images. That includes thermal imaging, good buddy—means you can't bang a broad, take a dump, or pick your nose behind closed doors no more. And here's a flash, there's a bill going through the Senate, gonna give Fed funding to city and states to buy the systems, with discretionary access to the Fed agencies. I'm talking fascist networking, here." Bubere sighed, then added, "What you paying?"

Swag removed a fat roll of bills. "Five hundred francs for an analysis."

"What you want to know?" Bubere asked, straightening himself on the couch. "Stocks, futures, market trends on the eighteen- to twenty-year-olds? What?"

"A couple of names," Swag answered, peeling off five hundred francs and tossing them to Bubere.

Bubere caught the money and lifted his shades cautiously, revealing a pair of small, deep-set eyes surrounded by dark circles. "Yeah, what kinda names?"

"Whole bunch of dead ones and a couple of live ones."

The glasses dropped back into place. "What? City, state, fed? Criminal background, financials, credit lines, tax returns, education, age, residence, or former residence, as the case may be?"

"Norman," Swag said, coming in lower, "I need everything. The works."

Bubere threw his head back and rubbed his hands along the legs of the filthy pants. "Yeah, sure," he said.

"When?" Swag asked, inching closer.

Bubere reached into his pocket, pulling out a two-inch stack of credit cards secured by a thick, red rubber band. He snapped the band off and began dealing through the cards, Amex, Diners, Eurocheque, Banc Swiss, and Eurotel. It looked like every piece of plastic made.

The two women watched intently, shifting uneasily as Bubere kept shuffling. Finally he pulled two cards from the deck and handed one to each woman. "Disappear for a couple of hours," he told them. "Buy a coupla things. Take a nice lunch, ya know?"

The women nodded agreeably, took the cards and vanished quickly from the room.

"Nice girls," Bubere said when they had left. "They've been a comfort in my time of need."

"I can imagine," Swag answered.

Bubere was on his feet, stretching, working kinks from his back. "No you can't," he said finally. "Come on, I got my equipment set up in the other room."

The other room looked like it hadn't seen maid service since just after the Boxer Rebellion. Cases of soda and piles of newspaper covered the floor. Every surface in the room, from the dresser to the three chairs, was littered with disassembled lap-tops, computer cards, technical documentation. Shopping bags overflowed with printed circuit boards and liquid crystal displays of all sizes. Even the bed could not escape the chaos of Bubere's technical clutter. Across its rumpled, unmade surface, Swag could see hints of women's and men's clothing, lurid paperbacks, a partially disassembled keyboard, and no less than half a dozen empty Coke cans.

At the opposite side of the room was a writing desk, also covered with debris of more soda cans, disk drives, and an ancient turkey club sandwich, still with the toothpicks stuck in its quartered sections.

"Sorry 'bout the mess," Bubere said, wiping most of the desk's clutter onto the floor to reveal a lap-top at its far end. "Maid hasn't been up for a while."

"That's too bad," Swag answered, stepping around an overflowing shopping bag and several circuit boards to reach the desk.

"Yeah, I like them little mints they leave on the pillow," Bubere answered, clearing a space on the chair and sitting down.

It took two hours to download the files. Bubere was efficient, working every computer file he could think of, and siphoning the material through the switchboard of a Japanese bank. When he'd finally finished, he pulled a disk from the mess on the desk and loaded it into the lap-top. "This is a little ditty I dreamed up myself," he said. "Used to use it for betting sports. Compares anything, and finds the trend."

Thirty seconds later the portable printer was spitting out paper. "Ah now, this is interesting," he said, pulling the sheath of paper up and studying it through the dark lenses of his glasses. "They're all dirty."

"How you figure that?" Swag asked as he started to read the data.

"Look, they all took busts within the last ten years," Bubere answered. "Fourth line from the bottom."

Swag skipped to Kat's name. The fourth line from the

bottom of the thick graph read: "Charged: Att. Mrder, felonious asslt, unlawful disch. firearm. Convicted: Unlawful disch. firearm. Sentence: suspended. Fine: $200."

"Anything else?" Swag asked.

"Offhand, I'd say they're still dirty," Bubere answered. "Look, they all got chauffeur's licenses. If half the drivers with licenses were on the road, this city would freeze solid with gridlock. You want I should run the companies they work for?"

"No, I think I already know," Swag answered.

"Hey now, this is interesting," Bubere said, a low whistle escaping his mouth.

"Yeah, what's that?" Swag asked.

"They all got their licenses renewed within the last six months," came the answer. "All done here in the city."

chapter eighteen

SEYMOUR WAS THE WHITE HALF of Sandy's matched set of physical therapist goons. And now he could feel them closing in. He wasn't sure who it was, except it had something to do with that bitch, Sandy Mann. It began just after that deal with the dead Englishman. At first it was just a feeling something wasn't right. Then came the letters and the phone calls. A few days later he could feel them ghosting behind as he walked the streets. First he thought it was in his head, something stress related.

Then he spotted the woman with a cast on her arm four different times, and he knew there was something behind his paranoia.

His partner, Louie, had vanished, just after they quit Sandy. Now he was on his own, ducking shadows and losing sleep over whoever was following. If he wasn't careful, he'd end up on some locked ward at Bellevue. And it wouldn't be like it was for Sandy Mann either. They'd toss him into some dorm and dope him to the gills. He'd be doing the Prolixin shuffle, or watching the world behind Thorazine eyes faster than you could say NDO—Ninety Day Observation.

The main thing—the most important thing—was to keep moving. If he stopped moving, even for a day, he was dead.

"But you stopped, didn't you?" he asked himself, staring

dead on at his own image in the bathroom mirror. "Been in here almost a week."

Seymour took a rare look at himself. Unwashed and stinking, without even a clean T-shirt. His mouth tasted like a Ninth Avenue gutter during a trash strike in August.

And after almost a week the empty cans and TV dinners were beginning to build up in the kitchen, spilling out over the sink and garbage pail onto the floor. He spent his days—and nights, for that matter—watching television and cleaning his gun.

Then there was the impulse call he made to the phone-in radio talk show, trying to get the threatening phone calls to stop. "Uh, this is, uh, Tommy," he said, cleverly assuming a name. "And I think someone or something's trying to kill me."

The host wasn't any help, saying, "Well, that sounds like quite a problem you got there. Anyone got any advice for Uh Tommy?" A lady from Queens called in and said, "I heard Tommy before, and I know. Something's trying to kill all of us. It's called life. Get with the program, buster!"

The threatening calls had stopped after that, but only because he yanked the phone from the wall. At night he watched from the floor as the red pinpoints of a laser sight danced at his window shade.

Now it was nearly noon and an eerie stillness settled over the studio apartment. Forcing himself to open the door, he left the apartment to leave his trash stacked neatly in the hall. When he returned, he looked cautiously out the window of the sixth-floor walk-up on East 23rd and felt a jolt of panic. There, lounging at the curb, was the girl with the cast on her arm. She was leaning against a white Japanese car, a Debonair Executive, if he wasn't wrong, and reading the morning paper.

Seymour opened the window, leaned out and shouted, "Hey, fuck you, bitch!"

She looked up with mild interest, then returned to the paper, idly turning the page.

Running back to the far end of the room, he grabbed

the Smith & Wesson 9mm off the television, checked the action and tucked it into the front of his pants. He was halfway to the door before he thought of the knife. It was an old Legionnaire's boot dagger, which he found in an aluminum tray that once held a Big Guy Turkey Dinner. Cleaning off the gravy and bits of processed cranberry sauce, he fitted the knife in its boot sheath on the outside of his right leg.

"Okay, fuckers," he said to himself. "Let's go. Party time."

Checking the window again, he saw that the woman with the cast had vanished and so had the white car.

Seymour took the six flights of stairs at a run, feeling the gun and knife riding comfortably as he moved. It was the front door that stopped him cold. Someone had jammed the lock. He tried pushing it out a half-dozen times, wedging his shoulder into the wire mesh over the smashed window, but the thing wouldn't move.

It was the same story on the basement door. The panic set in full force then. He was trapped.

By the time Seymour reached the roof, he was panting and a light sweat had broken out on his face. Pulling the gun from his belt, he pushed against the roof's steel door and edged his way out into sunlight. He'd cross over two roofs and down through another building. Whatever he left in the apartment, including his physical therapist certification and clothes, he'd call a loss. The whole city was a loss as far as he was concerned.

He was completely out of the door before he saw the old woman. She was hunched over just to his right, dressed up in a Japanese silk bathrobe.

"What the fuck you doing up here?" he asked, lowering the gun.

When the old woman turned, the silk robe fell to the tarpapered roof. That's when he saw it wasn't a woman at all, but a little Japanese guy, done up in robes and armor, with a steel breastplate. Seymour had no way of knowing that the armor, which he now saw included a pointy helmet and sword, were meticulous reproductions of originals from the early Tokugawa period in which the shogunate ruled and the samurai were in full flower.

"What the fuck are you supposed to be?" Seymour said as he began to draw his gun.

He felt a pinch then, at the back of his arm, just above the elbow. Turning, he saw a flashing glimpse of the woman with the cast as she vanished behind a waist-high wall on the opposite roof. Then the arm went numb, like it was shot full of novocaine.

The little Japanese guy bowed, according to bushido custom.

Seymour tried to pull out his piece, but his hand was frozen, like it had a bad cramp. Panicked, he hit it twice with his fist, but couldn't feel a thing.

Then the little Japanese guy bowed again, and pulled out the long single-edged sword of the samurai.

"Oh fuck," Seymour said as he fumbled left-handed for his piece.

The little Japanese guy raised the sword and took a small step forward. Seymour, bringing the automatic from his pants with his left hand, stumbled backward, feeling the edge of the wall against the back of his thighs.

The little Japanese guy muttered something as he brought the sword to its full height above his head.

"Okay, come on, asshole," Seymour said, getting the gun up. "Bringing a sword to a gunfight, how dumb can you get?"

Seymour pulled back on the trigger, but felt it lock up with the safety on. His thumb searched for the safety, but it wasn't a model with an ambidextrous safety. That's when the Japanese guy swung down with the sword. Seymour brought his gun hand up fast, and the razor-sharp blade cut through it at mid-forearm, severing flesh and bone in one swift downward motion.

The gun, hand, and arm clattered to the tar paper as a long curving flow of blood began. Seymour tried to raise his right hand to staunch the flow of blood, but the arm refused to move. The doomed physical therapist looked down at his arm and let out a wail.

The sword flashed again, and sliced straight through his neck, silencing Seymour's wail as he fell away backward and toppled off the roof.

Resheathing the sword, the samurai stepped forward and leaned over the wall in a half bow. Beneath, in the litter-strewn airway, was Seymour's body, the head resting at an impossible angle on the shoulder.

The woman appeared then, coming off from behind a brick wall on the building next door, moving quickly, even with her arm in plaster. She was carrying a large paper shopping bag, and crossed the narrow opening between the two buildings easily.

The samurai nodded at her approach. She bowed back, though lower in her tribute, then adding as she rose, "*Steki des!*" Excellent!

The samurai bowed lower, humble and polite, and appreciative of the compliment.

"*Amari jikan ga arimasen,*" the woman said, which meant, "There's not much time." Then she handed the samurai a carefully folded Burberry raincoat from the shopping bag and replaced it with the robe from the tar paper. Already she was heading back over the roof.

The samurai looked once more over the roof and followed her out. The raincoat fit neatly over his armor. Anyone seeing the helmet would more than likely take it for the latest in male haberdashery.

"There is not much time," the Japanese guy repeated in English, following the woman down the stairs of the apartment building.

"No, there is not. Your honorable Gulfstream twin-engine leaves in twenty minutes," she replied in flawless Japanese.

"*Wakarimas,*" I understand, he answered, falling back into Japanese as he huffed down the stairs, sword clanking through the raincoat against the metal handrail.

* * *

"I need a chauffeur's license," Swag said into the phone outside the old Equitable Building.

There was a long pause on the other end of the line, then Sam Narcadia came on. "That's not funny."

"It wasn't supposed to be," Swag answered.

"Tell me something funny," Narcadia said. "You know the rules."

Swag thought a moment. "How do lawyers practice birth control?" he asked.

"I dunno," Narcadia answered.

"By personality," Swag said.

But Narcadia wasn't laughing. "I heard that one," he said.

"Then why didn't you say so?"

"I forgot," Narcadia answered blandly. "Tell me another."

"What's black and brown and looks good on a lawyer?"

"I dunno," Narcadia answered.

"You're sure now?" Swag replied, certain that Narcadia was hustling him for a free joke.

"Yeah, I'm sure."

"A Doberman," Swag said.

"Okay, come on up."

Swag knew the procedure. Wait for the scan, then lock the gun in the plastic drawer. And there was Narcadia, ugly as ever, sitting behind his huge gray desk, ruling a domain of constantly monitored phone lines.

Narcadia buzzed Swag through the clear plastic door and spread his remarkably untumored hands out on the desk. "So, what's this about a license?" he asked. "Career move or what?"

"I just need one," Swag said.

"Fifty in European," Narcadia answered. "Give me a photo and dissolve for an hour, I'll have it for you."

"That's not exactly what I need," Swag said. "What I need is a sponsoring company and the preliminary paperwork. I'll get it myself from the DMV."

Narcadia raised a section of tumors that Swag took to

be an eyebrow and lifted his hands over the desk, as if trying to heal it. "Ahh, I see," he said.

"You do, huh?" Swag asked.

"You need another cover," Narcadia said. "Maybe you're not so clean anymore. Maybe got a little discretionary income, needs washing before you bank it?"

"Yeah, that's it," Swag said. "Can you do it?"

"Go stand in line down at DMV," came the answer. "I'll have the kid bring down the papers."

"I want it with one of these companies," Swag offered, handing a sheet of Bubere's printout across the desk.

"Ahh," Narcadia sighed, scanning the names with hidden eyes, his overgrown head bobbing with grim satisfaction. "These are the bottom of the barrel. No questions asked whatsoever. I can do better."

"Just do what I want," Swag answered, peeling off money and laying it on the edge of Narcadia's desk.

The fixer rose heavily from his chair, his face sagging noticeably with the pull of gravity as he leaned far over the desk to scoop up the money, then disappear it into a drawer. "Corruption in all its wondrous and infinite variations is a funny thing," he said, musing. "I wonder why you're exploiting your obvious talents so late? Don't fear, though, I'll be calling you. You'd be surprised how often I get a call for someone like yourself. Maybe someone willing to bend a law here and there."

"Don't bother," Swag answered.

"You'd be surprised how easy it gets," came the answer. "It'll get easier all the time." Narcadia did the most astonishing thing, he laughed. For just an instant a pair of very human lips twisted up under the mass of tumors, revealing the briefest flash of white teeth and a gray tongue before being swallowed up again.

As the phone began to ring, Swag headed out of the office.

chapter nineteen

THE DEPARTMENT OF MOTOR VEHICLES was downtown, near the courts, city hall, the new Tombs prison complex, and old Hall of Records. This was the granite and limestone heart of the machine. To get caught in the Byzantine workings of any of those government buildings meant that you could easily spend a lifetime trying to get untangled.

Bureaucrats bred like mice down here. Invisible fiefdoms were founded, flourished, and withered silently within the gray walls of the government buildings. Government workers in cheap suits and stained ties studied memos and directives, divining the subtle ebb and flow of gray-steel-desk-windowed-office-power. The hidden workings of city government ran on a diet of greasy doughnuts, acidic coffee, and whispered rumors. And next to tourism, government was the biggest employer in the city.

The DMV was housed in a bland state building with granite walls and brass doors. Swag took the steps at a reluctant trot and entered the ancient coolness of a battered government lobby. For reasons no one was ever quite certain about, the riots that touched nearly every building in the city—from luxury office buildings to prisons and courtrooms—had left the DMV unscathed. Swag had his own private theory: nobody wanted to go into the DMV on their own accord, not even for purposes of looting.

Swag spotted the line just inside the door and took his place. Before him the monster line snaked its way forward through a maze of battered velvet ropes, plastic yellow chains, filthy clothesline, anything that could be secured to the chipped chrome stanchions. The line curved back on itself no less than a dozen times, filling the entire room with a coil of shuffling people. Far to the left were twelve windows where the line split, like a sectioned snake, into smaller lines of ten or twelve.

Behind each of the twelve windows, DMV employees shuffled as slowly as those in line. They strolled casually from service window to computer terminal to coffee machine to mysterious back room and back again. They moved at the same lethargic pace as bureaucrats everywhere, immune, hardened, or blind to the constant stare of three or four hundred pairs of eyes.

Perhaps they fed off it, Swag thought, actually enjoyed the line; like a troupe of deranged actors in the midst of some obscure piece of performance art, unwilling to relinquish their audience. Though Swag knew the truth was much more sinister. They enjoyed the power over the line— willing it through thought and action to creep along at their pace. Like bureaucrats everywhere, they enjoyed calling the tune, even if it wasn't their own.

Young boys worked their way up and down the line, hawking newspapers, soda, cups of water from ancient thermoses, and sandwiches of dubious content. To leave the line, for any reason, meant losing your place. Often you could pay a couple of bucks to the person in front or back to hold your place for a quick trip to the phone or men's room. Sometimes you could even buy a place midway up. But neither practice was recommended. Fistfights, knifings, and the occasional shooting were not unheard of, if not generally anticipated as a break from the boredom.

The greatest fear, of course, was that some form or piece of documentation was lacking when you finally arrived. To stand for six or seven hours in line, only to be turned back to repeat the process because a form was filled out incorrectly or a piece of ID wasn't current.

"You want a paper?" the waist-high voice asked.

Swag, looking down, saw the kid. No more than eight or nine. "No thanks," he said.

"Yeah, you do," the kid answered, eyes forming slits of utter contempt for such obvious stupidity.

"Okay, sure," Swag said, reaching down for the tabloid. But the kid held on. "That's a D mark," the kid whispered.

"I only got francs," Swag answered.

"Any easy'll do it," the kid said, then watched greedily as Swag pulled one from his pocket.

The kid took the cash and released the paper reluctantly.

Swag opened the paper and began reading. When he reached the business section, he found the documentation was glued to the second page in an office envelope from the You Talkin' to Me? Cab & Livery Service.

The company was immediately recognizable. Sandy, apparently, had a thing for cute names. Unlike the fronts of old times, which aimed deliberately toward the bland, Sandy Mann's operations features such memorable names as the Hot Enough for Ya? Cabs; You Call That a Tip? Car Service; and Don't Go to Brooklyn Livery.

Included in the envelope were three glowing character references from people Swag had never met; a patently fictitious address with Con Ed and telephone bills to back it up; a letter promising employment from You Talkin' to Me?; and a nearly perfect score on a hack test given that day. The test was stamped with initials, time, and date.

It took three hours for the line to move enough for Swag to see the counter where the clerk processing hack licenses stood. He was lounging behind the glass partition, drinking coffee and reading a racing form. The sign in front said NEXT WINDOW, and the only problem was that the next window was attached to a door that led back out to the street.

The guy was a round-shouldered weasel with thick glasses, a pasty face, and thinning hair. He was wearing a shirt that might once have been white, but had faded to sweat-stained yellow, the color of old newspapers. Swag put

his age at between thirty and fifty—he had that kind of
face.

When a good twenty or thirty people—mostly men, but
a few women too—had gathered in front of the hack clerk's
window, he brought the "Next Window" sign down and
stashed the racing form.

Swag started watching the clock then. It was just short
of four in the afternoon. If he didn't make it to the window
by five, then he'd be back again tomorrow. Miraculously,
the line began shuffling forward with a barely perceptible,
minute-hand progress. By the time he reached the window,
it was ten to five.

"So whattaya got?" the clerk asked, not looking up to
make eye contact.

"Letters, proof of residence, application," Swag
answered. "Completed test."

"Congratulations," the clerk mumbled, hauling in a pile
of papers. Eight minutes later he was still reading.

Swag looked down at the ink-stained fingers and dirty
nails that snaked their way slowly over his papers. But what
held his attention was the watch that was strapped to the
nearly hairless wrist. It was an Audemars Piguet Automatic.
Swag studied it carefully, right down to the alligator band.
Day, date, month, and moon phase. It was the kind of
watch a Japanese or German tourist would wear, but stash
in a hotel safe at night. And it looked real enough to cost
what a DMV clerk would take home in a year.

"You got a problem," the clerk said at last with monu-
mental disinterest.

"What's that?" Swag answered.

"See this sheet here," the clerk said, pointing a grubby
finger to the letter from You Talkin' to Me? "I can't read
the signature."

"The guy's name is right under," Swag answered, already
knowing what the game was. "See, it's typed."

"You coulda signed it," the clerk answered, bored, but
raising his eyes about an inch. "And it's almost five. Another
two minutes and I'm outta here."

"Look, I'll show you my signature," Swag said, pulling out his wallet and handing over an ancient library card with ten francs folded under it.

The clerk took the card and studied it carefully. When he handed it back, the francs were gone. "I guess I can trust you," he said lazily.

"That how you got that watch, trusting people?" Swag asked.

"It was a gift from my mother," the guy answered. "You gonna call me a liar at two minutes to five?"

The line behind Swag dissolved in a grumbling of hopelessness. He was alone at the window. All around, people began to wander off in a slow shuffle, beaten by the clock.

"That's a nice mother," Swag answered. "Let's get on with it."

"Yeah, I'm the apple of her damned eye," came the slow response. "Step over there, get shot and printed, then come back. And you better make it in one minute twenty."

Swag made it just under the clock, but it cost him another two francs for the photo and three for the prints, which were clicking out in hardcopy on the clerk's terminal as Swag returned to the window.

The clerk checked the photo, studied the prints, and punched the key that sent both into the computer. Swag knew that beneath the counter was a machine that barcoded and laminated the final card. But the clerk rose heavily from his stool and slowly walked to the back room.

"What's the deal?" Swag called when the clerk had taken a few steps.

"Machine's down," the clerk called back without turning. "Don't bust my stones, I'll be back in a second. Maybe."

The room was empty. The service windows were closed, the last of the line dissolved through the doors and back into the street. It was two minutes past five.

The clerk returned at six minutes past five, throwing the laminated card across the counter. "Congratulations, you're a cab driver," he said, then turned and left without waiting for an answer.

* * *

Louie, the black half of Sandy Mann's physical therapy
team, paced the corner of 52nd and Fifth. He'd been waiting half an hour and hoped he was doing the right thing.
The fact that he was always considered the smarter half of
the team was little comfort, especially after he'd heard about
Seymour. Officially, it was being called a suicide. But
Seymour, dumb as he was, wasn't the type to take a header
off a roof. And the hell of it was, he knew what and who
was behind it. The whole thing began with that Sandy
Mann job. The way he had it figured, a bunch of heavies—
maybe even irate franchisees—were after the both of them
for the killing of the fish and chips guy.

Louie looked at his watch and saw that it was five-ten.
Tourists were hurrying back to their hotels, a scattering of
rush hour traffic was creeping down Fifth. That was all
good, just the way he wanted it, with a lot of people
around.

The light changed again, and he looked up the street,
toward the Plaza. If they were coming, that's where they'd
be coming from—Provisional Provost Headquarters. The
way he had it set up, he'd talk to the provosts, lay out the
deal with Sandy, Seymour, all of it, and then ask for protection. But he was flexible there, he'd bargain with the provosts for either protection before and during the
investigation and the trial or enough money to split town.
That way it was a good deal for everyone involved.

When the car, an unmarked Plymouth, came up beside
him on 52nd, he wheeled around, surprised. Inside were
three provosts—two in back and one in front—all in plainclothes, but looking like cops just the same. The mirrored
shades were the tip-off. The mirrored shades and the
DeaWoo automatic assault rifle that rested across the front
seat, barrel aimed at the passenger door.

"Louie?" one of the men inside the car asked.

"Who's asking?" Louie answered.

"Major Aston Martin, Provost Command," came the
smiling answer as the young major slipped off his shades.

Louie ran the play through his head fast. The thing didn't smell right. Three guys in an unmarked car. It looked like a disappearance crew.

"You called us, remember?" the major said, still smiling. It was the smile of some Cali surfer after the last good wave of the day. But the eyes were flat as plate-glass, with lots of white showing below the washed-out hazel. Louie, a student of Far Eastern martial arts and philosophy, knew these to be the eyes of an unbalanced soul—maybe even a fucking maniac.

"Got the wrong guy," Louie answered definitively and began to turn, heading against traffic on 52nd.

"Oh no," the major answered, his words drawn out, as if he were talking to a child. "We *got* exactly the right guy."

Louie took one step before he felt their hands on him. Four guys, dressed like tourists, comfortable shoes and all, but strong.

"You got the wrong guy," Louie said, struggling. Then the hypo went in, hitting him high on the thigh. The last thing he saw before the drug hit was the Plymouth's rear door swinging open.

chapter twenty

THE DMV CLERK CAME OUT THE SIDE door. He was alone, walking quickly, hunched over and carrying a cheap plastic briefcase. He walked to the subway and joined the crowd of office workers streaming underground.

Swag followed the clerk down, hanging back at a safe distance, keeping track of him on the platform. When the train finally came, the clerk entered through the car's rear door. Swag hustled into the front door and took up a position where he could see the guy at the opposite end of the car. The clerk kept his nose buried in one of those slick commodity tout sheets. The kind that were always printed on nice coated stock and included five or six computer-generated charts to plot the gold, silver, pork bellies, and petroleum futures. All scientific as hell and with a name that screamed either old money or new science. The only problem was, they were wrong with a consistency that baffled the mind. This particular sheet offered tips on wheat futures.

The clerk stepped off the train in midtown, staying with the swell of passengers who pushed their way out through the turnstiles. As he headed up the stairs he unexpectedly picked up speed, and Swag now had to run to keep up, only to get caught in a push of commuters. Jogging up the stairs in the twilight, the clerk vanished from sight.

Swag barely noticed the woman that he jostled, on her way down into the subway, noting only that she had a cast on one arm. He didn't notice that she was carrying a plastic briefcase that was not only identical to the one the DMV clerk had held, but in fact was the same one.

She noticed Swag with an unpleasant shock of recognition and easily controlled professional panic.

When Swag caught up to the clerk, he was turning into a bar on East 54th Street, the kind frequented by wealthy tourists looking for a safe haven from shopping, sightseeing, and crowds. The clerk paused for a moment at the doorway. Examining his reflection in the black glass, he straightened his tie, smoothed down the pill-balled lapels of the cheap baby-blue summer sport coat, then wiped his lips across its greasy sleeve.

It was only then that Swag noticed that the clerk was no longer carrying the briefcase.

Taking up a position across the street and a few yards down the block, in front of a gray-shuttered driveway to an abandoned office building, Swag lit a cigarette and waited. Three kids, none older than fifteen, lounged by the corner, watching the traffic and passing a plastic jug of water around. They were dressed in French and Spanish gimme T-shirts and torn jeans. The shortest one, a wiry kid, was talking fast, using a lot of hand motions and trying to get the attention of the bigger and no doubt older kids. The other two listened with bored expressions. Every two or three minutes they cut Swag a hard stare, sizing him up.

When the trio abandoned the corner, they walked toward Swag slowly, strolling in as they looked for the clue that would classify him as either tourist, cop, or citizen. Whatever he was, he didn't fit into the two important categories—victim or trouble. Nothing registered behind their eyes. He was out of place, as sharp a contrast to the bland citizens and tourists as the loud greens and reds of his Hawaiian shirt against the gray steel of the entranceway's door.

As they came closer, the three kids fell into a loose pattern. The shortest one up front, walking point, the two others behind, acting as backup. Swag threw down the cigarette he was smoking without grinding it out. He waited until the kids were ten or fifteen yards away, then reached up behind his back with his right hand. Just to let them know about the Custom 10 in the back holster.

As the three walked by, something clicked in their collective mind. It was then that the clerk emerged from the bar. Now he was carrying the same briefcase.

"Come here," Swag said as the kids passed him.

The three kids were still walking. They were maybe ten feet past Swag and heading west, the same direction as the clerk. They turned, two still moving and the third, and largest, coming to a complete stop to face Swag.

"You looking to get paid?" Swag asked.

"The man don't pay shit," the big kid said.

"You think I'm Provost?" Swag asked. "Or what, P.D. maybe?"

"You look like P.D." the kid said. "Don't dress like P.D. Nobody'd wear that shirt, not even a cop."

The two others laughed nervously. Swag let it pass; the clerk was almost to the corner.

"Blind cop, maybe," the little one said, setting off a new chorus of laughs.

"So, what are you?" the big kid asked, breaking in and silencing his buddies. "We didn't do Jacques shit."

"See that guy up there, with the briefcase. I'm the guy that's gonna pay you a franc to bring me that case." Swag said, nodding to the leader.

"You settin' us up?" the kid asked, now squinting. "What kind of lame shit is this?"

The clerk was stopped just short of the corner, studying a collection of Japanese electronics in a store window.

"He turns that corner, he's gone," Swag said. "So's the offer."

The kids stepped back, conferring with one another quickly.

"He just has to get it?" the big one said finally, indicating the smallest of the group.

"Just bring it to me," Swag answered.

"If he does it, you don't have shit. It's a veg special, no beef at all," the leader warned. "Une, he's a minor. Deux, it's entrapment. And trois, let's see the easy, asshole."

Swag pulled out a single bill, waving it slightly in front of him.

"Make it ten," the kid said, bargaining.

The clerk was moving again. Not turning the corner, but waiting for a light.

"I'll make it two," Swag answered, then brought another bill from his pocket.

The three were moving in now, trying to surround Swag, squeeze him to the slightly recessed wall of the garage door. Swag stepped away from them, toward the curb, his hand coming up to his back. "You know the difference between easy money and hard money?" Swag asked.

"Nothing's hard when the odds go in your direction," the big one said, edging forward, getting right in Swag's space.

This was bullshit and Swag knew it. The whole thing was a bad idea from the jump. Now he was going to end up with a problem he didn't need. "Okay, let's do it," he said, resigned, his hand now around the butt of the gun.

The big one took a step forward and Swag slid the Colt out smoothly, holding it low but pointing it directly at the leader's stomach. From out of the corner of his eye he saw the two others, hands frozen now, midway to their pockets. Razors or butterfly knives, he thought, or little summer guns; .25s, maybe.

"Hey man, don't get nervous," the leader said, stopping short as the other two followed his lead. "We don't want any tension. None whatso-fuckin'-ever."

The other two kids were spread out on either side of Swag, but he kept the piece trained on the leader. "See this, now we got a situation," Swag said. "I'm not going to get my briefcase, you guys aren't getting paid. And somebody maybe is going to get hurt. All because of attitude, *dis*-respect, and *mis*-communication."

"Okay, let's just all ease back and relax for a second," the leader said as he brought his hands up cautiously, palms out. Swag thumbed the hammer back, strictly movie stuff that wouldn't impress anyone over twenty.

"So, what's the next thing to do here?" Swag asked.

"Look, he's gonna go get the case," the leader said, nodding his head sideways toward the youngest one.

Swag cut a fast look toward the corner, where the light had changed and the clerk was crossing the street, beginning to vanish in a crowd. "He better hurry," Swag answered.

The leader nodded again and the little one took off. "Come 'round like before," the leader yelled. "At the restaurant!"

The three of them watched as the kid ran, head down, dodging pedestrians, legs and arms pumping, heading for the corner. In another lifetime, maybe fifteen or ten years before, he'd be running J.V. track and thinking about cheerleaders.

"We'll meet him around," the big one said.

And Swag followed them around the corner.

This is the way it went down. The two older kids walked east, across Lex, with Swag following. Then they headed down the narrow stairs of an abandoned basement restaurant. Swag waited at the top of the stairs, the Colt now wedged into the front of his pants.

When the young kid finally appeared, he was wearing a different T-shirt. It was a standard petty thief move. They used to call them "throwaways," before nobody threw nothing away. Now they wore the second shirt under the top one. It made the ID harder. The top layer would be something flashy and easy to remember, red or orange. The second one a dull gray or white. Some street kids were so adept, they could make the change at a full run, switching a stolen purse from one hand to the other as they dodged traffic or headed down from an alley.

When the smallest kid came up, holding the briefcase out to Swag, he was breathing hard and smiling. "He yelled

a whole lot," the kid said. "Said he was a state official. That
true? He's not Provost or anything?"

"He works for the DMV," Swag answered.

"Fuck him, then," the leader said, grinning.

Swag set the briefcase down between his feet, nodded
to the street and the two older kids coming up the stairs,
worried looks on their faces.

"Here's the two," Swag said, handing the leader the
money with one hand and keeping the other close to the
Colt. "Start walking."

They walked off slow, checking over their shoulders every
three or four steps. When a taxi headed down the street,
Swag flagged it. So it's come to this, he thought to himself,
shaking down kids to do your work.

He told the cabbie to head downtown, and he opened
the case. Inside were four money wraps, indicating francs,
D-marks, dollars, and escudos. There was also an envelope,
empty, but bearing the company name, Fantaisiste Tours.
There wasn't a street address under it, but rather the slogan,
Facta non verba. Deeds not words.

If there had been cash inside, it was now in the pockets
of the three kids. But Swag doubted it. The youngest one
wouldn't have jeopardized the other two for a quick score.
And if he had, even a kid wouldn't have left wraps in the
case. More than likely, the clerk had already pocketed whatever money the case held.

Colonel Bammer was sipping champagne and smiling. The
champagne was the color of old urine. The smile was the
too white shine of cheap caps. He was in full dress uniform,
which meant plenty of gold. And that was good, because
he was hosting a party in one of the Plaza's smaller ball-
rooms, which featured an abundance of gold-leaf trim. The
party was for a minor dignitary from Washington: a polit-
ical appointee, which meant either money, influence, or
inside information. Officially, his title was Divisional Direc-
tor of Auditing and Budget Services.

The room was packed. Twenty small groups of four and

five uniformed provosts and civilians gibbered away, meshing and unmeshing like gears of some huge chattering small-talk machine. Bammer wanted a larger banquet room, but Dobbs put the kibosh on that idea. Small rooms made it seem like more of a crowd. Better for the photographers.

Across the room he could see Dobbs. The guy was wearing a tux as if he was born in one and holding court with three young women and the guest of honor. Bammer recognized one of the women as a high-priced pro. The other two were probably whores too, but you couldn't prove it by their looks. And Bammer knew, with that kind of expensive talent, you couldn't prove it by their talk either. It amazed Bammer how Dobbs dug up these girls. It went beyond pimp. The colonel had no doubt that if he crossed the room and asked Dobbs to dig up a one-legged redhead fluent in esperanto, the guy would be on the phone and have her standing in the doorway done up in a requisitioned Scassi and Harry Winston inside of twenty minutes.

Bammer squinted his eyes and studied Dobbs closely. Now what in hell do you talk about with three whores and a Washington pencil pusher? he thought. Dobbs was telling a joke, gesturing slightly with his hands. Bammer knew when the joke ended, he could hear the laughter from across the room.

It must have been some joke; the four were nearly doubled over with laughter. The pencil pusher reached out and patted Dobbs affectionately on the shoulder. By next week the joke would be all over Washington—maybe even on a sound bite, if it was clean.

"Colonel, you were in the middle of a story?" one of the women in Bammer's group asked.

Bammer snapped out of his daze, a little unsure of how the punch line of his own story would go over. Would anyone in this group slap him on the back? Would they laugh at all?

"So, I said to him, I said straight out. . . ." Bammer was

saying as Aston Martin approached, weaving his way through the room to stand like a puppy at Bammer's elbow.

The group of civilians surrounding Bammer nodded, smiling and encouraging him to continue. The women, Bammer noticed, were all pretty good-looking—for their ages, which fell between thirty-five and a perpetual thirty-nine. That is to say, they had some mileage on the old meters and looked a little tense, wore those strained expressions that were the result of one too many snip and stretch jobs. But the men, well, they were horrors. Balding, liver-spotted trolls done up in tuxes, like prom night at Grimms' fairy tales. Bammer knew these were money guys. Collectively, they ran nearly every sweatshop in the city, turned out everything from stuffed, plush toys to silk-screened T-shirts, and employed nearly twenty percent of the total workforce.

"So, I said to him, not pulling any punches, 'cause I know him *that well*," Bammer continued, "I said . . . what the hell is it, Major Martin?"

The group gave a little start, then smiled. The joke had been on the good major, a uniformed subordinate.

"Sir, there's a matter that needs your immediate attention," the major replied crisply.

The small group turned serious, clearly impressed. This was official business happening before their eyes. *Official Provost Business.* The sudden change was not lost on Bammer.

"Major Martin is group leader of our tactical squad," Bammer said, as the major entered into the circle.

"Sirs, ladies," the major said, stiffly, with a slight nod. Then he shook hands all around, clearly impressing the guests with his competent manner and firm handshake. If any of them noticed the dark moons of fresh blood under his fingernails and cuticles, or the smudged glaze of it across the plastic crystal of the provost-issue military watch, none of them said anything.

"Now, if you'll excuse me ladies, gentlemen," Bammer said. "I have a small piece of business to attend to." Unable to resist, he John Wayned it up, swallowing the remainder of his drink in a gulp. A manly brace of liquor, albeit domestic, to fortify him for the job ahead.

There were eager assents all around as Bammer stepped away, purposefully grim-faced, the major following close behind.

When they reached a secluded spot by the curtained French doors, Bammer said, "What can you tell me?"

"We located the owner of the Jag that drove Hollowbutton off the FDR," the major reported. "We found the leader and one of the participants."

"Good work, then, bring the fuckers in," Bammer said.

"I'm afraid that's impossible now," the major answered. "At least for the participant. You see, he led us to the organizer. He didn't survive interrogation."

"Is it possible he died in a shoot-out?" Bammer asked.

"Negative. We choppered what was left out to Jersey," the major answered. "To the French fertilizer plant."

Bammer held the bridge of his nose with two fingers and squeezed tightly, as if he expected it to fall off. "Are you telling me that a key suspect in a high-profile murder is going to be dumped on frog grapes? I don't think you want to tell me that. In point of fact, I seriously doubt it."

The major hesitated, like a little boy done bad. "Sir, in all truthfulness, there wasn't a lot left of him," he managed to get out. "Postinterrogationwise, that is."

Bammer released his nose, eyes searching for a uniformed waiter with a silver tray of drinks. "What about this other one?" he asked. "This Mr. Big."

"Ms. Big, sir," the major corrected.

"Now, you haven't ground *her* up into plant food?"

"No sir, we know exactly where she is," the majored answered.

"And where would that be?"

The major squirmed uncomfortably, his eyes darting around the room. "Actually, sir, she's in the suite directly above your own."

Bammer stood in shock for a full five beat while he

digested this information. Finally he answered. "Get me Dobbs," he snapped. "Instantaneously."

Two minutes later Dobbs had been apprised of the situation. He stood deep in thought for a full ten seconds, eight seconds longer than it usually took him to reach a decision on almost any matter.

"Well?" Bammer asked.

"Shut off all elevators," Dobbs said. "Six men go in low-profile. All weapons, anything that goes through the door, is fitted with a suppressor. When you bring her out, she comes directly to me. Is that understood?"

"Yes sir," the major said, answering the public relations guy.

"What about the others?" Bammer asked. "There must be others in the room."

"Put everyone else in an unmarked van. That includes yourself, Major, and the six members of your team," Dobbs instructed. "Drive them around the city. Stop for no one."

"For how long, sir?" the major asked.

"Until you hear from me," Dobbs snapped back. "You are to drive no more than a twenty-block radius, maintaining a complete radio silence. And don't think for an instant I won't have comm center monitor."

"Yes sir," the major answered.

"Is this a good idea?" Bammer asked. "I mean, we must have every major daily and all the television people here. They have mobile units outside."

"It's perfect," Dobbs said with a sly smile. "When else will you ever know where they all are? We have total control of all media access. How long will this operation take, Major?"

"Twenty minutes, thirty at the far outside," the major answered. "That's from the time I leave the room."

Dobbs brushed his hair back with one hand, then adjusted his glasses. "Leave now, then," he said. "Colonel, can you keep everyone in this room for twenty minutes?"

"If I had a speech," came the answer.

Dobbs reached into the inside pocket of his tux, removed a single sheet of paper and handed it to Bammer. "This is a toast," he said. "In three languages, phonetically typed by alternating lines. Wait two minutes, then read it from the podium."

Bammer took the speech and began reading.

Dobbs turned angrily on the major. "Are you still here?" he snapped.

"Sir, the battering ram makes a bit of noise," the major said. "Explosives make more. There are other guests on that floor."

Dobbs fixed him with a steely, unforgiving stare. "Has the thought of knocking ever entered your mind?"

Ten minutes later six men of the tactical squad were lined up in the hall, kneeling, crouching, and taking up defensive-offensive combat positions along the walls on either side of the doors. Their Steyr rifles were fitted with silencers and aimed in the general direction of the double gold-trimmed doors of Sandy Mann's suite.

It was Major Martin who pressed the ivory-colored buzzer, giving it three quick bursts before he took up his position off to the left side of the doors.

"Who is it?" a male voice inside the suite called.

"Room service," Martin replied.

Martin could hear a short, muffled conversation within the suite. Then another male voice said, "Nobody ordered nothing."

The major, thinking fast on his feet, shouted, "It's a complimentary fruit basket."

And that's when the door opened.

chapter twenty-one

"SHE'S OUT," O'NEAL SAID FLATLY over his battered desk in the detectives' squad room. He moved to stub out a cigarette into the overflowing ashtray, but couldn't find an opening. Couldn't make one either, not without spilling butts and ashes over the paper clutter of the desk. He settled for the floor, grinding out the smoke under his heel.

"Out, how?" Swag asked, settling into the steel chair at the side of the desk. There wasn't any sense in anger, not now, and not until he heard the whole story.

All around phones were ringing. At the phones that weren't ringing, detectives were working. The squad room hadn't changed in years, mostly because all funding went into provost operations. The furniture, phones, even the assignment blackboard remained the same, worse for the wear, tear, and occasional violent episode.

"Out, as in not here. As in gone," O'Neal answered. Then added, "Out as in about."

"I thought we had a deal," Swag asked, reaching for his own cigarettes, then thinking better of it after glancing at the ashtray. O'Neal's ashtrays had always been packed, but this one was the Mount Fuji of ashtrays. Somewhere near the center a cigarette smoldered against the filter of its neighbor, sending a fine acrid string of smoke into the air.

"We had a deal," O'Neal answered, sorting through past burglary reports, then laying the hard copies down to check a battered handheld field unit. "I don't know what kind of deal she was working. Kicked the night officer in the balls and bolted."

"Shit." Swag sighed, deciding to light up regardless of the ashtray. "She say anything?"

"I believe she said something to the effect of 'Fuck you, motherfucker,' if that has any special meaning for you. It should, by the way."

Swag lit the Thai cigarette off a pack of matches from the Dead Banker and took a long pull. "Is the officer around?" he asked, letting the smoke out. "Maybe he can fill me in."

"He's down at St. Vin's with blood clots in his balls," O'Neal answered, squinting into the field unit's fuzzy display, then fine-tuning it with a knock against the edge of the desk. "You visiting him, that would really make his day. Take him some flowers, why doncha? Maybe a nice stuffed animal, huh?"

"Sarcasm?" Swag asked, releasing an ash to the floor. "Is that sarcasm?"

"Look, I'm real busy here," O'Neal said, punching in a seven-digit number on the handheld. "You remember the way out, right?"

Swag took another slow drag on the cigarette and watched O'Neal sort through paperwork, looking for a report that matched the handheld's readout. He'd been a good detective once. Now he was stuck on a shit assignment like past burglaries.

"The man's talking," someone shouted, and a tall patrolman reached up to turn up the volume on the set that had hung unwatched from the ceiling.

All eyes flashed to the set as Bammer strode through the Plaza's hallway, face fixed in an air of determination. Beside him was a short little guy in a suit trying hard to look important. A small squad of provosts and civilians trailed in their wake, filling the hall, wall to wall. The provosts wore mirrored aviator shades, blank expressions, and carried Steyrs. The civilians carried microcassette records, pads, and 35mm cameras. And they weren't doing as good a job as the provosts at keeping their faces blank. The Plaza press corps were smiling as they always did. The smiles were eager and currying, almost giddy, in the face of power and the prospect of a buffet luncheon.

The cameraman was doing a good job, walking backward as Bammer and the little guy came forward.

"Colonel, do you anticipate more federal funds for provost operations?" one of the reporters shouted.

Bammer acknowledged the unseen reporter with a slight nod. "Alex, as you know, Washington has always given us everything we need to do the job," Bammer answered, careful to address the reporter by name.

"Are the rumors true that provost funding will be cut come budget time?" came another question. "And will this spike the crime numbers significantly?"

Bammer stopped at this question, the short guy coming up alongside. "Marge," Bammer began, again using the questioner's first name. "I think that's best answered by our guest, don't you?"

The little guy stammered for a second, sweat breaking out on his face. "We have every confidence in the colonel and his operations. Need I say that his word carries considerable weight down in Washington?"

A howl went up from the squad room as a couple of balled up forms hit the screen.

"And if tourism drops off?" one of the reporters asked.

"Are you worried, Stan? Hotels are booked to seventy-five percent," Bammer said, smiling. "That's seventy-five percent. And gentlemen and ladies, those are darn good numbers, darn good, where I come from."

"You come from Jersey, you fuck!" someone in the squad room yelled.

Then it was the little guy's turn. "I can only add that New York is once again Fun City," he said, trying to muster enthusiasm. "And I speak not just from above-the-line statistics, but from personal experience as a tourist over these last few days."

The reporters applauded their appreciation as Bammer

and the little guy smiled. While the squad room hissed and cursed, Bammer shook hands with the little guy from Washington and started walking again. This would have been the closing shot, but the cameras kept rolling, tracking the two down the hall.

"What about the Hollowbutton case?" one of the reporters shouted. It was a woman's voice.

The question brought Bammer up abruptly. "That's on ongoing investigation," Bammer said, suddenly stern-faced. "And I'm not about to comment on ongoing investigations."

"Isn't the unsolved murder of a tourist worth a word?" the reporter persisted.

"I don't believe I know you," Bammer said, singling out the reporter, squinting through he crowd, as if at something minuscule. Then just for a second his face lost all composure, turning into a scowl of such pure nastiness and unmasked hate that it silenced even the squad room.

The reporter's response was deleted out on the delay.

"Well, little miss," Bammer began, his face recovering from the scowl to one of his four hardline looks of rigid determination. "You don't know me either. But I'll tell you something about me right now. And about my men. We're a short hair away from bringing in those people. Closer than even they can know. Do you understand me? Nobody kills a tourist in my town! It won't be tolerated. I won't have it! Not ever!"

The reporters applauded again with wary appreciation. Then a commercial came on. What neither Swag, O'Neal, or anyone watching the broadcast heard was Bammer turning to the uniformed provost directly to his right and saying, "Find out who that cunt is. If she's foreign, run everything on her, tickets, wants and warrants, visa, every-fuckin'-thing, understand? If she's domestic, call the station. Next time I see that bitch, I want it to be snapping gum and flagging down cars for half-franc hose jobs on Ninth and Thirty-three."

"Now there was a little peek, huh boyo?" O'Neal asked, meaning Bammer's scowl.

"Just for a second," Swag answered. "Won't be noticed." But he was worried. Bammer's little piece of video ugliness hadn't been scripted. And if it wasn't scripted, then maybe, just maybe, he was talking truth.

"Look boyo," O'Neal said, his voice carrying a renewed calm. "I gotta finish this bullshit paperwork. Maybe next week we'll get together, right?"

"Yeah, sure," Swag answered, dropping what remained of the cigarette. "Listen, did Kat pick up her pocket litter?"

O'Neal raised his head slightly. "I'd have to say no," he said. "She kicked out a hall window and went down a fire escape. And seeing that she was never here, officially, in the first place—"

"You mind, then?" Swag asked.

Exasperated, O'Neal pulled the manila envelope from the desk's center drawer and tossed it to Swag. "Now, really, good bye."

"It's been fun," Swag answered, coming out of the chair.

"Is that what it's been?" O'Neal asked.

Henri Esterhazy stood in the center of the empty entrance-way thinking. The house was empty from top to bottom, not a single stick of furniture remained. For most people, there is an echoing sadness in an empty house. The unfurnished rooms and barren walls call up the past ghosts. But for the French travel agent an empty house was different. There was potential in it, like exposed film, upon which he could capture any image flawlessly. In the hands of Henri Esterhazy, the stripped-down town house on the East Side was a film of unlimited ASA and infinite exposures, and he was the Japanese-camera-toting tourist with an itchy shutter finger.

As he waited, thinking, in the entranceway, the young woman crossed the street, dodging between cars halted for a light. She was wearing black cycle leathers, the large-toothed zipper on the jacket undone just enough to expose a hint of white lace brassiere. The young woman walked quickly, swinging her arms freely as she approached the building's entrance.

Esterhazy recovered from his trance when he saw her at the door, hand already raised toward the intercom. Walking slowly across the marbled hall, he quickly negotiated the complicated lock system on the inside door, then the less difficult locks on the steel-barred outside door.

"Ah, they've removed the cast," he said, greeting the young woman.

"A day early, but it won't matter," she said, flexing her arm; the one holding the helmet. "Surgical dressing comes off in a few days."

"Ahh," Esterhazy breathed. "Are we ready for the next assignment, *ma petite poupée?*"

"I suppose," she answered, somewhat bored. "What will it be this time? Italian? Another Englishman?"

"Ah, but this time is different," he said.

"Different, how?"

"This time we have two. A German and a Spaniard."

"A junket?" Erica answered. *"Pourquoi?"*

The French language annoyed the young woman only slightly less than the French themselves. It was an insidious language, not only spoken as if you had a mouthful of snails, but infectious as well. After an hour with a frog, you could find yourself speaking, if not actual French, then at the very least with an accent. Extreme cases were defined by slipping in phrases such as *mon chère, très bien, oui, n'est-ce pas,* and *mais où sont les neiges d'antan?* But detox was fast, she discovered. French left the system as quickly as cheap beer.

"The *prévôt* are everywhere. The unfortunate demise of Monsieur Hollowbutton has captured their attention. And the other target, the woman, in police custody. Yet no record of her arrest. And the man, vanished. None of it's any good."

"The provosts, sure they're around," she said. "And the others, they probably split."

"Something isn't right," he said, suddenly losing the accent.

"So, this is the last score?"

"Yes," he replied. "This is the last. We still have several days to monitor the official investigations."

"And if it's still too hot, what then? Refunds?"

Esterhazy stiffened, eyes narrowing. "We never give refunds," he said curtly. "Never."

It was then that the furniture arrived. Two trucks pulled up in front and men began unloading beds, nightstands, and dressers. Erica noted that there was nothing special about the furniture. It was the generic type of furnishings a not too high-ranking executive might find in a chain hotel. Every piece was done up with a veneer of the same patently bogus, artificial wood grain.

There were paintings as well. The workmen quickly unloaded the chrome-framed reproductions of Motherwell, Jasper Johns, DeKooning; abstracts whose dominant colors were suspiciously close matches to the variety of polyester bedspreads and drapery that followed.

The movers filed in through the doors at an orderly pace, transforming the nineteenth century town house into something very much like a Holiday Inn.

"Planning on a hasty departure?"

"Why not prepare for the worst?" Esterhazy replied. "If we were to leave under hostile circumstances, there would be no great loss."

"And you're expecting the worst," the woman said after the movers had been at it for a time.

"Not to worry," Esterhazy replied calmly, in a voice free of not only accent, but inflection as well. "By this time next week we shall be where? In London, overlooking Chester Square?"

The woman shook her head, somewhat sadly.

"A villa in Barcelona? Marbella, perhaps?" Esterhazy continued.

Again she shook her head.

"Ah, then," Esterhazy said, a light coming to his eyes, "the house in Switzerland, then. A villa on Lake Lugano?"

"Perhaps," the young woman said. "Isn't Lugano the city with all those banks. Italian, isn't it?"

"Yes, Italian," Esterhazy replied, hopeful.

"Good, anything but Romansch," she said. Then added for a reaction, "Or French."

"Think on it, then," he said. "But while you're thinking, could I interest you in a game of backgammon?"

The woman shrugged and followed Esterhazy into the kitchen, the only room where the furnishings had remained unchanged.

chapter twenty-two

BAMMER DIDN'T LIKE IT. HE didn't like it one damned bit. But it had been Dobbs's idea to bring the woman down to the suite and treat her like a guest no less. If Bammer had had any say in it, he would have marched the bitch out in cuffs and hung the whole mess on her. Over twenty murders, with motive. All with the best motive—money. Records showed that most of the vics were operating under one of her holding companies. Maybe she was cheating them. Who knows and who gave a good hot damn? She was dirty. All they had to do was say that she accidentally ran Hollowbutton off the road into the river during a failed kidnap attempt. They had their perp for the Hollowbutton hit. So just throw the crooked bitch into the system and let it grind her down.

But Dobbs saw it differently. The way he saw it, they needed a male perp. How could they parade some five-foot-three-inch woman out in front of the press as the cold-blooded killer of the tea bag? She'd start crying and carrying on, Dobbs explained, and pretty soon there's a public opinion shift swinging down on you like an axe. On one side there's a good-looking 'merican girl just trying to make a buck, and on the other a fat guy who dresses up like a flounder and quotes Churchill.

Now Bammer was in the middle of it. Staring out at the darkened park while Dobbs interrogated the woman. Shit, it all used to be so easy. Scumbags on one side and his men on the other. And bullets in between.

"More coffee?" Dobbs asked, leaning over the low table that sat between him and Sandy Mann.

"Just a warm-up please," she said sweetly, proffering her cup.

Dobbs took the cup graciously, set it back down on the saucer with its double-P Plaza logo, and began pouring from the silver service that squatted low and shiny on the table. "Say when," he said.

Major Martin stood at ease in one corner, a lopsided sneer plastered across his face that said he sure as hell knew how to make a broad talk. And it wasn't by pouring her coffee either.

"When," Sandy Mann said. "And some more cream, please."

When Dobbs had finished, he handed the cup and saucer back to the woman, who sat primly on her chair, like a girl at some boarding-school tea, the small dog curled at her feet. "Now, we've got a situation here," he said in a professionally-concerned voice. "We have ourselves a real humdinger of a situation."

Now he was saying "Humdinger," Bammer thought to himself. *Hum-fucking-dinger*, for Chrissakes! Just being folksy as hell. Shit, Bammer thought, folksy crap wouldn't play with this bitch. She was off the street; money and fear were what she knew. But then, Dobbs never cursed. There wasn't a word in his vocabulary that wasn't printed in *Webster's Unabridged* or listed in *The New York Times Manual of Style and Usage*.

"What do you mean, we?" she asked, taking a dainty sip, then reaching down to scratch the dog behind the ear.

Dobbs stared at her, turning on those wide college-boy eyes to little effect. "I mean you and me," he answered calmly, keeping up the Mayberry act. "We both have a situation. But I believe, sincerely believe, we're in a position to do each other some good. A fortunate turn of events, wouldn't you agree?"

"Do you see a lawyer in this room?" she answered sweetly. "Until you see a lawyer with my retainer check in his pocket, I'm afraid it wouldn't be in my best interest to say a thing. Wouldn't you agree?"

Bammer wheeled from the window, his face sunset red. "Listen, you little bitch!" he screamed. "You know what happens to people who piss me off? You have any idea what you're playing with here? That bodyguard of yours is dead as you're going to be if you don't start cooperating."

"Fuck you," Sandy said, not so sweetly. The tiny dog at her feet snarled.

"Fuck me?" Bammer screamed, storming away from the window. "No! Fuck you!"

"Hey, fuck you!" Sandy yelled back. The dog was up on its feet, its tiny paws dug into the carpet.

Bammer began to sputter, his hands clenching and unclenching at his sides. "Fuck you, bitch!" he shouted.

Dobbs broke in before Sandy could make the predictable reply. "I'd like to suggest we take this dialogue in a different direction," he said placidly. "Something that can advance the interests of all concerned parties."

"Start talking, Dobbsy," she said. "You start and I'll just jump in when it gets interesting." The dog was down again, resuming its relaxed position.

"This is bullshit," Bammer said. "Bullshit with a bell on it."

Dobbs ignored the colonel's remark. "This is where you stand," he said, addressing the woman, then reaching down to scratch the dog's hind end. "We can prosecute on the murder. Don't hold any illusions about that. We can prosecute and maybe win a conviction. Odds could run sixty-forty in our favor. We have your cars. They were pulled from the river this morning. And there's a positive paint match from the Bentley on both."

"Keep talking," Sandy said, sipping her coffee without emotion. She knew that if they were going for a conviction on the murder charge, they wouldn't have hauled her down

194   L.S. Riker

to Bammer's suite. The deal was still to come. They were going to serve it like dim sum.

"We can prosecute on a continuing criminal enterprise charge," Dobbs continued, breaking off a small section of butter cookie from the tray and feeding it to the dog. "And we can win that one too. The odds on that would run ninety-ten, our favor. Maybe that earns you three or four years working for the state. But you'll lose it all—we'll grab every asset we can find."

"Don't feed the dog that shit. Cholesterol and all," she advised as she set her coffee down. Then, almost as an after-thought, she said, "The question is, what can you do for me?"

Dobbs took his glasses off then, and leaned across toward her with great sincerity. "We can let you walk. Your little enterprise still intact," he said. "We just need a little cooperation."

"For instance?" she asked calmly.

"Who else was in the cars?" Dobbs asked. "Give us the driver and the shooter. Do that and you'll walk. Right after you testify. And believe me, those are the best odds you'll get."

"There were my bodyguards in the limo," she said. "One's dead, he was that guy in the alley with his head sliced off. The other disappeared. His name was Lou Birney. A black guy."

"Birney's dead," Bammer injected.

She greeted this news with a slight shiver. "You seem pretty sure," she said.

"I goddamned well oughta be," Bammer shot back before returning to the window in disgust.

"Give us another name," Dobbs asked.

"Kat Jones," Sandy said quickly. "Works for me at the Dead Banker."

"That a man or a woman?" Dobbs asked with some interest.

"Woman," came the answer.

"No good, we need a man," Dobbs said, coaxing.

"Look, this is boring and it's where I step off," Sandy said as she started to rise. "Let's get my lawyer in here. I'll take my odds with a trial."

"You just don't get it, do you?" Dobbs said. "You just aren't reading from the same page we are."

"I get that this is lame," Sandy said. "And I've—"

Before she could finish, Dobbs's right hand shot out, grabbed her around the throat, then forced her back down into the seat. The dog began snarling, but as Dobbs rose he brought the right Gucci down hard, severing the animal's spine. It let out a small yelp, then began shivering and convulsing on the floor.

"No, I'm afraid you don't get it," Dobbs said, his voice still calm as he leaned over the woman, his foot pinning the now dead dog to the floor. "But I'll explain it again, and we'll all get up to speed on this thing. If you don't give up someone within the next twenty seconds, you'll be dead. I'll give you excellent odds on that."

Even Bammer was amazed by Dobbs's sudden use of force. He watched in grim fascination as his media guy continued to strangle the young woman with one hand that closed mercilessly around her throat. His mouth was set into a thin-lipped expression of concentration. Not an ounce of strain showed on his face, save for a slight twitching of one of his jaw muscles. For all the world he looked as if he were typing up one of his famous speeches or pouring coffee. Still, something had changed about him. Suddenly he didn't look all that young anymore.

Both of her hands were up, clutching at Dobbs's wrist, trying to free herself. Her mouth was set half opened, struggling futilely to pull air down into her lungs. Kicking out, she overturned the table, sending the coffee service crashing to the floor.

In the corner, unnoticed and forgotten, Major Martin lost his straight-backed composure. His eyes glowed at the sight as he licked his lips.

Just as Sandy Mann's eyes began to lose their focus, she

stopped struggling and began nodding, panicked. She had been just a few seconds from unconscious and knew it.

Dobbs released his grip, smiling as he stepped back. "See there, I had every confidence in you," he said, straightening the cuff of his suit coat. "What's the name?"

"You killed my dog," she managed to get out. "You fuckin' killed him."

"Nasty animals. I prefer cats myself," Dobbs answered without remorse. "What is the name?"

"It's this guy off the street," she said, gasping for breath and rubbing her throat, imprinted with Dobbs's finger marks. Her eyes were glued to the dog corpse on the floor. "A real loser. His street name's Swag."

"Sonofabitch!" Bammer screamed as he lifted a lamp and hurled it across the room to smash against the opposite wall. Instinct sent Dobbs and Sandy Mann into a crouch as it flew overhead. "Goddamned sonofabitch!"

"You heard of him?" Sandy asked, still rubbing her throat.

"Apparently," Dobbs cordially answered as he reached for his coffee cup, which had overturned on the floor.

Swag made one stop, at Narcadia's, before returning to the DMV. While he was talking to the DMV clerk, Narcadia would be running the name of the travel agency. With any luck, they'd finish at about the same time.

He smoked one of the Thai cigarettes as he waited behind the building at the employee entrance. He'd follow the clerk again and try to catch him in a secluded place.

Employees started filing out the door at two minutes after five. The DMV clerk was among the first out. It took about half a second for the clerk to make Swag. The little man's eyes darted around in a panic, then he took off at a run, dropping the new plastic briefcase as he sprinted down the street. Swag dropped the cigarette and followed. By the time the little guy reached the corner of the building, he was already winded and losing steam.

A group of provosts were clustered across the street. The

clerk saw them and darted away. So, he's dirty, Swag thought as he stopped to pick up the clerk's briefcase. A citizen in danger runs to the provosts, not away.

Swag caught up with the guy near a city courts building, the one that held small claims court. The little guy was puffing hard, bent over, supported by one pudgy hand against the large plate-glass window that looked into a barren lobby.

"Here, you dropped this," Swag said, offering the briefcase.

"Okay, you got me," the little guy said, still puffing, but straightening up some. "How much you want?"

What was this now? Swag thought to himself. The little guy thinks I'm a cop?

"How much?" the clerk asked again. "Fifty, a hundred?"

"Talk to me." Swag asked.

"Here, take the watch." the clerk said, slipping the watch from his wrist and handing it out to Swag. "You like it so much, take it."

"You remember me?" Swag asked. "That's good."

"I knew you were heat, I just knew it," the guy said, shaking the expensive timepiece in Swag's face. "Come on, take the watch."

"Let's just talk here a minute," Swag said. "I'm looking for a friend."

"Try a personal in the paper," the guy said, suddenly toughening up as the realization that Swag wasn't Provost or NYPD dawned on him. The watch vanished into a pocket.

"Am I hearing an attitude here?" Swag asked.

"You ain't hearing shit," the guy said.

City workers were now pouring out of the building from elevators. The lobby was packed with witnesses.

The clerk tried to move away, indignant. Swag shot a hand up, palm against the glass, blocking him. The little guy turned, heading in the opposite direction. Swag shot another hand up.

"You're not heat," the guy said. "You're just a fuckin' cab driver. So what you gonna do? Look at all those people."

Swag leaned into the little guy, getting right in his face. "I can put your head through this window," he whispered.

"Fuck you," the guy said, drawing out the word. Then he tried to pull Swag's left hand down from the glass.

Behind the little clerk a security guard stared suspiciously at the scene. Swag figured he had maybe thirty seconds before the guard got curious enough to come out of the air-conditioned lobby and see what was up. "You know this girl?" Swag asked, pulling Kat's hack license from his pocket and holding it a few inches from the clerk's eyes. "You tell me who's after her."

All color drained from the guy's face as a look of genuine fear took hold. Suddenly he turned and tried to pull Swag's hand off the glass again. When that failed, he tried going under.

"Who's after her?" Swag asked.

"Get it away," the clerk stammered, panicked. "Get that thing the fuck away from me."

"You know her, don't you?" Swag asked, holding the license closer.

"Get it away!" the guy said. He'd managed to slip under the left arm. Swag caught him by the belt and spun him back into the glass, bowing it badly with the impact.

The guard was moving now, walking quickly toward the east doorway.

Swag held the card close with two fingers, bringing it right up to the clerk's eye. "Who's got her?"

"Get that damned thing away!" the guy shouted.

That's when it hit Swag. He waved the license close to the clerk's face. "What? You're afraid of this?"

The guard was coming down on them. He was moving cautiously now, across the front of the building, his left hand planted on the butt of the ancient .38 service revolver. The holster was unstrapped.

Swag let his arm fall, and the clerk took off at a run. Even at a labored crouching run, he blended instantly with the crowd of office workers.

The guard was right on Swag then. "You got a problem here?" he asked.

Swag pocketed the license, smiled and brought his hands up, showing empty palms as he turned to face the guard. "Misunderstanding," he said.

"Looked that way," the guard answered, keeping his distance.

"Guy owed me some money," Swag said. "No big deal."

"It won't be if you vanish," the guard said. "Like instantly."

chapter twenty-three

SWAG HEADED UP TO EMERY CHEN'S because he wanted a contact that wasn't well known and because Chen was close—his Canal Street factory just a few blocks from the DMV. Swag figured that maybe Chen would have a connect in Chinatown that knew about documents, forged, altered, and otherwise. Something about the hack license, a wallet-sized laminated card, scared the clerk a hell of a lot more than a six-foot-two lunatic in an Hawaiian shirt chasing him around Foley Square.

It took a full three minutes of door-pounding and threats to get into the workshop. Somewhere above him in the shadows of the stairwell a young girl sighed and ratched back the slide of her pistol.

When Chen finally opened the door, wearing an electric-blue suit, cadmium-yellow flowered tie, and blue suede cowboy boots, he was already midway through a slow burn of barely concealed anger—if conceal is what he was in fact trying to do with it.

"Nice outfit," Swag said, throwing gasoline on the fire. "That like a road safety thing, for night?"

"These rags cost more than you'll see in a year, Jack," Emery said, offended. Then added, significantly, "Italian."

"Shoes and all, huh?" Swag answered.

Emery gave his shoes a quick look, checking for stains. "You couldn't trade a kidney for these."

"Well, I always figured you for a blue suede kinda guy."

"Look, this is total fuckin' wacko," Emery answered. "Come in here insulting me."

"You got a paper guy?" Swag asked.

"No, I don't have no paper guy," Emery shot back, sarcastic. "I'm a legit businessman, a total fuckin' citizen, which is more than some people can say. You, for instance."

"Maybe there's someone in the back, huh?" Swag said. "Someone with a cousin."

The layout was changed since the last time Swag had been there. The maze had been altered subtly.

"Swag, we're trying to do business here, do you understand that?"

"American dream and all that," Swag said.

"Yeah, exactly," Emery replied, reaching for the door. "I'm a hardworking guy, trying to make my immigrant dreams come true. Now get the fuck out!"

Swag blocked the doorknob and locks with his body. "I've been hearing that a lot lately," he said. "Maybe I'm not going about it the right way. Maybe fifty francs is a better approach. What do you think?"

Emery froze, then brought his hand down. "Fifty and the promise not to come back. Not that your promise is worth shit."

"Deal," Swag said.

It was then that the old Chinese guy came hustling through the maze toward the door, arms and legs working inside the baggy pants and shirt. He was moving faster than Swag would have thought he could. And he was talking fast, saying, "Hot, hot, hot!"

Emery turned, frowning. "What's hot?" he said.

"Hot, hot, hot," the old man repeated with much arm waving.

"Check it out," Emery ordered. "Get the box."

"Check out! Check out!" the old guy said definitively, nodding. "Hot!"

Then Emery and the old guy launched into a heated discussion in Chinese. Emery was trying to keep calm. The old guy kept nodding or shaking his head.

When the old guy vanished back into the maze, Swag said, "Complaint about working conditions? Worried 'bout OSHA, are you?"

Emery wheeled back on him, his face fearful, not even pissed-off anymore. "This ain't no joke," he said. "We got a hot load somewhere."

"Like hot, how?" Swag asked.

"Like radio-fucking-active," Emery said. "Got a load in two years ago from Jersey. Scrap metal for castings. Now I got two guys in a clinic, their hair falling out. There were pellets all over the shit. Some ignorant asshole out in Jersey broke open medical equipment."

Swag let the enormity of it sink in. The expression must have shown on his face.

"That ain't so funny now, is it?" Emery said.

Swag shook his head. "Holy shit."

"Holy shit is right. Those pellets fucked up everything they touched," Emery said, whispering the story. "Plus we melted them down."

"What happened?"

"On the street, man," Emery murmured. "Cast into product. All sold. Gone to tourists. After that I had the place wired. Anything hot comes through that door, a light comes on over the workbench."

The old man returned then. He was holding a small Geiger counter, about the size of a cigarette pack, painted sandy tan and labeled as French military issue. The thing was clicking like crazy, registering rads on a red digital display that was turning over like a pinball game. And the closer it got to Swag, the faster it clicked, and the faster the numbers turned over.

"What the hell you holding?" Emery asked, backing away. "You got a thermonuke in your pocket?"

"No, I'm just happy to see you," Swag tried, but the joke fell flat. The old man was running the counter over Swag, head to toe. The clicks became a sustained tone at the midsection.

"The wallet, man," Emery advised.

The old man ran back to the bench and retrieved a lead apron, the kind that X-ray techs wore. Swag dropped Kat's and his wallet in the center and folded it up.

"What kinda shit did you step in?" Emery asked.

"How much to find out?" Swag answered.

"Hundred and fifty," came the wary answer. "But I'd pay *you*, just to leave."

Swag pulled the roll from his pocket and peeled off the franc notes.

Emery took the money warily, passing it under the Geiger counter to make sure it wasn't hot. Then the three of them made their way back through the maze, Emery following at a safe distance. When they reached the locked door to the back room, Emery waved Swag off and passed a magnetic card key just left of the door at chest level. There wasn't a click, but when Swag pulled, the door opened.

There was a small chamber between the two doors, most of it occupied by an immensely fat Chinese guy, who sat propped on a bar stool with an assault shotgun across his lap. He barely acknowledged the trio as they crowded into the small cubicle. When the door behind them clicked shut, the guard reached down and produced what looked like a pair of binoculars attached to the wall by a thick spiraled cord.

"Old time Eyedentify system," Emery said, bringing the unit up to his eyes. "Scans blood vessels. You don't have my blood vessels, you don't get in." Then he clicked down on a small button on the side of the unit and the door clicked open.

The three filed into the lab, but they might as well have been walking into another world. The lab was immaculate, done up in white tile walls and a hard-surface white floor. A dozen or more guys in white and gray lab coats busied themselves at tables, gently prying gems from their settings under jeweler loops and high intensity lights of magnifying glasses. Others worked with small files and vials of acid, for testing gold quality.

The tables were arranged in work stations, and each one

was equipped with a digital scale with settings for grams, pennyweight, ounces, and carats. The jewelry was broken down, then sorted into a series of clear plastic trays. There were also small keyboards and monitors, where they recorded their findings.

At the far end of the room was another door, locked. Swag guessed that's where the smelting and casting operations took place.

But what really held his attention were the workers. None of them wore a stitch of clothing under their pocketless lab coats.

When Emery noticed Swag's raised eyebrow, he said, "I hate pockets. Get rid of pockets and there'd be no more thieves."

It wasn't the first time Swag had seen layouts like this. Old-time drug dealers used to hire young girls and old women from the neighborhood, whom they'd known all their lives, to package dope. They'd work naked at clear glass tables, cutting, weighing, bagging, and stamping for a hundred bucks a day. Undercover tapes were filled with gossip and small talk, recipes, and jokes from the places.

"Bingo!" Emery called, and immediately a young blond kid came over. The kid had bleached-blond hair down to his shoulders and he walked with a steady, loose-limbed shuffle, like he was listening to music no one else could hear.

"Yo, boss-dude," the kid said, with an accent that fell clearly on the sands of some southern Cali beach.

"Bingo, look at this," Emery said as the old man set out the lead vest on the table.

The kid, who Swag now saw was around thirty, flipped the ends of the vest open. "Like it's a wallet, man," he said.

"Yeah, it's a wallet," Emery said. "It's also hot."

"No shit," the kid replied. "Far out."

"Go get your stuff," Emery said. "Do a workup on it."

"Sure thing, man," the kid said, and vanished to the back of the room.

"What's he on?" Swag asked.

"High on life," Emery replied, shaking his head. "Creepy kid. Left Brooklyn for post grad at Cal Tech, physics, chemistry. Came back like this. Would you believe it if I told you he rides the subway out to Coney Island to surf?"

Swag watched the kid gather equipment from a cabinet in the corner. He was still nodding to music. "Probably."

When the kid returned to the table, he was holding a counter and wearing lead gloves. He removed the contents of the wallet with some difficulty, then began passing the counter over them and sorting through the pocket litter.

"Weird shit," Bingo said. "This hack license and this one are hot. Nice-looking babe, though."

"How hot?" Swag asked. "Dangerous?"

"Ever like go to the dentist and like get an X ray?" the kid asked, looking up.

Swag nodded, hopeful.

"Yeah, well, ever get like two hundred X rays at the dentist?" the kid asked. "'Cause you got some serious rad action going on here. You want I should categorize the isotope?"

"How bad?" Emery asked.

"You carry this shit around a month, and you ain't gonna need no pension," the kid said.

"Where'd it come from?" Swag asked.

"Like who knows," the kid said, slipping on the lead vest to protect himself. "You been hangin' in Jersey lately? Maybe hitting some of the clubs?"

Swag shook his head.

"Well, like somebody dosed your paper, dude," the kid answered. "Dosed this babe's too. Like you're one dosed dude, dude."

"Can you do an analysis?" Swag asked. "I know who did it. What I need to know is why."

"Yeah, well, like let me run it," the kid answered. Then he was moving, heading for one of the scales. "Like we'll do this right."

He set one of the licenses down on the scale and wrote

down the readout in pencil. Then he slapped his sides and said, "Like boss, you got a license?"

Emery produced his license reluctantly and handed it over.

When the kid placed it on the scale, it weighed less.

"Whoa, bogus man," he said. "Like this ain't like a real license."

"Yeah it is," Swag answered.

The kid weighted the other hack license, Kat's, and it came up heavy too.

"Totally like weird," Bingo said. "Let's see what's in 'em."

From one of the tables Bingo retrieved a razor knife, used for prying stones from settings. Working under a magnifying glass, he slit the laminated seal of Swag's license and peeled the paper away from the plastic. It only took him a second to study the plastic before he went to work on the paper.

Swag and Emery watched at a safe distance as the kid worked in the heavy gloves with the knife. The paper finally yielded and he tore the layer away.

"Whoa, dudes, like look at this," he said.

Swag moved a few steps closer. Wedged between two pieces of paper, in a yellowish-white center, far up in the left corner, was a tiny brown square.

"What, what did you find?" Emery asked, beating Swag to the question.

"Like this is heavy, man," the kid said, setting the dissected license down. "This is like a tracking system."

"That little box?" Swag asked.

"Naw man, like you don't track with that," Bingo said. "That's a passive radio microchip. Like in the stores, you know?"

Swag did know. They'd been using radio units for years. Just circuits that didn't transmit or receive, but when you walked between two posts that did, they busted up the signal. They used them in stores for concealable products. Two posts at the exit, and anything in your pockets with the chip on it set off the alarm. Lately, manufacturers had begun installing them at the factory, inside the packaging.

"You been getting busted a' lot?" Bingo asked. "Setting off alarms?"

Swag shook his head no.

"Yeah, well, you can set 'em up for different frequencies, like, make 'em like proprietary," Bingo answered. "Companies use 'em, like to restrict access to certain floors like. They implant 'em, like, on ID cards. I know a dude'll do a frequency analysis. Tell you this, though, you and this babe's been triggering something."

"How would this unit work, if you were using it?" Swag asked.

"Wow, like you could do anything," the kid replied.

"Gimme an example," Swag said.

"Well, like say you were after some dude," Bingo began, conspiracy etched in his voice. "Like you wanted to know where he was, like always. You followin' me, dosed dude?"

"Okay," Swag said. "I'm following."

"So, like you put in a couple of the radio dealies. Like small units, say they look like tape with a little box. Maybe not even a box, you could like run power and transmit off like something the size of a watch battery. Something that looked like a screw or nail," Bingo said. "Spike 'em into some doorway, 'cause you gotta hook them parallel—send receive, like. But like you could do it for a whole building. You could wire a block—or two blocks. You could do the whole city. Some dude walking around tripping receivers every time he crosses a street, you know, it registers like someplace else. Whoa, that's heavy, man."

"Then why the hot stuff?" Swag asked.

"Whoa there, dude," Bingo said. "Like you can't really wire like a whole city. So like you wire a couple of blocks. Once the dude or dudette, as like the case may be, crosses a perimeter, the alarm trips. Then you kick in with the hot stuff—that's your yellow powder there. You could keep track of someone for like two, three blocks away. Say, like a half mile."

"What kind of shit is this, Swag?" Emery broke in.

"Paranoia-city, man," Bingo said, awed. "Like you can' *move* with this thing. Somebody always knowing where you are. Heavy, man, *awesomely heavy.*"

"So what do you want, Swag?" Emery said impatiently "You want me to dump this thing? Ship it to Jersey?"

Swag thought a moment, then said, "No, wrap it in lead I'll take it with me."

"Whoa man, like heavy," Bingo cut in.

Kat Jones had gone to ground. She was staying low, riding the subways, walking the streets only at night. A friend had loaned her a 9mm Sig, but it was little comfort. And what's more, the money she lifted from the guard was running low.

And now the provosts were after her. She felt them out there closing in on her when she was in the P.D. cage. Then she heard Bammer—saw his grim face speaking out from a pile of discount televisions over on Ninth Avenue. It was like he was speaking to her when he said, "We're a short hair away from bringing in those people. Closer than even they could know."

Not two hours later her picture began showing up on televisions all over the city. A grainy, bleached-out photo from the DMV. As soon as she saw the photo, the thing made sense. It was a provost frame from the go.

Riding the Number 6 train up and down Manhattan, she thought of her next move. She could probably take out a store, maybe a liquor store or a bar, but that wasn't her style Besides, anything worth robbing—anything with easy currency in the register—was alarmed into Provost HQ.

No, she didn't need that kind of heat. That's the move they'd be waiting for. Then they'd drop her in some alley.

As the train screeched into the East 86th Street stop, a smattering of rush hour commuters crowded the door When the doors hissed open, they hustled through, moving for the stairs. And there, for just a second, before the doors

hut again, was a poster. It came into sharp focus, only for
n instant.

MAD AS HELL?
RIPPED OFF? INJURED? CHEATED?
DO SOMETHING ABOUT IT!
MAKE THEM PAY!

t was a poster she had seen a thousand times before for
chain of storefront lawyers. She didn't even have to read
he company's motto, which was, "Even If You Think Law-
ers Are Beneath Contempt—Remember, Nobody Is
Above the Law! CALL TODAY! MAKE THEM PAY!"

The poster itself was an omen, but what held her atten-
ion now was that someone had scrawled kill! kill! kill! in
vhite chalk across the blue and white poster. A double
>men if ever there was one.

"Yeah," Kat whispered to herself as her pocketed hand
ightened around the gun's grip and she thumbed off the
afety. She was one Jersey girl who wasn't going to run. If
hey were gonna get her, then she was going to take a
hitload of them with her.

Then the doors hissed shut, and the train was moving
again.

"As you understand, we'll be working very closely
ogether," Dobbs said.

"Believe me, I have absolutely no problem with that,"
Sandy answered.

They were sitting in the Palm Court of the Plaza, eating
unch. The string quartet was just finishing one number and
egueing into another. It had been a long time since Sandy
had been out and about. Now she was dressed in a slinky
French item. She wore jewelry borrowed from the hotel's
hops, and every inch of her, from pedicure to hairstyle, had
>een seen to by a small army of hotel employees, paid for
>ut of provost funds.

"You understand, there'll be a grand jury investigation?" Dobbs continued. "And then there's a small matter of a trial?"

"It all sounds so very high profile," Sandy said, smiling sweetly as she raised the water glass to her lips. "But the thing that worries me is that I never know what to say. There'll be a lot of press around. And with me going in and out of the car, well, they only want a sound bite. Is that the word for it?"

"Sound and sight bite," Dobbs answered. "If you're worried, I can have something prepared." He noted then, for the first time, she had the most remarkable blue-gray eyes.

She smiled her appreciation with a small nod. When she brought the water glass away from her lips, there wasn't a trace of lipstick along its rim. A fact not lost on Dobbs. "How sweet," she said. "But nothing cheap. I wouldn't want to come off like a bimbo or an airhead."

"You'll be perceived as a hardworking woman with solid intelligence," Dobbs answered.

She smiled again. "And honest. Honesty is very important, isn't it?"

"Someone too smart to lie," Dobbs added. "A woman strengthened by an irrefutable knowledge that she is in the right. Speaking off the top of my head, I would say that you had no prior knowledge—no idea at all—that this Swag-person would attempt to spoil your job interview and late supper with Mr. Hollowbutton. Why, you were excited about the prospect of bettering your fortunes, and probably mentioned it while at work. You had no reason to suspect a kidnap attempt by this drifter Swag-person and his accomplice . . . Kat, is it?"

"Yes, Kat Jones. I believe that's just the way it happened. You know, I do remember him *lurking* around the bar at all hours. Lurking is the right word, isn't it?"

Dobbs considered it and nodded.

"He drank heavily, especially in the mornings. I remember, because he never tipped. And he never seemed to have a job," Sandy continued. "But the way you just summed it all up was great. I bet if I had something written down—for the grand jury—I wouldn't be so nervous about it."

"I'll have something prepared," Dobbs said offhandedly.

"And I'll need a clothing allowance," she said. "Nothing too flashy, you understand. Day clothes, of course. A dozen salt-of-the-earth outfits. And maybe one or two gowns, for evening wear. Keeping up appearances for something like this is important, isn't it?"

"Of course," Dobbs said.

"And, those companies of mine," she said, broaching the subject carefully. "There's no need to bring them up, is there? They are, after all, perfectly legitimate."

"I don't see why," Dobbs agreed. "You are, after all, a waitress by profession. I don't imagine how it's anyone's business if you want to tuck a few francs away in Luxembourg."

"For my retirement," Sandy added.

"Of course," Dobbs said, a small smile breaking out on his face.

"And I'll need full protection," she continued. "Perhaps a room here, something with leg room."

"As it happens, there's a suite we use for protective custody," Dobbs answered. "Very comfortable. It's the one next to my own, so I should know."

"How convenient," Sandy sighed, then reached across the table to touch his hand lightly with her fingertips.

chapter twenty-four

NARCADIA LEANED HEAVILY OVER THE gray metal desk, the weight of his tumorous head pulling him down. The watch and ring glistened dully on his hand. When he finally spoke, it was like a voice from a tomb. "Get the fuck outta town, my friend."

"That's advice. I wanted information," Swag said, reaching for a cigarette.

The phone on the huge desk buzzed and chirped unanswered. Narcadia didn't seem to notice. "That's the best information you'll get, ever. This thing you're on to, it's outta your league."

"How far out?"

The tumorous mass twitched with frustration and annoyance. Suddenly the small office seemed much smaller. "You don't get it, do you?"

"Why don't you fill me in?" Swag tried, lighting the cigarette.

"You came to see me about that guy, *Easy*. That's fine, that's the kind of job you're cut out for," Narcadia said. "Well, he doesn't figure into it anymore. The kinds of questions you're asking. You don't have enough money to buy the answers. And you don't have enough weight to do anything with them. Now just be a good boy and leave town."

"And if I don't?" Swag asked.

From some drawer deep in the desk, Narcadia pulled a fat envelope, then tossed it across the Formica expanse. It skidded to a stop with one corner just off the edge, pointing at Swag.

"Take it," Narcadia said. "I'm making it as simple as possible, understand?"

Swag studied the envelope, which he now saw was air mail variety. The engraved face of a Swiss franc showed through the thin paper indistinctly. "What's this, your mad money?"

"I'm not an animal," came the response. "That's your only chance. Take it."

Smoke from Swag's cigarette filled the room. "You ugly asshole, you're working the other side, aren't you?"

"I'm working *the only side*, mine," Narcadia answered. "Now take the damn money."

"Fuck you," Swag answered and got up to leave.

They caught him as he was leaving the lobby of the Equitable Building. There were four of them, and later he'd tell himself that if he hadn't been so pissed off at Narcadia, he would have seen them coming. But in truth, it wouldn't have helped.

"Okay, right there," the leader said.

Instinct brought Swag's hands up, palms outward. He recognized the leader's uniform as that of a major from a Provost Tactical Unit. Narcadia had set him up. Probably was on the phone to Provost hotline right after inviting him up.

"That's a good boy," the major said, then nodded his head toward Swag, and one of the four patted him down. When he found the Custom Colt 10, he trotted back to the major with his find.

"We're not going to have any problems here, are we?" the major asked, tucking the Colt into the front of his uniform.

"No problems," Swag answered.

"That's good, because you have a lunch date."

Then they were walking Swag out to the car. They moved in a tight detail, two in back, one in front. The fourth ran ahead to open the provost Range Rover's door.

"Am I meeting anyone in particular?"

"Does it matter?" the major said, ushering Swag into the car before taking a seat up front. Of the three remaining men, one slid in behind the driver's seat and the other two flanked Swag, Steyrs pointed at his head.

"I'm a little particular about who I eat with, you know? I may have to check my calendar."

"You're having lunch with the colonel," the guard to Swag's right chirped in.

"Bammer?" Swag asked. "You know, I think I'm already booked for today."

"You have something against the colonel?" the guard on Swag's left asked.

"Ever eat with him?" Swag answered. "Makes you sick to see it. Guy chews with his mouth open. Orders red wine with fish. Doesn't know the silverware layout for shit."

"Keep making jokes," the major snapped back. "Go ahead, keep on joking. It isn't often I meet a dead man with a sense of humor."

It was a long ride up to the Plaza, and it gave Swag plenty of time to think out the situation. If this was a disappearance squad, then why would they be hauling him back to provisional headquarters? If they were going to vanish him, they'd be turning right, heading west toward the river so he could die with a view of Jersey.

"He's real funny, ain't he?" the major said. "A reg'lar laugh riot."

The other men grunted lackey approval as the car continued uptown.

The plan went something like this. Swag was to be hauled in so that Bammer could gawk at him for a bit. For years he'd been after Swag, but there was always something. One time it was a tourist with pull in D.C. Another time the hit squad just fucked up. But this time Bammer had Swag nailed, and what was better, it was all going to be public.

Dobbs had organized the thing down to the last detail. First they'd dose the lowlife with a shot of a hypnostimulate to make him look crazy for the cameras when they pulled him out in cuffs from an East Side squat. There was already a makeup guy on call, just to add the finishing touches—dirt under the nails and darken up the beard a bit. Dobbs even suggested knocking out a few front teeth, which was okay by Bammer, who would be in the forefront of the capture party, taking command.

Once they had Swag in custody, they'd throw his raggedy ass up on a prison ward at Bellevue. They had a doctor on the pad there that'd diagnose paranoid schizophrenia and feed the press anonymous quotes regarding his condition. "Violent." "Intractable." "Florid." "Psychotic." "Organic brain disorder." These were the terms Dobbs had outlined for the leaks.

Dobbs figured it would take two, maybe three days to indict, but they could maybe stretch it out for a week—running from Tuesday to Tuesday—depending on whether it was a slow news week or not. He knew he could count on above-the-fold, lead coverage for at least that long.

The actual hit would take place in the court's parking garage. Dobbs had run the ancient film of the Oswald hit more than a hundred times, and there was no doubt about it; the Oswald killing was more than a history lesson, it was great television. Except you couldn't buy guys like Jack Ruby anymore. Swag would have to try to escape.

Bammer was sitting in the Palm Court at his usual table. An elaborate pastry and a cup of coffee were set out before him, but he could touch neither. Just too damned excited. Checking his watch, he wondered what was taking Martin and his men so long. They'd promised Swag to him within the hour. Now, it had been more than an hour, and there was still no Swag.

Across the room a small group of German tourists nodded and smiled graciously—there was genuine respect for power in their manner. Bammer returned their greeting with a distracted air, something the Germans fully appreciated.

"Fuck it," Bammer said to himself. "I'll call." Signaling

a waiter over with a broad hand gesture, he ordered that a cellular be brought to his table. It appeared nearly at once. He didn't have to go through the comm center for Martin's vehicle number, he knew it by heart.

The phone in the cruiser rang once before the driver picked it up.

"That for me?" Swag asked, and got a rifle barrel jammed up hard under his chin for asking.

"Where in hell is that delivery?" Bammer's voice boomed over the car's handset.

"On our way now," the driver answered. "ETA inside of two minutes. We'll deliver around the side, as planned."

"You do that," Bammer said, then punched the phone's power off. He lasted nearly ninety seconds from the time he hung up to when he rose from his table and left the Palm Court.

This was too good, he thought to himself. I got to see them drag that sonofabitch from the car. They'd be walking him in low profile, like some service guy, but still, he just had to see it.

Bammer was descending the thickly carpeted steps when he saw the cruiser pull up. He pushed past the armed doorman, taking up a position just inside the entrance, on the other side of the double glass doors, where the view was better.

And by God if Swag wasn't in the backseat. Hot damn if that wasn't a sweet sight.

When the car pulled up at the side of the Plaza, Swag could see the colonel himself on the other side of the door, looking like a kid on the wrong side of a candy store's window.

"This is where the fun starts, asshole," the major said, opened the front door, and slid out.

"Haul out the rubber hoses," Swag said.

"No more rubber hoses," one of the men said. "They do it with transdermals now, not even a needle mark. A little patch on the neck and maybe a couple hundred volts in the right place."

"And that's just to soften you up, tough guy," the major added, grinning.

Swag, his hands tied with plastic restrainers in front of him, waited for the provost on his right to open the door, then followed him out. As they crossed the sidewalk toward the side entrance, Bammer, looking for all the world like a smiling doorman from Hell, opened the plate-glass door.

Hesitating a second on the sidewalk, Swag felt the Steyr's barrel urging him along.

When Swag heard the first shot, he dropped fast, first to his knees, then on his back. Looking up, he saw the provost immediately to his left wobble slightly, the entire side of his jaw blown away.

The next four shots came fast, before the other provosts could turn to bring their weapons up. The first two hit the other enlisted man in the legs, just below his Kevlar vest, the third caught Martin in the left arm. And the fourth went wild, streaming just above the heads of the two falling provosts, out toward Fifth Avenue.

Swag rolled, facing west. For the briefest instant he caught a flash of Bammer, running back up the stairs and colliding with the doorman, both of them falling to the carpeted floor. Then he saw Kat Jones, right in the middle of the sidewalk, ten yards away, a small automatic held in a two-handed combat stance, her black raincoat streaming out behind her in the light summer breeze.

The major let out a wail of pain and reached toward the nylon harness of the tactical holster for his weapon. Kicking out, Swag hit the major hard at the ankles just as he fired off two rounds at Kat, who didn't even duck as the bullets ventilated the raincoat under her left arm.

Kat fired again, catching the major high in the chest and dead center of the threat-zoned Kevlar vest. The impact knocked him back, and Swag scrambled forward to grab the Colt still tucked in the waistband of his uniform.

Swag turned and rolled, firing before he aimed. The first shot caught one of the enlisted men in the shoulder, just below the vest's protection, knocking the rifle up into the air for a three-round burst of full-auto. The second round caught another enlisted man on the hand, spraying blood and bone across the shattered plastic grip of his rifle and knocking it from his useless grasp.

Kat was walking forward now, her eyes wild. She fired twice more, the shots so close to Swag's head, he could feel the air pushing out in front of them. The first hit the guy with the ruined hand square in the stomach, cutting short his cries of pain. The second exploded into the head of the last remaining guard, sending bits of skull and brain flying toward Fifth Avenue as he collapsed backward, the rifle still locked in his dead fingers.

"Die, you motherfuckers!" Kat yelled, moving forward, gun out in front of her.

The major came up fast then, lunging for the Colt. Swag turned on him, fired once and again caught him in the stomach. The major let out something like a wheezing sigh as his second rib splintered with the impact.

Kat was right over Swag then, the gun sited in directly at his head. "You too," she said.

"Kat, it's me!" Swag tried, not bringing the gun up.

He could see Kat think it over for a second, then her eyes narrowed, aiming.

"It's me!" Swag yelled, raising his cuffed hands in front of him.

She was pulling back on the trigger, standing over him like some angel of death with that damned black raincoat spread out like wings in the humid breeze. There wasn't even time to bring the colt up.

Kat's eyes twitched slightly, then she turned, pivoting on one foot as she fired, sending the doorman back into the hotel with a shot that blew out his left eye and exited somewhere just north of the gold braid of his uniform's collar. The small Mac 12 fell from his hands and clattered down the carpeted outside stairs. He was dead before he hit the ground.

When she turned back to Swag, the alarms were sounding. They were deep, bass two-note European alarms. And Kat's eyes unnarrowed, as if coming out of a trance.

"We gotta get outta here," Swag said, coming to his knees, then his feet.

Kat gave a quick nod, her eyes darting desperately around. Up on the corner on Fifth a wary crowd was starting to gather. Swag saw several of them look off to the right, toward the hotel's front entrance, then point. No doubt doormen were pouring out, armed with Mac 12s, and provosts with them.

"Come on," Swag yelled, and they began running west toward Broadway as the bullets bit into the concrete at their feet and sliced through the air around their heads.

They reached Sixth Avenue at a dead run. Swag struggled for balance with his hands bound in front. Then they turned left, slowed to a fast walk, and vanished into the subway.

chapter twenty-five

A LIGHT RAIN BEGAN TO FALL in late afternoon. The sun made its way down toward the western horizon unnoticed, like a junkie working his way down a fire escape to an unlocked window. Esterhazy took his time dressing, carefully selecting a silk Italian suit, flashy Spanish tie, and nearly new pair of custom John Lobb shoes. He might have been mistaken for a European businessman on his way to a meeting, had it not been for the button he wore pinned to the Burberry raincoat. Made of ceramic and eighteen-carat gold, the small button might in fact have been mistaken for a Japanese company button, unless you looked close enough to see the design, which read "J' ♥ Jerry."

As he walked east toward Lexington Avenue, Esterhazy checked his watch and saw that he was late. The light rain turned into a downpour when he hit Lex, and the cabs vanished almost immediately. Esterhazy walked faster, feeling the substantial drops hit his face and hair. It would not do to be late, not at all.

Swag and Kat stayed on the train until the mid-nineties, then got off and caught a train downtown. As Swag explained the situation, he could see the tension drain from her face, though the bone-weariness remained. She seemed to calm down, her strength gathering quietly somewhere behind her clear eyes.

"So it was the license?" she asked.

"Yeah, whoever was after you was tracking you by your hack license."

"Well, goddamn," she said, her voice barely audible amid the clatter of the ancient subway car. "You almost bought it there. Until I saw the handcuffs, you know."

"What were you going to do, just blow away as many provosts as you could?"

Kat smiled sheepishly. "Yeah, something like that," she answered. "So, where are we heading now? Or don't I want to know?"

"DMV," Swag said. "That clerk's our only link to the bad guys."

Kat, huddled in the raincoat, let out a sigh. "What makes you think he's still down there?"

"He's in public service," Swag said. "Besides, he probably thinks I'm dead by now."

They got off the train at the City Hall stop and walked across Foley Square toward the building that now housed the DMV. It was a quarter to five and raining hard. They wouldn't have to wait long.

"You sure this is going to work?" Kat asked as they took up their positions by the back entrance.

"Believe me," Swag answered, and handed Kat back the Sig. "Nothing scares the guy more than a pissed-off lady with a gun. It's the ultimate dick shriveler."

"Well, I'm really pissed off," she answered.

At exactly five after five the clerk came out the door. He was leading the way for an entire group of employees, who hesitated just long enough to blossom open cheap umbrellas inside the door or cover their heads with that morning's newspaper.

Swag opened the conversation with a sharp blow to the guy's side. The punch sent him bouncing off the granite wall of the building and halfway to his knees, umbrella falling to the ground. In a flash Kat had the Sig out of the raincoat pocket, where he could see it, and leveled it at his head.

"You," the clerk said. "It's you!"

"Surprised?" Swag answered, stepping closer and grinding the umbrella's chrome ribs and nylon skin under his boot.

The other employees were scattering now, breaking away from their small chatting groups and heading in all directions. Not one stopped to help their coworker.

"Where's the tour agency?" Kat demanded.

"Why you want to know?" the clerk asked, using the wall as support as he came uneasily to his feet.

"I'm planning a vacation," Swag answered, then backhanded him against the wall.

"Fuck you," the clerk said, a thin line of blood running from the corner of his mouth.

Kat triggered off a quick round that bit out a small chunk of granite from the side of the building. The shot seemed very loud, the report bouncing off city, state, and federal walls up and down the street. They were only a couple hundred yards from the prison; if they didn't get what they wanted fast, they'd be a lot closer.

The rain was coming down harder now. The clerk's hair, which had been combed with great care to cover a bald spot, was plastered to his head. The cheap cloth raincoat he wore offered little protection.

"Where's the agency?" Kat demanded, moving in closer.

"The cops, provosts, the whole world's gonna be here in a second," the clerk said, sensing he could hold out that long. "You're assaulting a civil servant."

"Then they'll have a murder on their hands," Swag answered. "Where's the agency?"

"Get lost, you ain't gonna do shit," the clerk answered as he began to get up.

"Do him," Swag said casually, then turned his back.

Kat nodded grimly. Although only a couple of feet divided the clerk from the barrel of the Sig, she took her time sighting in at the center of the guy's head. She wanted to give him a good long look at the 9mm abyss staring him in the face.

Kat took a deep breath and eased back on the trigger

with a slim finger, the knuckle growing white with the tension.

"Okay, okay," the clerk said. "It's a French guy, Esterhazy, up on East 68th, just off of Fifth. Get this crazy bitch away from me, willya?"

Swag turned, smiling. When he'd walked back to stand next to Kat, he saw the clerk's face had changed into a mask of fear.

"Pull the trigger," Swag said.

The clerk made his mouth into an anguished O, and Kat pulled back on the trigger, grinning. The hammer clicked down on an empty shell casing.

Swag had unloaded all but one live round from her gun.

"So, you'll hit your mark here on the steps, and here with the flag behind you, and here, just inside the rotunda," Dobbs said, pointing to a detailed map of the courthouse grounds and floor plan. The map was laid across the peach silk sheets and was equally supported by Dobbs's and Sandy's knees beneath.

On the other side of the suite's window, it was storming. The rain beat against the high-impact glass, beading across the chemically treated pane and forming odd rivulets that distorted the streetlight-lit green view of Central Park.

"And if they come in around the back?" Sandy asked.

Dobbs let his side of the floor plan free and it curled across the sheets into Sandy's grasp. "No chance. There'll be a half-dozen provosts blocking all angles except for the designated shots. Do you remember the sound-bite sequence?"

"Why, of course," she said, then turned her back on him to set the paper baton of the floor plan at the side of the bed. "Outside, I do the bit about being afraid, but determined. Faith in the justice system and the provosts."

"Right-O," Dobbs answered, removing his glasses. "The pillars will be behind you. Don't stop walking to answer questions until you're at least ten steps up the stairs. Then you reach out and touch the provost on your right at the elbow. The entire detail will stop when they see you do that."

"Okay, sure. Inside, I do the pissed-off thing," she said. "About how maniacs have guns, but I have justice on my side. Then I point to the statue and say, 'She might be blind, but I can tell you for a fact, she ain't dumb.' Then I pause and say, 'After all, this is still America.'"

Dobbs smiled. "And the last?"

"Coming out, I do my satisfied-with-a-job-well-done routine, with the flag in the background. I thought all the flags were stolen?"

"There'll be one on the park's pole tomorrow," Dobbs assured her. "Just make sure you stop exactly fourteen steps down at the center handrail. If you keep going, you'll run right into the detail, and the flag won't be in the picture."

"Shit this is corny," she said, reaching under the covers. "Whyn't you just dress me up like Miss Liberty and give me a couple of apple pies to cart around?"

"These are sound bites," Dobbs explained carefully. "Timed for ten, fifteen seconds. Nobody will *notice* the courthouse arch. They won't remember seeing the flag. Hardly anybody will remember what you say. But it'll register. Now, I want you to remember this—don't answer any questions directly. Nothing, not even your age, name, nothing. Do the lines and move on."

"What about that guy, Swag?" she asked as she continued to move her hand under the sheet.

"They'll be bringing him in through the back," Dobbs said, with some difficulty. "He won't be able to answer questions. They'll have him dosed with a transdermal and fitted with distorting contact lenses. He'll look nuts as hell."

"When they catch him, you mean."

"They'll catch him," Dobbs answered, leaning back on the pillows and closing his eyes. "Two days, tops. No problem."

"I just have one, tiny problem," Sandy said, rolling over and kissing the soft spot on Dobbs's neck. "My former financial advisor. He knows too much. That package he sent up this afternoon could blow the whole thing."

"That doesn't represent a problem,' Dobbs answered, smiling. "It's being taken care of now. Your financial advisor, the French. Everything."

"The colonel, he goes along with it?" Sandy asked, burrowing farther down under the sheets, her head now at Dobbs's stomach. "After all, my advisor did provide that tip."

"Bammer? He does what I say," Dobbs answered. "I'm the one you have to worry about."

From beneath the sheets Sandy answered, "I was hoping you'd say that."

chapter twenty-six

THE DOWNPOUR SHOWED NO SIGN OF letting up. Swag caught a cab only by waving a fistful of soaked franc notes on Broadway, just below Canal. It would cost them four francs for the trip up to the East Side. For the first time he was paying tourist rates, but didn't mind.

"So what do we do now?" Kat asked, settling back in the seat.

"You mean, like a plan?" Swag asked, as the cab nosed its way through the gridlock on Canal.

"Something like that."

"We play it by ear. Knock on the door and see what happens."

"What if they don't answer?" Kat said, looking out the window. All along Canal the last of the street vendors and tourists were hustling to get out of the rain.

"Then it's your turn to come up with a plan," Swag answered, digging in his pocket for a cigarette and finding only a water-soaked mess of tobacco and papers.

It took the better part of an hour to reach the town house. The city seemed locked up in the sudden shower, each cross street a horror of hopelessly stubborn drivers seeking small advantages as they edged their vehicles slowly into the crosswalks and avenue traffic or overheated to block streets altogether. Nobody was giving an inch as the steamy rain continued to fall.

When the cab finally pulled up in front of the East

68th Street address, the cabbie switched off his Off Duty sign and eased his way back into traffic. Swag was relieved to see the light on in the town house, which in itself was a good sign.

"Well, go up and ring the bell," Kat instructed. "I'll back you up."

Swag took the stairs easily, found the small metal button and pushed it. There was a slight click as the video intercom came on, followed by a minute hum as its lens adjusted for a full-body image of the visitor.

Then there was another click and a louder humming sound. Swag and Kat watched as every window in the place sealed itself shut with alloy shutters lowered quickly behind the glass.

"Good plan," Kat said. "You have another or what?"

"How 'bout you go up and say you're delivering a pizza?" Swag suggested.

"This is bullshit," Kat answered. They were standing on the sidewalk in front of the town house, both of them soaked through. Swag could sense that Kat was getting tense again, and it scared the hell out of him.

Narcadia was laughing to himself inside the hermetically sealed room. For the second time in as many days, the phones were left unanswered. The huge gray desk was plastered with documents: computer printouts, fax transmissions; newspaper clippings; customs entry records; and over twenty Medical Examiner reports with accompanying crime scene photos. But of all the paperwork Narcadia reviewed, nothing struck him quite as humorous as a detailed synopsis of the rules governing "*Établissements financiers non bancaires*" in Luxembourg from the Institut Monetaire Luxembourgeois.

Narcadia lifted his head heavily toward the ceiling, pinched two fingers into the fleshy, tumorous folds of his eye sockets and wiped away a few mirthful tears. Who could have guessed that such a bland document would be the solution to all his problems—particularly that persistent problem about having to work for a living.

When he looked back down at the paper, he once again read his favorite part, Article 16 of the revised Grand Ducal decree for banking secrecy laws: ". . . under the criminal code, directors, managers, and employees of banks are prohibited from disclosing confidential information," unless of course to shareholders holding at least fifty percent of a company's assets.

It was a bit of luck, really, Narcadia thought to himself as he gathered up the papers. Two weeks ago he had moved more of Sandy's money into that venture capital fund in Luxembourg. He'd put Sandy into the thing a couple of years ago because he could maybe spin off some cash for his own little businesses—a little international quid pro quo. He knew it was crooked from the start—even the prospectus was wacky—but the guys he was dealing with understood the game and that was all that mattered.

Surprisingly, the fund spun off a nice chunk of change, both for him and Sandy, so he started buying up more and more shares. It wasn't until he got his position up to 50.86 percent that he really took an interest in the company's portfolio. When the president refused to talk beyond Eurocratic babble, Narcadia went to the fund custodians at the bank who transacted. "Hey, I own the joint, now start talking," he told them. But even then he got nothing but a lot more of the same shit.

Narcadia began leaning on the bank managers then. And when word got back to his partners, they came clean. Sure, there were a bunch of hardworking software designers, creative clothing manufacturers, and experimental flavoring operations—just like the prospectus said. But the real stuff, the meat of the operation, was financing every low-down immoral piece-of-shit business in the world. Sex clubs in Thailand; silicon sweatshops in Korea; hazardous waste disposal in Jersey; they even had a division that turned out counterfeit watches in Hong Kong. It was, in short, Narcadia's type of business.

But the thing that would really pay off was this package tour company incorporated in Paris. Sure, it looked like any other tour company, until you looked at the rates. A guy could live in Monte Carlo for a year for what a two-week jaunt with this outfit cost. And nothing in New York cost that much—nothing. It took Narcadia three days to piece it together, and about six seconds to figure out how to make it pay.

And the thing that was ironic wasn't that Sandy Mann, hustler extraordinaire, had unwittingly financed her own attempted murder, but that now, with her the state's witness in the Hollowbutton hit—which she also helped finance— she was about to take a bath in her choicest investment. First she pays to have herself whacked out, then she rats out her own operation.

For Narcadia, the whole thing was beyond irony—it was opportunity. He'd already sent copies of the paper trail up to the Plaza and out to the fund managers. Shit, he could turn them fuckers upside down and shake their pockets clean.

Narcadia chuckled again and arranged the original papers into a neat pile. Altogether, the pile was maybe four inches thick, each item neatly labeled in his own stylish writing. He was so caught up in his plans, he didn't see the unmarked provost helicopter swing by the window. Certainly he wouldn't have heard the small craft through the triple layer of five-inch-thick polycarbonate glass.

The chopper spun by the window quickly, then banked two or more blocks away as it drew in more slowly. In the doorway were two snipers, their armor-plated seats, swung out in combat position, in the open doorway. A touch of the pedal at their feet would swing them back into the doorway when they were done. Their weapons were identical: .50-caliber silenced, gyrostabilized Browning M-2s, fitted with 30x thermoimaging, night-vision scopes. Their faces were nearly identical pictures of concentration as they studied the images in their scopes—set up for daylight action, the computer-enhanced imaged displayed a clear view of Narcadia's broad back. Just to his left in the gunners' sights, a digital readout provided distance as the video cross hairs fluttered into alignment.

They were not wearing provost uniforms; in fact, the tail and belly numbers identified it as a traffic helicopter from one of the local television stations.

As the chopper hovered just outside Narcadia's window, the fixer turned, swiveling in his chair with that odd feeling that someone was watching him. The chopper was close enough for him to see the slightly turned-down lips of the two shooters and the building's windows in the reflection of the copilot's mirrored aviator glasses.

"Holy shit," Narcadia moaned. The phone rang then, and instinct brought his hand to the button to punch up the call. "Talk to me."

Someone on the other end of the phone said, "Did you hear the one about . . ." as four explosive rounds took out the window, sending heavy chunks of shattered plastic back at Narcadia, blowing the headset from around his head and sending him back across the desk. Three more rounds hit him in the face, chest, and belly, and splattered the better part of him against the clear plastic of the cubicle, whose walls miraculously held, though now they looked much like the clear glass of a blender.

The two gunners swung back into the hatch as the chopper rose quickly, then headed up Broadway. Far below on the street a handful of glass fell like hail among the raindrops.

Two of the messengers stared, gaping up as the chopper vanished in the distance. "What do ya think? Someone scram the boss?" one of the messengers asked, still staring in the direction where the chopper disappeared into the low clouds.

The other one had already counted floors. "It was a good job while it lasted."

"You don't wanna go up, check it out?"

"Hell no!"

"He could still be alive, maybe."

"What, you joking me? He's history, and so are these jobs."

chapter twenty-seven

"THIS REALLY SUCKS, I MEAN big-time," Kat said. They were standing across the street from the town house, rain still coming down. But the rain didn't matter anymore, they were already soaked through. Up and down the block doormen and security people were giving them suspicious looks.

"We can wait them out," Swag answered. "Phone them up, what do you think?"

It was then they heard it. Barely audible under the hiss of the rain and blare of car horns was the sound of a chopper. When it was so close that it drowned out the rain, instinct told Swag to beat feet. He grabbed Kat and headed east, ducking down the stairs into the service entrance of an ersatz palazzo.

The chopper was close now, practically over their heads, but still high up. Looking up over the iron fence, they saw the chopper make a quick sweep of the street, turn, and head back.

"News unit, must be an accident," Kat said, venturing up on the stairs.

Swag pulled her back down, catching the sleeve of her raincoat in his hand. "Provosts. Every station in the city has Bell choppers, that one's French."

"Pretty sure of that, huh?"

"You tell me, what news station needs twin turbos for traffic reports?"

"Looking for us, you think?" Kat asked.

"They wouldn't have passed," Swag answered. "They could pick us up with thermosensors."

When the chopper came in again, it was moving slowly. Just before it reached the town house, the door gunners swung out, weapons pointed straight down. The dual machine-gun burst was so fast, if you weren't listening for it, you wouldn't have heard it. Neither would you have seen the small ball that dropped from the chopper's door down two hundred feet into the shot-up roof of the building.

The chopper took off then, lifting straight up and banking gracefully toward the park and the West Side.

"What was that all about?" Kat asked as she escaped Swag's grasp and hurried up the stairs.

Swag followed warily, sensing something about to happen. They were halfway across the street when something did happen. The blast rocked Swag backward, against a parked car. Kat, who was farther ahead, was knocked to her back, as every metal shutter in the town house billowed outward like thin plastic, releasing a thick cloud of acrid smoke. For a split second the entire Beaux Arts facade seemed to expand like a balloon, as pieces of it fell like icing from a week-old birthday cake. Up and down the block windows shattered with the punch of the shock wave.

Swag pushed himself off the car and ran to Kat. "You okay?" he asked, ears ringing and his own voice sounding very far away.

"Holy shit," Kat said. Then, discovering she was partially deaf, elaborated. *"Holy-fuckin'-shit!"*

Swag helped her to her feet as the smoke began to drain from every window and door in the town house. The steel shutters now hung bent and distorted in their tracks; smoke poured from every opening.

They were still watching the smoke coming from the house when the front door opened. Far-off sirens began to scream as emergency vehicles bullied their way through traffic.

Swag and Kat watched as the young woman, her face and hands smoke-blackened, wobbled uneasily out through smoke that continued to billow from the front door. She was dressed completely in black—lightweight biker leathers and black French running shoes.

Up the street Swag caught a glimpse of a blue Con Ed emergency vehicle, yellow lights turning on its roof. That's how he knew the provosts would play it—like a gas leak.

Kat was still steadying herself on her feet as Swag pulled her forward. "Come on, we have to get to her," he yelled, grabbing a fistful of raincoat and pulling.

"What?" she answered, dazed and trying to shake the ringing from her ears.

Swag pointed, his entire arm extended toward the young woman who was now leaning on the hood of a parked car. Every window in the car was blown out. "We have to get her," he shouted, pulling Kat behind him.

"What?" she asked again, then saw where Swag was pointing and followed.

They reached the woman as she was just looking up to survey the damage to the house. "It just blew," the woman said, her voice numb.

"We gotta get outta here," Swag yelled.

"What?" the young woman asked.

"Come on, we gotta split!" Swag tried, raising his voice.

"Who are you people?" the woman asked, dazed.

"What?" Kat asked, still twitching the ringing from her ears.

"What?" the woman asked back, her smoke-stained face staring intently forward in question.

"Huh?" Kat asked. "What'd'ya say?"

The Con Ed truck pulled into the street, edging its way around double-parked cars. From its loudspeaker someone shouted, "You people, freeze, right there!"

Swag recognized the voice immediately; maybe not the guy, but the voice. It was the voice of a cop. The eastern end of the street was already blocked off with plastic sawhorses and yellow tape. They were just getting the sawhorses in position at the opposite corner.

Swag pulled the Colt from his back holster and stuck it under the woman's chin. Kat saw the plan and pulled her roughly by the elbow. All three were in a jogging run down the puddled street when the first rounds pinged off the sidewalk at their feet.

For some reason the bogus utility workers hadn't blocked the eastern end of the street with their truck. All that barred their way were a few sawhorses.

Swag, holding the young woman up with his right arm, leveled the gun left-handed in front of him and began firing. A few of the half-dozen workers scrambled, reaching toward hidden tactical holsters for weapons. The rest bolted back for the safety of the truck, somewhere just around the corner.

Kat was firing too, her right arm extended, her left holding up the woman. Swag timed the shots, five steps and fire, five steps and fire. If he worked it just right, he'd empty the clip as they reached the corner.

By the time they reached Madison Avenue, they had chewed up the sawhorses pretty bad and stopped all uptown traffic on that street.

Swag released the empty clip and slapped in a new one. The woman was still dazed, but able to walk. Switching the Colt to his right hand, he motioned to Kat. "Take her across the street," he instructed. "I'll go up on the left. When they pop out, take them."

Three rifle shots sounded behind them as the Con Ed shooters came up the street in the bogus utility van. They were shooting provost-issue Steyrs, but not well. The rain was probably screwing up their aim. Swag triggered off a shot, taking out the window on the driver's side, but the truck kept coming, the two gunmen walking behind it, using it for cover.

Swag serpentined up the sidewalk as the Con Ed shoot ers let go with a short burst of automatic fire. Kat was almost to the corner, sticking close to the building, turning only to trigger off a round at the Con Ed guys behind her. The young woman was edging up close behind. A small automatic suddenly appeared in her hand, and she let go with three rounds that sent the Con Ed marksmen ducking back behind their truck.

You take help where you can get it, Swag thought to himself, and ran toward the parked car on the corner. Poking his head up fast, he fired twice, hitting the window of the second truck.

His shots were returned by a hail of automatic fire, then Kat popped out around the corner and took out the shooter at close range.

Edging his way out around the front of the car in a duck walk, Swag lifted himself up again and let go with two rounds. Again one of the phony utility workers opened up on full-auto.

Kat nailed him, angling her shot through the open back door he was using for cover.

Behind him, the Con Ed truck was close. The young woman was timing her shots, making each one count. But the little automatic she held was no match for Steyrs.

Swag jumped up and ran. Splashing through an ankle-deep puddle, he bolted toward the truck parked in front of him. As he passed Kat, she followed, gun out in a combat stance. The young woman was walking backward, capping off her last three rounds as she turned the corner and got a hail of automatic fire for her trouble.

There had been only two men on the second truck. Both lay dead, their blood draining off with the rainwater. One got it in the neck, the other shot through the eye. Kat hadn't lost her touch.

Picking up one of the Steyrs, Swag ran to the corner, edged it around without looking and emptied the magazine on full-auto at the approaching Con Ed Truck. As the

ruck came to a halt, Swag ducked back around the corner,
dropped the empty rifle and ran, following Kat and the
woman down Madison Avenue.

They were nearly two blocks down the street before the
woman began falling behind in a lurching run.

"Swag, she's shot," Kat said.

The three ducked into the doorway of a French bou-
tique.

"Where'd they get you?" Swag asked, propping her up
against the glass.

"My back, aw shit," the young woman said.

A few of the sales clerks were rushing the door, but Kat
held them back with a wave of the Sig.

"Who do you work for, bitch?" Kat snapped.

"Easy," Swag said, turning the woman around. There
was a smudged bloodstain across the window's glass as she
moved away. When he lifted the end of her jacket, he saw
she wasn't wearing a shirt underneath. The bullet hole was
just to the right of her spine, a few inches above the black
belt of her leather pants. There was a whole lot of blood
that wasn't immediately apparent against the black leather.
And there was an exit wound at the front, just above her
hip. She was a mess. The bullet could have hit anything,
the way she was bleeding.

"Is it bad?" the woman asked, groaning.

"It's bad," Swag answered.

"It's not as bad as your brains splattered across this
year's designs," Kat spat. "Which is what it's going to be
if you don't start talking."

"Who are you people?" the woman moaned. "Why did
you bomb my house?"

"We didn't bomb your fuckin' house," Kat offered,
pushing the Sig's barrel up under her nose, but the
woman shook it off with an angry turn of the head.

"What is that, a Sig P-228?" the woman said through
much pain. "That last shot was your fourteenth. You're
empty, sister."

"So you can count, big fuckin' deal," Kat answered removing the gun.

"Look, it can go like this—you tell us who you work for, we'll split, and you get medical treatment," Swag said. "Or we have a nice long talk while you leak out over Madison Avenue."

The woman considered this. "What do you want to know?"

"Who do you work for?"

"Travel agency," the woman grunted.

She was getting heavier. Swag was having a hard time propping her up against the glass. "What kind of travel agency kills people?"

"An expensive one," she moaned.

"Who's the boss?" Kat snapped, still brandishing the empty gun.

"Esterhazy," she said, fading out. "Henri Esterhazy."

Swag tucked the gun into his pocket; he needed two hands to hold her to the window. "Where is he? Was he in the house?"

"No, he went out," she answered. "To the movies."

"Which movie?" Swag asked.

"Jerry Lewis retrospective," came the answer.

"Which one?" Swag asked. It was true—since the influx of French tourists, there were no less than three Jerry Lewis film festivals running at all times. They'd been running continuously for years.

"The good one," the dying girl answered. "The quintaplex downtown."

"Shit, the place must be crawling with frogs," Kat put in. "What does he look like?"

"Tall, black hair, dark raincoat, lapel pin says, 'J'aime Jerry.' *The Nutty Professor* is his favorite."

Swag eased the young woman to the ground. "Call 911," he shouted to the clerks gaping out wide-eyed through the glass.

"A fuckin' Jerry Lewis film festival," Kat said disgust-dly as she holstered her piece. "A Jerry Lewis fan tried to whack me out."

The young woman groaned, then said, "He's French, they love Jerry Lewis, you know." Those were the last words she would ever say.

chapter twenty-eight

THE QUINTAPLEX WAS A FAIRLY new building down in the
East Twenties. It wasn't hard to spot, not with its brushed
steel exterior, two miles of neon, and fifty-foot inflated
sculpture of Jerry Lewis anchored to the roof. The sculpture had been commissioned from the same firm that did
many of the floats for the Thanksgiving Day Parade—it
stood now as a landmark. Postcards of it were available.

The building itself was four floors connected by esca-
lators, with concession stands on each floor. Once upon
a time it was strictly first-run, offering Hollywood's
newest in staggered showings. Now, all its screens were
dedicated to Jerry Lewis. The features ran continuously,
with tourists moving from theater to theater for the
price of one ticket.

Swag and Kat took some strange looks at the ticket
office, but brazened it out, walking stiffly into the
lobby. At the back of the lobby was a small museum—
(foam-core mounted) vintage photos of the Newark,
New Jersey neighborhood where Lewis grew up. Lewis
in Las Vegas, hamming it up on a golf course. In New
York, sticking straws up his nose at a deli. And the
largest one of all—Lewis in front of the Eiffel Tower,
simply pointing and smiling. Scattered around were
life-sized cutouts of Lewis during his film career—
beginning with *My Friend Irma* (1949).

A cartoon balloon rose from one of the more dramatic

itouts of Lewis holding a mike: "When the light goes on
i the refrigerator, I do twenty minutes."

Each floor included nine or ten oversized high-def
ionitors that ran video loops of the highlights of years of
·lethons. Here was Lewis singing. Another one offered
im dancing. The remaining six, lined up in perfect sync,
iowed carefully selected years of him jacketless and
weating through tux shirts.

"Swag, this is really creepy," Kat said as they rode the
scalator up.

"Just another reason to hate the French," Swag said.
'll check out *The Nutty Professor*. If I'm not out in ten,
ome in after me."

wag paused just inside the door to let his eyes grow
ccustomed to the light. On screen, a hairy hand was ris-
ig above a breaker-strewn lab table. Then Lewis
ppeared, transmogrified into the suave, ascot-wearing
·uddy Love. The crowd let out an appreciative scattering
f applause, and several whispered, "Fantastique" and "'ee
ased zee chareeter on Dean Marteen, you know."

Pulling the Colt from the holster and thumbing off the
afety, Swag made his way down the aisle. It wasn't going
) be easy, finding a Frenchman in a Jerry Lewis film fes-
val. But Swag figured he had the advantage; the French
ated to go to movies alone. He'd simply look for a guy
itting by himself.

When Swag reached the front of the theater, he
urned and looked toward the rear. Illuminated in the
ickering light were fifty or more frogs, their attention
astened at the action on the screen. Their faces moved
1 a weird rapt unison of half smiles and laughs, obliviÂus to Swag.

Then he saw him. Two rows over, near the back of
he theater, a single man rose, grabbed a raincoat off
he back of the seat in front of him and headed for the
xit.

Swag started up the aisle at a trot, but before he was

halfway there, Esterhazy opened the door, letting in
thick slice of light. Even before the theater door swun
back into place, there were four shots. The small diamonc
shaped pane of glass on the door shattered and an arm c
light burst through as three more thinner fingers of ligh
appeared around it.

Esterhazy, small automatic in his hand, backed his wa
through the door, fired twice into the wood and bega
running forward, toward the screen and Swag.

"Hey, you!" Swag yelled.

Esterhazy answered with a shot in Swag's direction an
kept running. Every head in the theater was ducke
beneath seat level.

"Get that fuckin' frog!" Kat yelled as she burst throug
the shot-up rear door.

But Swag was already running, sprinting down th
aisle, as Esterhazy hit the front of the screen. For a
instant he remained frozen in the glare of the film—th
lower portion of Buddy Love's silk smoking jacke
imprinted across his face.

"Freeze, right there!" Swag yelled above the soun
track.

Esterhazy fired again, the shot going wild, far abov
Swag's head.

Kat fired twice from halfway down the opposite aisle
the jacketed hollowpoints blowing large holes in th
screen, which distorted the lower right-hand image of a
idyllic college campus.

Esterhazy's face was a mask of panic, his gun hand mov
ing from Swag to Kat then back again. When Kat wa
within ten yards he faked right, triggered off a shot a
Swag, and dived left. Beneath the cover of front-row seat
he scrambled for the emergency exit.

"Get him!" Swag yelled to Kat as he ran for the fron
of the theater. But he didn't have to say a word a he passec
the front row and turned left; she was pushing open th
door and following Esterhazy out. Three seconds late
Swag was through the door.

Two more shots echoed and ricocheted in the gray cinder-block stairwell as Swag took the stairs two at a time. On the second floor landing Kat waited, slapping a new clip into the Sig.

"He's gone," she said.

"Where?"

"He didn't go all the way down. Must be one of these two doors."

"You go right, I'll go left," Swag instructed.

Swag pushed through the door and came out near the screen where *Way . . . Way Out* was playing. Lewis, dressed like an astronaut, was getting bombed on instant vodka—or wodka—with Russian cosmonauts on a moon station.

At the rear of the theater a door swung closed. Swag headed for it. He came up on the right side of the double swinging doors slowly and carefully pushed it outward with his foot. The door had moved about six inches before the top half was shattered by a blast from a shotgun that pushed it back with sudden force.

Up on the screen, Lewis was ingesting a wodka pill, water, then jumping up and down to mix it as a Russian cosmonaut looked on.

Outside, three fast rounds from a pistol sounded, followed by another shotgun blast in the lobby. A television screen shattered. Swag dived through the door, rolling into a prone combat position. In front of him the kid at the snack counter was slumped over the glass case, his brains splattered across the popping corn that spilled from a shattered glass box.

Kat was already through the door, gun held out in front of her. "He took the kid's shotgun," she yelled.

Swag scrambled to his feet. "Which way?"

"Down the escalator!" Kat answered, already moving.

Outside, sirens were beginning to wail. Two provosts were coming through the front door, Steyrs raised, as the red-jacketed usher met them. Esterhazy couldn't have left,

Swag thought as they rode the escalator down. The provosts would have gotten him.

They took the escalator to the floor below, where two more theaters greeted them. "Go left." Swag pointed, indicating the theater where *The Bellboy* was showing. Swag ducked into the other theater, where Lewis was wowing them in *The Disorderly Orderly*.

Swag moved down the aisle cautiously. He kept the Colt against one leg. He was at the screen and about to turn and work his way back up toward the exit when he caught a flash of movement to his left.

Too late to turn, he ducked behind the first row as Esterhazy came up from the center row of seats, a combat-grip Ithaca riot gun raised to his shoulder. As Swag hit the floor, the painted wall of the screen exploded. The blast drowned out the sound, hitting the wall in an explosion of cinder-block chips and distorting Lewis's agonized face as he suffered sympathy pains for a nursing-home patient played by Alice Pearce.

Somebody began yelling in the audience as Swag crawled on elbows and knees across a floor made sticky by years of spilled soft drinks. When he came up again, at the aisle, Pearce was on the screen. Swag aimed over the top of the seat as Esterhazy, a lone standing figure, scanned the room with the shotgun.

Swag fired off another round, but it went wild, striking the rear wall. The Frenchman returned fire, the shot plowing through the seat two rows up from Swag.

"The provosts are here, there's nowhere to run!" Swag called from the floor as he worked his way back to the center.

"We shall see, my friend, whoever you are," Esterhazy called back, punctuating the threat by pumping a new shell into the chamber.

Swag was dead center of the screen when he popped up and fired, his shot muffled by a simultaneous blast from the shotgun. The big 10mm jacketed slug went high, very high, shattering the projectionist's window dead center.

Then it punched through the ancient projector's lens, slicing neatly through the film, film guide, rotary shutter, reflecting heat shield, and smashing into the mechanism that secured the twin carbon arcs.

For a split second the screen was illuminated by a brilliant flash as the film's audio track groaned to a halt—then it blacked out and light poured through from the projectionist's booth as the flattened slug pushed open the mirrored rear of the projector. The superheated carbon rods, hot as a welder's torch, scattered out its back end.

The projectionist, a fat guy wearing nothing but boxer shorts in the stifling room, had been listening to music on headphones and reading the paper. As the rear mirrored back of the projector's door burst open, he was temporarily blinded, then felt the fragments of hot carbon across his chest. Dropping the paper, he staggered from the booth screaming, even as the sports section ignited over a small fragment of carbon.

Swag fired again, and Esterhazy let go with another 12-gauge blast. Patrons were screaming now as the room was cast into near total darkness. Swag tried to judge where Esterhazy stood, but couldn't. Already, frightened moviegoers were running for the back exits—the light from the open door blocked by their crowding.

Taking off up the aisle at a crouch, Swag drew no fire and rose up, running for the door. Both exits were crowded with panicked French, and Swag holstered the Colt and mixed in with the crowd. When he hit the lobby, the crowd heaved toward the escalator, then back again as two provosts barricaded the way with rifles. The frightened audience from *The Disorderly Orderly* was soon joined by the audience from *The Bellboy* as word of the disturbance filtered back into the theater.

Swag let the crowd carry him first left, then right. Somewhere in the building a provost had cut into the Muzak on the public address system and was making announcements. Over the heads of the frightened mob

Swag saw Kat. She was at the opposite end of the lobby, hand raised above her head, signaling frantically toward the exit at Swag's end of the theater.

Swag acknowledged her signal and turned for the exit. He was still five or ten yards away, his movement blocked by frightened French. Behind him Kat was slowly shouldering her way through the turmoil. As he reached the exit he saw the provost on guard. He was a skinny guy, his rifle held up across his chest in a threat that cleared a small portion of rug in front of him. As Swag pushed his way into the semicircle, the provost tensed, eyes narrowing as he motioned Swag back with the barrel.

"Look, you don't understand," Swag said.

The guy gaped for a split second at the unexpected sound of English, which was all the time Swag needed. In an instant he had the rifle's foreshortened barrel in both hands and was turning it in the provost's hands. Then there was a shot—Kat firing at the ceiling. The crowd pushed forward under a rain of busted glass. Swag felt the mob at his back and let them push him forward, carrying him and the young provost through the exit.

As the provost reached the edge of the stairs, he gave up, surrendering the rifle to Swag and taking the steps three at a time at a running retreat. The crowd jammed the exit behind Swag, but he had a good four steps on them. When he reached the exit door on the floor below, he pulled it open. Another provost turned, and Swag caught him across the chin with the polymer butt of the Steyr, sending him backward into the empty lobby. The panic apparently had not spread this far down. But above, the fire had spread through the projectionist's booth up to the ceiling and crawl space leading to the roof. Fire codes had clearly not been obeyed.

Swag brought the rifle back up and lunged through the first door as automatic fire from the guard on the escalator ripped a jagged line across the wall.

Inside, the theater was nearly empty. *Jumping Jacks* was on the screen, and Lewis was standing in the hatch of a plane, parachute on his back. A grizzled jumpmaster was saying something to Lewis as Swag came down the aisle, but before he could answer, Esterhazy jumped up from the front row and fired off three shots from the shotgun.

Swag hit the floor and came up, thumbing on the Steyr's laser site. He pinned it on Esterhazy, who was now running across the screen. Swag clicked the rifle on full-auto and let go with a ten-round burst. A jagged line of fire ripped in Esterhazy's wake, destroying the screen as Lewis fell into space and let go with a madcap scream.

Esterhazy made the exit an inch in front of the Steyr's fire as the last of the audience ran for the back exits, effectively blocking the provosts who were coming in. The smell of smoke was everywhere now, carried by the ventilation system. All eight theaters were emptying, people running in a blind animal panic.

Swag made for the exit and caught it just as the fire alarm sounded. One flight down the stairwell was filling with French. Pushing through, Swag made it to the ground floor; the front exit door was opened, a warm breeze blowing in. He was about to go through when he felt the cool barrel of the shotgun at the back of his head.

"Hold it right there, my friend," the Frenchman said in an unaccented voice.

Swag froze, bringing the Steyr up one-handed to shoulder level.

"Now, if you'll be so kind," Esterhazy said, relieving Swag of the rifle and Custom Colt.

For an instant the shotgun's barrel left the back of Swag's neck, replaced by the smaller barrel of the Frenchman's little automatic. The Colt clattered to the concrete floor. Then Esterhazy dropped the shotgun behind him, but kept the rifle, holding it in his free hand.

The first of the crowd came down the stairs then. Esterhazy fired a shot into the concrete wall just in front of the leader, and they retreated back up in a confusion of panic.

A provost stationed on the sidewalk rushed to the sound of gunfire and the opened door. Esterhazy moved the little automatic a few inches to the left and shot him in the face. The provost staggered backward a few feet and collapsed near the curb.

Swag's ears rang with the shot. "What're you going to do me now?" he asked.

More people ventured down the stairs. The smell of smoke was getting stronger, and this only served to fuel their fears. Esterhazy turned at their approach and fired again, driving them back up. "I need you, my friend," he said.

Outside, the night clicked into day and every news van in the city pointed its lights away from the spectacle of the burning roof and down toward the exit door. A dozen reporters, minicam operators, and sound guys jockeyed for position, forming a loose semicircle around the action.

"Like a hostage, huh?" Swag asked.

"Exactly like a hostage," Esterhazy answered, nudging Swag out through the door into the glare of the cameras.

The half circle of news crews backed up, but not so much so they wouldn't get the shot.

"Listen to me, you people," Esterhazy said. "I have a hostage! Let me through!"

"Who are you?" one of the television reporters shouted. "What do you want? What are your demands?"

"I want to leave!" Esterhazy snapped, nudging Swag forward.

"But who are you?" another reporter shouted back.

The media people were moving forward now, feeling safe behind their cameras and blinding lights. Esterhazy triggered off five rounds straight up with the Steyr in his left hand, but the reporters wouldn't budge—not until they got their story. At the perimeter of the press circle, now six deep, provosts were trying to move in. Above, a helicopter hovered, its searchlight spearing through the sky into the small circle of light surrounding Swag and Esterhazy.

The Frenchman, trapped, tried to retreat, pulling Swag by the neck with the hand that held the automatic, to escape back in through the door. But the door was blocked with escaping theatergoers.

"Who are you?" a reporter repeated. "Can you tell us why you're doing this?"

"Does it have something to do with Jerry Lewis?" another called.

"Are you French?" someone shouted.

"He's the guy that killed Hollowbutton!" Swag shouted back, hoping to create more confusion.

"Shut up!" Esterhazy hissed, the little automatic pushing up into Swag's chin.

"Is that true?" a dozen reporters shouted at once, edging their way closer.

"Ask him," Swag shouted back. "He whacked out Hollowbutton!"

"Who are *you*?" someone shouted.

"Just a guy," Swag answered.

"Shut up!" Esterhazy said, his voice high-pitched.

"I can prove it!" Swag shouted out into the glare of cameras and jumble of boom and handheld mikes.

When Swag saw the provosts at the edge of the crowd, he made his move. Turning his head sharply to the left, he grabbed up at the little automatic with one hand and elbowed Esterhazy with the other arm. The Frenchman fell back as Swag turned and pulled the rifle from his hand. Swag brought the Steyr up fast, but Esterhazy recovered quickly, catching Swag in the sites of the automatic.

Esterhazy was smiling, a death look in his eye as he pulled back on the trigger. "Adieu, my friend," he said.

Three provosts burst through the press line, not knowing where to point their rifles as an awful groaning sound of splitting wood filled the air. Swag looked up and saw the giant Jerry Lewis head leaning outward precariously as the metal supports and steel wires ripped away from the burning roof. The top and rear of the head were in flames, but it still looked very much like Lewis.

Esterhazy's smile faded as his eyes followed Swag's skyward. Comprehension had just sunk in when the fifty-foot balloon sculpture came plummeting to earth, its lightweight plastic pulled down by three thousand pounds of steel struts and support cables.

Swag felt the rusted metal of the strut pass by his arm as the world vanished in a flesh-toned sheet of plastic. The flaming and melting plastic top of the balloon caught Esterhazy square on the head as he let go with a sustained burst of automatic fire straight up. For an instant his agonized face emerged from the flaming plastic, then he was swallowed in a billowing sheet that ignited instantly.

Struggling from under the plastic, Swag tripped, fell, and landed on a provost who had been knocked unconscious by one of the struts. Grabbing the guy by the shirt collar, he hauled him out from under an edge into the glare of news cameras.

The reporters had moved back to the curb, searching for that wide-angle shot. Panting, Swag turned and saw the dim outline of Esterhazy's writhing body under the melting inferno. Two firemen broke through the crowd and covered the mess in foam from handheld extinguishers, but it was too late. Esterhazy was dead.

One of the Frenchmen in the crowd whispered, "Deus ex machina" at the grim spectacle.

At his side, Swag saw the kid he'd hauled out from under the plastic. A huge gash was opened up on the side of his head, and he was bleeding badly, but he was regaining consciousness. A second later Swag looked down and saw a pair of boots standing next to him. When he looked up, he saw the smiling face of Major Aston Martin.

"Hold it right there, scumbag," Martin said. He was standing slightly lopsided and in some pain because of his broken rib. He wasn't holding a weapon, but the three provosts surrounding him all had their Steyrs pointed at Swag's head. In their midst he caught sight of Kat. She was already in cuffs.

"Sure, why not?" Swag answered.

chapter twenty-nine

"THIS IS THE BIGGEST BUNCH OF bullshit I've ever heard," Bammer thundered.

"You can do it your way," Dobbs said. He was speaking calmly, his glasses riding ever so slightly down on his nose. "In theory, you can do whatever you like. But just let me play the video again." Without waiting for an answer, Dobbs hit a button on the remote. Instantly the screen came to high-def life.

Bammer turned reluctantly, a disgusted look on his face as he watched the video—made himself watch it again. There was Swag held hostage. Then Swag fighting off his captor. Then finally Swag pulling a young provost out from under the burning plastic.

Swag, sitting at the opposite side of the room with Kat, watched as well. A small smile played across his face.

Dobbs switched the screen off when the newscaster started calling Swag a hero. "Would you like me to rewind? We can watch it again."

"I might like to hear that hero part again," Swag said.

"You, both of you, shut up," Bammer roared. "You're both about two seconds from a trip to the West Side Highway."

"I don't think so," Kat offered. Her voice was relaxed.

"May we speak privately?" Dobbs asked Bammer.

Bammer nodded stiffly, and the two men walked to the master bedroom and shut the door behind them.

"I say we call it a lie and go with the original plan," Bammer said, trying to make his voice sound reasonable, and failing. "We just call it a lie."

"But it wasn't a lie," Dobbs said. "It was on television—*no image is a lie*, even the lies; you should know that by now. And when people start talking about it . . . then it's gospel. And believe me, people are talking about our friend here. We took a spot survey today, and his recognition index is off the board."

"But we, you, can explain it," Bammer begged angrily. "Whatever happened to spin control?"

"What part, exactly, would you like to discredit? Perhaps where he saves one of your own men?"

"Everything, tell them the truth!"

"We . . . can . . . not . . . tell . . . them . . . *everything*," Dobbs said in a voice most frequently used by teachers of small children. "Full disclosure is repugnant—to me, to you, and most assuredly to the general public."

"Tell them what we need to, so we can at least lock this scumbag up," Bammer countered.

"Once again, I'm forced to lecture," Dobbs said wearily. "We cannot plant an idea in the public's mind that does not already exist there. They may already believe it or they may *want* to believe it. *Image is reality.* People want to believe that one soap is better; that politicians care about them; that a fast car will deliver them that all-important carnal conquest; that single-malt scotch is worth the money. People want to believe in heroes. Bless their television-watching eyes, *they want to believe*—it's like a hunger. They starve for it. But they want it fast—served up with a side of fries and a large soda. Luxembourg is not a side of fries."

"Let's make Martin out there the hero," Bammer said hopefully. "Discredit the film."

"Martin isn't a hero," Dobbs said. "If he wasn't in that uniform, he'd be in a padded cell taking interviews for European psychiatric journals."

"Oh, he's a good guy," Bammer pleaded. "Just too enthusiastic. . . ."

Dobbs was silent, one hand already on the gold-plated door handle. The lecture was over.

"We can still go to trial for the Hollowbutton murder," Bammer screamed. Now he sounded like a little kid being dragged home from the amusement park, as he walked from the bedroom and fixed Swag in a steely stare of thousand-watt hatred. "I just know this bastard did it. Didn't you, you slimy sonofabitch?"

Swag shrugged an answer.

Major Martin, who had been silent, standing at one corner of the room, joined the small gathering that approached Swag.

"Listen, I can make them disappear," he said, talking to Bammer but looking at Swag and Kat. "Since when do we bargain with scum, huh? People disappear all the time."

Dobbs removed his glasses and rubbed his eyes wearily. They'd been at it for nearly an hour, and he thought it best to ignore the major entirely and direct his voice of reason to Bammer. "Sure, take it to the grand jury. Get an indictment. But do you want to gamble on a high-profile trial—which is what it will come to now. And remember, this tape is going to be played every day the trial goes on."

Bammer was shaking with rage, his face the color of sundried tomatoes as he crossed the room to Swag. "You did it, didn't you? You killed that fat tea bag. Ran him into the river, didn't you?"

Swag shrugged again and reached for a pastry on the table in front of him.

Martin drew out his service automatic and pointed it menacingly close to Swag's face. Swag brushed it away with one hand and took a bite of the pastry. "I can shoot him now," Martin said, nodding and looking eagerly to his boss for the slightest hint of approval. "Shoot 'em both now and take 'em out under a couple of room service dollies."

"Calm down," Dobbs said. "Let's look at our options, shall we?"

"This scumbag only has one option," Bammer snarled.

Dobbs ignored the comment—he was going to have to

spell it out for Bammer. "On one side, we have a half-baked story about some renegade travel agent, a couple of dozen unsolved murders, Luxembourg corporations, and psychotic tourists. One hell of a story—but a little too complex, don't you think?"

"All the talk shows want him," Kat added. "French, English, Italian. One of the maids tells me there was a guy looking to cut a deal on movie rights."

"Only movie he's gonna be in is *Death of a Scumbag*," Martin shot back, holstering his piece.

Kat smiled sweetly and said, "Real wit you got there. Bet you just knock all the girls dead."

Dobbs continued without a change in tone. "On the other side, we have a burned-beyond-recognition anonymous maniac. Taped footage of him *not denying* the murders. And . . . a hero. Simple, to the point, and above the fold without a jump line. A three-minute lead for the nightly news."

Martin had come to Bammer's side and was nearly snarling, trying to stare Kat down without success.

"Oh now, that's really attractive, the way you twitch and make your eyes float back into your head," Kat cooed sarcastically.

Martin suddenly turned the full force of his wrath on Kat. "You got some set of balls, don't you?"

"Yeah, I keep 'em in a jar on my dresser," she answered calmly. "Why, you wanna borrow them sometime?"

Bammer, bending down, got in Swag's face. Rage had turned his face from red to white, except for the veins in his narrowed eyes, which seemed bursting. "Just give me a confession," Bammer asked, his voice a nasty needling whisper. "Say something, you bastard."

"Give me a reason," Martin added, waving the gun.

"I'd like to make my statement to the press now," Swag said.

"You miserable goddamn—" Bammer hauled back to take a poke as Swag leapt off his chair, overturning it as he came up.

In a flash Dobbs was between the two men. "Okay, this is the way we're going to play it. There won't be any statement to the press. And there won't be any movie rights or talk shows. And no book deals, no interviews, and absolutely no product endorsement or licensing arrangements. Do you understand? You are to disappear. Vanish."

"I'm as good as gone," Swag said, heading for the door.

"Not quite yet," Dobbs said softly, laying a friendly hand on Swag's shoulder.

They couldn't get Swag out of his Hawaiian shirt or cowboy boots for the ceremony, though Kat looked great in the Scassi gown.

The Plaza's Grand Ballroom was packed as Swag took the stage with Bammer to receive the framed citizen's citation. Looking out over the guests, news crews, and provosts in dress uniforms, Swag vaguely heard the prepared text of Bammer's speech, which he knew would run exactly six minutes on the miniprompter.

". . . therefore it gives me great—no—extraordinary pleasure and pride to present this award to one of our city's finest and certainly most courageous citizens."

Swag accepted the oversized framed document, and flash units exploded in front of him.

"How does it feel, being a hero?" one of the reporters shouted.

Swag smiled for the first time during the ceremony, ignoring the scrolling words that rode up on the prompter in front of him. "All I can say is, receiving this award can't be more of a thrill for the colonel than it is for me."

There was a smattering of applause at that.

"He wasn't supposed to say that," Bammer whispered through a frozen smile to Dobbs, who was standing next to him on the stage. "He was supposed to say it was an honor. I hate that fuckin' guy."

Swag stepped back and gave Bammer a hearty handshake.

Bammer pulled his hand quickly from Swag's grip and

retook the mike. "Now, if I'm not mistaken, we all have a wedding to go to."

Half an hour later Dobbs was married to Sandy Mann. It was Bammer who gave the bride away. And Dobbs who wrote both their vows.

Swag and Kat weren't invited. But as the wedding party left through the Plaza's front door, through a shower of rice toward the limo, Bammer felt an unusually hard handful of rice strike him across the face. He ignored it, kissed the bride good-bye, and closed the car's door himself. Turning, he saw Swag and Kat, standing just behind the barricade, smiling, another handful of rice already flying through the air.

Provost Maj. Slain
German Tourist Held

NEW YORK—Major Aston Martin, a highly-decorated five-year veteran of the Manhattan Provost Command and leader of an elite Special Tactical Unit, was killed late yesterday. Held in the apparent murder is Hans Schiller, a 53-year-old CEO of Mitteleuropa Ltd., a company with trans-Europe interests in microbreweries and walk-in psychiatric and family counseling facilities.

The murder, which took place yesterday afternoon, following the wedding of an aide to Provost Col. Mortimer Bammer (see Society Section page 12 col. 3), has puzzled authorities as to its motive. Martin was gunned down in a lower level rest room of the Plaza Hotel as he opened a gift presented to members of the wedding party's attendants. The gift, a Hermes wallet (see Best Buys Section page 78; col. 2), is said to have contained no currency, but rather a Class II driver's license bearing a fictitious name and photo of the entertainment personality Jerry Lewis.

"The major went into the stall, and the next thing I know this other guy followed him in and started shooting. Made a real mess," said Sid Cartin, the rest room attendant and sole witness to the murder.

Schiller was apprehended at the scene, a silenced handgun in his possession. He offered no resistance and according to sources close to the investigation appeared in a genuine state of confusion at his arrest.

Official reports indicate no previous contact between Schiller and Martin. Schiller, who had arrived in the country two days ago, is currently under observation at Bellevue Psychiatric Center.

"This is truly a tragedy, in every sense of the word," said Bammer. "This senseless act is a tragic loss for the Provost Command as well as myself, personally. But most importantly, it is a loss to the city. He was a damned fine soldier and good New Yorker. It's a genuine pity that he was killed in the city he loved so much." In the prepared statement, Colonel Bammer stressed that the murder is "categorically not linked" to the recent accidental death of a Department of Motor Vehicles' clerk hit by a Spanish tourist later last night.

Acting head of Mitteleuropa, Georg Schnitzler, said that he had no knowledge of Schiller's intentions when he last saw his boss at the Hamburg airport. "He told me only that he was off on holiday," Schnitzler said. "I fear that a terrible mistake has been made."

The aide, whose wedding Martin had attended, was not available for comment, as he is currently honeymooning in Mustique (see Travel Section, page 49, col. 4).

**Here is an excerpt
from *Kill Crazy*—
Book 3 in the
incredible
Swag Town series by
L. S. Riker:**

The two guys were closing in on Jim Bob. Swag could see it. The one on the opposite side of the street was picking up his pace. There were maybe twenty yards between Jim Bob and the pink shirt.

When the guy in pink made his move, reaching for the holstered piece, Swag pulled out the Colt and shouted out, "Hey asshole, got a match?"

The guy turned, bringing the gun up, and fired. The shot didn't make a sound. But just to the left of Swag a store window shattered and turned to dust. Up and down the street people took cover in store doorways.

Swag triggered off a round, the shot booming down the street and sending Jim Bob rolling into the entranceway of a bank. Swag's shot went wild, just to the left. But it caught the guy in the crook of his arm, blowing out the entire elbow and sending the gun flying.

The second round missed completely, the 10mm slug

burying itself in the closed newsstand on the corner. Then Swag heard it—the low rumble of a motorcycle coming up behind him on the sidewalk.

Swag fired again, moving closer to the storefront, and caught the guy in the chest, knocking him back a staggering step. From behind Swag came a blast. He felt the round push by at head level, cleaving the air like a hot knife. A second later, the wounded man's head exploded.

Spinning, Swag caught the motorcyclist in his sights before he saw it was the woman, Darissa, decked out in black leather on an old police Electra-Glide bike, her face partially obscured by a helmet.

"On!" she shouted. An autoloading shotgun with pistol-grips and laser-sight rested across the handlebars.

Jim Bob was pinned down in a bank's lobby, completely surrounded by broken windows. The guy in the blue shirt across the street was flattened against the opposite side of a street light, firing into the bank's shattered glass with a pistol. Jim Bob was returning fire with the .45 automag, the shots, incredibly, ringing off the thick aluminum post at chest level.

The bike hit the curb on the other side of the street at twenty-five miles an hour, Darissa bringing the big machine into a controlled skid that sent it sideways halfway across the sidewalk before she straightened it out.

"Shoot him! Nail that bastard!" she hissed, then began firing with the shotgun, sending three ten-gauge slugs down Fifty-Seventh before Swag had a chance to raise his gun.

They were picking up speed, moving fast down the sidewalk as Swag got off two rounds, then crashed into a jewelry store's window across the street.

A silenced round crashed into the headlamp, another sparked off the frame, and Darissa yelled, "Off!"

She was already lifting the shotgun from between the handlebars and stepping off the bike in a roll, before Swag realized she was jumping.

Swag hit the pavement, taking a chunk out of his

bare arm, and rolled. When he looked up, the woman was running low behind the bike, shotgun out in front of her.

Shooting around her, Swag got off two rounds before the bike began turning. From the corner of his eye, he caught a glimpse of Jim Bob, the .45 resting on the blown-out window frame. When he fired, the round hit the bike on the cylinder head, changing the engine's pitch. He fired again and the bullet slammed into the gas tank. The bike ignited in an angry flash of orange flame and inky smoke.

Momentum carried the flaming bike forward as Darissa ran up behind, shotgun at waist level. Now she was triggering off rounds as fast as she could, her booted feet moving lightly through the trail of burning gas the bike left in its wake. For an instant all Swag could hear was the sound of Jim Bob's big .45 and Darissa's shotgun.

Then the bike turned, its flaming body crashing into a storefront before coming to a sputtering stop. But Darissa kept running, staying close to the building, using the flames as cover. When she was right at the bike, she jumped through the flames enveloping the motorcycle, and vanished in the smoke.

A moment later it was quiet.

Swag rose from his crouching position and walked toward the flames. From across the street, Jim Bob appeared, stepping through the shattered window of the bank, gun at his side.

It wasn't until Jim Bob was nearly halfway across the street that Swag saw him—another guy, this one in a white shirt, stalking through the bank's shattered window behind Jim Bob.

Swag raised the Colt, aiming just left to Jim Bob's head. In an instant Jim Bob had the automag up, Swag trained in its sights.

When Swag fired, Jim Bob fell and rolled, coming up in a combat sitting position facing the bank. A second later the guy in the white shirt fell back, gun upraised as ten rounds from Jim Bob's automag and Swag's Colt caught him in the chest and head.

Looking back, Swag saw Darissa walking toward him. She was limping slightly and holding the lowered shotgun in one hand.

Far off, the Provosts' sirens wailed in the night.

Kill Crazy—the latest amazing offering in the *Swag Town* series—coming in May '93 from L.S. Riker and St. Martin's Paperbacks!

D. C. POYER

AUTHOR OF *THE GULF* AND *THE MED*

"There can be no better writer of modern sea adventure around today."
—Clive Cussler

The tight-lipped residents of Hatteras Island aren't talking about the bodies of the three U-boat crewmen that have mysteriously surfaced after more than forty years. But their reappearance has unleashed a tide of powerful forces—Nazis with a ruthless plan to corner the South American drug market, and a shadowy figure with his own dangerous agenda.

Whatever's out there, someone besides salvage diver Tiller Galloway is interested. Someone prepared to bomb his boat and kill any witnesses. And when Tiller finally meets face-to-face with his pursuers, it's in a violent, gut-wrenching firefight that climaxes hundreds of feet below the surface.

"I couldn't turn the pages fast enough!"
—Greg Dinallo, author of *Purpose of Evasion*

HATTERAS BLUE

HATTERAS BLUE
D. C. Poyer
_____ 92749-5 $4.99 U.S./$5.99 Can.

blindsight: residual vision following lesion
of the striate cortex. *that is, the ability
of a blind person to see.*

Guy Sullivan is slowly going blind. His only hope
lies in possibly dangerous experiments in
blindsight. But with each jarring headache that
heralds his coming darkness, Guy is haunted
by bizarre flashes of the future...a future that
beckons his son to a horrifying destiny....

M I C H A E L
S T E W A R T

BLINDSIGHT

"CHILLING!"
—Washington Post Book World

BLINDSIGHT
Michael Stewart
_____ 92264-7 $3.95 U.S. only